Unholy

by

Kathryn Amurra

Heart's True Desire

Cover Art by *Lea Schizas*

The Wild Rose Press, Inc.
PO Box 708
Adams Basin, NY 14410-0708
Visit us at www.thewildrosepress.com

Publishing History
First Edition, 2025
Trade Paperback Print ISBN 978-1-5092-6333-2
Digital ISBN 978-1-5092-6334-9

Heart's True Desire
Published in the United States of America

Dedication

To my husband, Ken, who has endured countless nights of falling asleep to the faint glow of my laptop so I could bring my characters into the world. I love you.

Prologue

In the last decades of the Ottoman Empire's rule in Bulgaria, there lived a jeweler in one of the biggest cities in the country. This man, a widower, had a daughter and a son—twins—and he loved them more than anything else in the world. On the eve of his daughter's wedding, the man wished to give his daughter something special to remember him by. He found a rare stone in his collection that he had obtained in a trade with another jeweler from the Orient years before, and he proceeded to make the girl a necklace. As he fashioned the chain and the mount for the stone, a thought occurred to him. He could not give his daughter such a gift without giving something to his beloved son, as well. So, he carefully cleaved the stone to obtain two similarly-sized stones. With one, he finished the necklace for his daughter. With the other, he made a ring for his son.

After getting the blessing of the parish priest on the gifts, the man grew to believe that the necklace and the ring embodied his unconditional love for his children. And just as he would do anything for his son and daughter, he believed the necklace and the ring now had the power to do anything his children asked.

The necklace and the ring were passed down from generation to generation. The necklace found its way to a young man in America, a descendant of the daughter whose father had fashioned the jewelry. The young man's grandmother, judging him worthy to possess such a powerful artifact, gifted him the heirloom and told him that whatever he asked of the necklace, it would grant to him because of the power in the stone. She warned him that he could only ask for one thing, the thing he most desired. So long as he kept the necklace, he would keep that which his heart desired most. Once he gave the amulet to another, however, he would no longer have the stone's power in his life.

The young man knew what he wanted—he wished for success—but although he achieved great wealth as the founder of a booming tech company, he felt that something was missing. It was only after he found the love of a kind and intelligent attorney who was hired at a crucial time for his company, and only after his love for her compelled him to give up the magical necklace and all its blessings so that she could have what she desired most, that he discovered the true power of the stone.

Chapter One

Lennox Engineering Hall, Freeman University, Upstate NY
Present Day

Beth D'Angelo let out a long, slow breath to manage her growing frustration. The bangs she was trying to grow out had escaped her ponytail and flew about in all directions. Mindlessly, she pushed them back behind her ears.

No matter how long she stared at the photos displayed on the computer screen in front of her, she could not figure out why the alignment was not right. Without the correct alignment, she couldn't measure the size of the fuel droplets. Without the data on the fuel droplets, she couldn't write her report. Without a finished report, she couldn't satisfy her senior research requirement, and she wouldn't graduate at the end of the semester. In fact, at this rate, it would take Beth just as long to get her bachelor's in mechanical engineering as it would take her peers to get their PhDs.

Letting out a groan, she plucked a pencil from the tin can sitting on the lab counter and flipped through her notepad, determined to go through the setup one more time.

From what she could tell, all the different parts of the experimental apparatus—the housing, the camera, the fuel source, and the igniter—were assembled correctly. The release mechanism also functioned the way it was supposed to—when she pressed the button on the controller, the housing dropped from its starting position thirty feet up in the air. The fuel droplet was generated and ignited as the housing fell, all at the proper timing, all according to plan.

The problem was capturing the whole thing in a series of photos. For some unfathomable reason, Beth could not get a picture of the burning droplet in the center of the camera's view. It was always off. She had tightened the camera to the housing, moved it to a different location, and rotated it. She had used a different camera, started taking pictures earlier, and at one point even tried using two cameras. No matter what she did, though, nothing seemed to work.

Brushing the hair out of her face again, Beth logged off the computer, then packed up to go home. Maybe research wasn't her calling. She certainly didn't seem to have the patience for it.

At this point, though, it didn't matter. There was no time to put together a different experiment. It was already February, and projects were due just before spring break in April. That left her with only two months to get the data she needed, write up her report, and present it. She had to finish.

Beth glanced at her watch as she put her arms through her puffy winter coat and wrapped a thick scarf around her neck. It was a few minutes past ten. The bar-hoppers and clubbers would be out in full force, enjoying another Saturday night of debauchery in Collegetown.

Slinging her backpack over her shoulder, Beth

walked out of the lab, locking the door behind her. As she made her way up the stairs to the main floor of the aging structure that housed the Borlyn Center for Mechanical Engineering, she admonished herself for staying so late. She hated being in the building alone at night. The halls were so quiet compared to the daytime hustle and bustle of students, and the periodic rumble of the heating system turning on as the late winter chill attempted to penetrate its walls always made her jump.

As she hurried toward the exit, motion sensors lit up one section of the hall at a time with a click. She tried to keep her gaze focused on the well-lit section she was in, refusing to acknowledge the darkness in front and behind her.

The creak of the metal door on its hinges as Beth pushed her way outside at last was disturbingly loud against the quiet backdrop of the empty building. Once outside, the sounds of revelry coming from the bar scene two blocks away immediately reached her ears, carrying well in the chilly night air, and she found the laughter and voices oddly comforting.

Beth had reached her car and was about to put the key in the door to unlock it when a woman's shrill squeal hit her ears. Startled, Beth almost dropped her keys. As she paused, listening for more, the squealing was replaced with girlish laughter, which was then followed by the voice of a young man saying something unintelligible, precipitating even more laughter from the girl.

Beth's gaze tracked the voices to the wooded area just past the parking lot, and she slowly shook her head, sighing. Drunk college students often wandered from the bars to the wooded area on the other side of the parking lot, seeking the secluded cover of the trees. It was foolish and dangerous, in Beth's opinion. In fact, one girl last October had almost died out there in those woods. The campus police found her on Sunday morning, unconscious and half naked with strange marks on the back of her neck. She had been very drunk, apparently, as she couldn't even remember how she'd gotten there or who had been with her. Of course, the guy never came forward for questioning. The girl had just been lucky that the weather had been on the mild side for upstate New York that time of year. She could have died of hypothermia.

Beth pulled out of the parking lot and onto the side road that ran from the Engineering Quad toward Central Campus, then took a left on East Avenue and made her way past the Arts and Sciences buildings and into North Campus, where many of the University's sorority and fraternity houses were located. Her apartment was a tiny one-bedroom on the second floor of a shabby-looking brick building nestled between two of the University's rowdiest fraternities. It was rather ironic.

As Beth pulled into her usual spot under a large tree in the lot in front of her building and turned off the ignition, her cell phone rang. It was her best friend, Xiaolin Feng.

"Hey, Lin, what's up?" Beth chose to stay in the warm car for a few minutes while they talked.

"Beth, where are you?" Lin was naturally terse, but her kind heart and quirky sense of humor had drawn Beth in from the moment they'd first met as freshmen in their residence hall. Neither got along with their roommate that year, and their mutual misery had made the bond between them that much stronger.

"I'm sitting in my parked car outside my apartment building. Why?"

"Can you come over?"

Beth let out a sigh she hoped her friend couldn't hear. "You want me to come over right now? I just got back from the lab and I'm tired. It's almost ten-thirty." She really didn't feel like doing anything other than taking a long, hot shower and falling asleep under a pile of blankets.

"Beth," replied Lin in an exasperated tone, "It's Saturday night, and you're not eighty years old. Most people our age don't even go out until ten or eleven on the weekend. I need to talk to you about something."

Beth leaned back in her seat, accepting defeat. "Fine, I'll come over, but I can't stay long."

"All right, old lady. See you in a few minutes."

Beth chuckled as she contemplated whether to walk eight minutes to the house Lin shared with some international exchange students or drive, but upon seeing drops of rain land on the windshield, she decided on the latter. She turned the key in the ignition, and the car hummed to life once again.

****

Thomas stood near the wall in the living room-turned-dance floor of Epsilon Delta Pi, a fraternity known for its loud parties and endless supply of alcohol. The rhythmic bass of the current song, which sounded a lot like the last song, pulsed through him, almost like a heartbeat. Holding a full bottle of beer, he gave an aloof but encouraging nod to a cute redhead who was looking his way. She smiled back at him. Then, as expected, she extricated herself from a conversation with two frat boys who were trying to sweet talk the pants off her.

Poor boys, Thomas thought, unsympathetically. They didn't stand a chance with him in the room.

"Hi," said the redhead, extending her manicured hand. "My name is Ashley."

"Hello, Ashley," he replied, taking her hand in his and rubbing his thumb seductively over her knuckles. "My name is Thomas."

He heard her suck in a quick breath at his touch and smiled warmly at her. *This is too easy.*

Up close, he noticed the thick layer of makeup the girl wore, like a mask on her face. She was insecure about her freckles, so she hid them with a generous amount of foundation. Her eyebrows were traced over with a dark shade of brown, and her eyelashes were obviously not hers.

Thomas breathed deeply, filling his lungs with the human scent of her. It was not just the smell of her blood—sweet with just a hint of minerality—that thrilled him. It was the smell of strawberries and pears that came from the shampoo she had used to wash her hair hours before; the fragrance of lilacs from the perfume she wore; the salty scent of that thin layer of perspiration beginning to form under her arms and in between her breasts as she admired his tall stature and perfect features. As all these scents mingled in his nostrils, his body stiffened in anticipation. To say he would enjoy his next meal would be a ridiculous understatement.

"It's pretty loud in here," said Thomas, leaning in close so that the girl could feel his breath across her cheek. "Do you want to go somewhere a little quieter so we can talk?"

Even before she spoke, the girl began nodding slowly, a smile spreading across her face. "Yeah, sure. That would be great."

Thomas detected alcohol on her breath, a mixture of beer and red wine. She was not falling over drunk, but she'd had enough that she would adequately enjoy what Thomas was about to do to her. More importantly, she would remember none of it in the morning.

Thomas reached down and took the girl's hand, then led her to the stairs.

"Do you live here?" she asked, doing her best to keep pace with him in her high heels and tight skirt.

"No, but I've been here before. I know where we can go."

Pulling her into an empty bedroom at the top of the stairs, Thomas closed the door behind them. He didn't need to look at her to know what she was feeling. He could smell it.

Without a sound, Thomas stepped toward the redhead, his movements smooth and catlike. She sat down on the unmade bed and smiled coyly up at him in invitation.

Second only to the blissful oblivion of draining the blood from a human, this was what gave Thomas the most pleasure—the dance between the hunter and the hunted, the taker and the giver. That was what all these humans were, after all—givers. They were made to produce blood, and he was made to drink it. This girl, whose lips parted in expectation as Thomas sat beside her, she wanted him to take her. Her body, her blood— it was all one and the same.

Her eyes followed Thomas' movements, wide and unblinking, consuming him even before he consumed her. Her hands were folded neatly in her lap, her fingers intertwined and moving restlessly against each other in a shallow attempt to hide the fact that what she wanted more than anything else was to touch him and have him touch her.

He didn't even have to try. All Thomas had to do was look at the girl and smile, and she was willingly and happily his. He was her master, and the realization of that thrilled him, time and time again.

Thomas ran his fingers slowly through her curly red locks. "I like your hair."

The girl blushed, though the mask of make-up she wore dulled the rising color in her face.

Then, without warning, she leaned into him and pressed her lips against his. It was an awkward, childish kiss, but it roused him just the same.

As she withdrew, seemingly embarrassed by her own boldness, Thomas cradled her head between his hands and drew her to him once more.

Perhaps the pleasure he derived from this foreplay was because of the anticipation of the blood to come, or perhaps it was instinctual, a natural mechanism for preparing his victim. He had learned over time that the more willing his subjects—the more enjoyable the experience was for them—the less likely it was that they would remember they were bitten. And this girl was just as willing as he was, without even knowing what she was submitting to.

The first kiss was not very sexy. Thomas kept his mouth closed, and it was brief, but the girl melted into him, nonetheless. She craved Thomas, almost as much as Thomas craved the blood flowing through her veins. She wanted him to want her, needed his validation. It didn't matter to her the reasons why. And he was more than happy to oblige.

When they parted, her hands moved to grasp the back of his head, her fingers burrowing into his thick hair, and this time it was she who pulled him in for another kiss.

Thinking about how her blood would taste on his tongue, Thomas tilted his head slightly, kissing her more deeply this time. She moaned softly and arched her back, pressing her breasts against his chest. She was his, and, knowing that, Thomas could wait no longer.

Slowly, he leaned her back until she was lying on the bed with him. Moving her thick hair out of the way, Thomas pressed gentle kisses along the curve of her neck.

"You have a pretty neck," he mumbled against her skin as he rolled on top of her. The girl's pulse quickened and her rib cage rose and fell beneath him in fast, shallow breaths of desire. The feel of the blood under her unbroken skin roused Thomas to the point of physical pain. He had to drink. There would be no carnal pleasure tonight. Only blood.

"Just relax, I'm not going to hurt you," he said softly into her neck.

She mumbled something and moved her head to the side to give him better access. *What a good girl.*

Drawing his lips back from his teeth, he bit into her neck and the warm, sweet liquid filled his mouth.

"Oh," he heard her utter, but she made no move to push him away.

As a reward for her compliance, Thomas put his free hand on the girl's breast and rubbed it a little, and she moaned again.

Time seemed to stop as Thomas filled himself with blood from the wound. When the girl grew quiet and stopped squirming beneath him, he parted his mouth from her flesh and looked down at his victim. Her eyes were closed, and anyone who didn't know better would think she was asleep, having the most wonderful dream. Placing his fingers on the other side of the girl's neck, Thomas felt for her pulse. It had slowed a bit, but not dangerously so. She would be fine.

Reassured, Thomas bent down again to clean the wounded area with his tongue, then picked the girl up and laid her more comfortably on the bed. The puncture wounds were at her hairline near the back of her neck, and, more likely than not, they would go unnoticed until practically healed. Even if his victim did find them, she wouldn't know where they had come from. She would not remember much about that night.

Licking his lips in satisfaction, Thomas stood up, and immediately the room spun a bit around him, the effects of the alcohol in the girl's blood, which now flowed within his own body. It was the closest he could ever come to the buzz of a stiff drink.

He stumbled over to the window and opened it, feeling the cold breeze against his now warm skin. The music from the party down below was still spilling out into the night, but it was time for Thomas to leave.

Despite his semi-drunken state, he jumped onto the ledge in one fluid motion and closed the window behind him. Looking around to make sure there was no one who would see, he leaped to the ground below, then started walking home in long, graceful strides, like a lion returning to its den, proud and victorious after a successful hunt.

Chapter Two

Beth dashed from her car to Lin's front door, her scarf wound about her neck and the hood of her coat cinched around her face in an effort to stay warm and dry. Lin opened the door after the second knock and pulled Beth inside, shutting the door quickly to keep out the cold.

"I hate it when it rains this time of year," said Lin by way of greeting. "It should be snowing instead."

"Only a couple of degrees colder and it will be." Beth took off her coat and hung it up on one of the hooks by the door, along with the scarf. "It'll probably turn into snow in an hour or two."

Beth looked at her friend in the dim yellow light cast by the small foyer chandelier overhead. Lin's short black hair was as straight as the bristles on a paintbrush and framed a pretty face with cheeks that looked like they wanted to be pinched. She stood four inches shorter than Beth but probably weighed about the same, though she always wore tight-fitting clothes that were a hundred times sexier than Beth's daily uniform of boot cut jeans and loose knit sweaters.

As Lin stepped away from the door, Beth saw the faint trace of a frown on her face. Lin really was worried about something.

"Do you want to go up to your room and talk?" Beth asked, taking a step toward the dark wooden staircase opposite the front door.

Lin shook her head. "No need. Everyone else is out tonight. It's only us two losers here."

She led Beth out of the foyer and into a sitting room, the centerpiece of which consisted of an ugly velvet couch in various shades of burgundy. An assortment of equally unappealing armchairs, end tables, cabinets, and shelving units were distributed throughout the room with no apparent thought to aesthetics or functionality.

Beth sat down on the couch beside Lin and waited for her friend to say what was on her mind.

After a few moments of silence, Lin let out a sigh and slumped back against the cushions. "I don't know how I get myself into these messes."

Beth took that as her cue to speak. "What messes, Lin? What happened?"

Still leaning back against the couch cushions, but now covering her face with her hands, Lin replied in a muffled voice, "I told him he could come over for a visit next weekend."

Although Lin hadn't said exactly who "he" was, Beth was pretty sure she was talking about the guy her friend had met online two months ago, a college student at NYU.

"No," Beth replied, shaking her head in disbelief. "You told Tyler, if that's even his real name, that he could come visit you? In person? Are you kidding me?"

Lin let out an anguished sigh, then sat up and looked at her. "I wish I were kidding, Beth, but I'm not. I was chatting online with him earlier tonight, and he mentioned that his one Friday class was canceled this week. He said he was thinking of renting a car and driving up to see me. I thought it was sweet of him to want to spend his day off driving six hours to spend time with me, you know? So, I said I thought it was a great idea."

"I see." Beth paused before continuing. "Where is he going to stay?"

At that question, Lin's eyes flashed briefly in Beth's direction. "Here. Where else is he supposed to stay?"

"Oh, Lin, I don't think that's such a great idea. Can't he stay at a hotel or something?" She could see Lin's face flush red, but she couldn't in good conscience watch her friend walk in front of a bus and not warn her, could she?

"You know, that's not the kind of support I was looking for from you."

Beth took a deep breath and tried again. "I'm just worried about you, Lin. You don't even know this guy. He could be a mass murderer."

"He's a college student at NYU. I've checked it out online."

"But still, you don't really know him."

Lin got up from the couch and began pacing. "I talk to him every night for at least half an hour. I like him. We share the same interests. He cares about what I think. I want to meet him. That's why I agreed."

"But now you're thinking I'm right, aren't you?"

Lin paused. "Not really. I can take care of myself. I'm just worried."

"If you're not worried about him being on the FBI's Most Wanted list, then what are you worried about?"

Lin stopped pacing and sat down again beside

Beth. "I'm worried about what he'll think when he sees me, in person. What if…" Her voice trailed off, but she didn't need to say any more for Beth to understand.

"You're worried he won't like you? How can you possibly be worried about that? I think it's more likely he's a mass murderer than it is that he wouldn't like you." Seeing Lin's eyes fill with tears, Beth leaned in and wrapped her arms around her friend, offering a reassuring hug, which was gladly accepted.

Pulling away, Lin sighed again and wiped the tears off her cheeks with palms of her hands. For as tough as she pretended to be, with her sharp tongue and sexy clothes that screamed self-confidence, Lin was just a girl on the inside—a girl who was afraid the boy she liked wouldn't like her back.

As she watched her friend collect herself, pushing her straight black hair away from her face and brushing the wrinkles out of her low-cut top, Beth grew more worried about something else. She knew Lin didn't share her views on religion or sex, but she also knew that Lin was still a virgin, just like her, which made Beth suspect that on some level her friend wanted to wait for the right guy, even if she wasn't married to him.

"You're not going to have sex with him, are you?" The question flew out of Beth's mouth before her brain could send the signal to her jaw muscles to bite her tongue.

Lin straightened her back and glared at her. "Not the first time I see him, but eventually, yes. I'm not like you, Beth. I'm not going to be a virgin for the rest of my life."

"I wasn't saying you should be a virgin for the rest

of your life." Beth could hear herself getting defensive, but she couldn't help it. "I'm not, either. I'm just saying you should be careful, that's all. You just don't want to make a mistake, not with that."

Lin sighed. "I'm sorry Beth. I'm just stressed out. I want things to work out with me and Tyler. I really like him."

Beth gave Lin's shoulder a squeeze. "It's going to be fine. Just don't let this guy pressure you into doing something you're not ready to do. You know you can have a boyfriend without sleeping with him."

Lin snorted. "Yeah, you can say that because you have the most patient boyfriend on the face of the planet. It's like he doesn't even have a sex drive. I don't think anyone else would be okay with going out with a girl for a year and not getting any."

Beth's face grew warm. She hadn't told her friend about the increasing pressure Ryan was putting on her to be more physical with him. The truth was, she could feel his patience running out, and she didn't know quite what to do about it.

"It's tomorrow, isn't it? February eighth?" Lin asked, interrupting Beth's thoughts.

"Yes, tomorrow. Our first date was a year ago, tomorrow." Beth hoped she sounded a little more excited than she felt about their milestone.

"Go on, get out of here," said Lin, leaning into her friend's shoulder in a tender gesture. "I know you want to get home. I appreciate that you came. You're a good listener, and it always makes me feel better talking to you."

They stood and walked back to the foyer. As Lin moved to open the front door, Beth gave her another hug. "No one in their right mind wouldn't like you. You need to remember that and just watch out for yourself, okay?"

Lin smiled as they separated. "Don't worry about me. I can take care of myself. And I've got at least one good friend to turn to when I mess up."

Beth bundled herself up once more, then shoved a hand inside her coat pocket to find the car keys. The sound of the rain outside had quieted, and when Lin pulled open the door, Beth's suspicions were confirmed—the rain had turned into sleet.

"Be careful," Lin called out after her as Beth clutched the thin metal railing and slowly took the glazed steps one at a time.

The ground was slippery under her feet as she skated quickly to her car and got in. Looking back to Lin, huddled in the doorway wearing only a long-sleeved blouse and tight jeans, Beth waved, then motioned for her friend to get back inside where it was warm. Nodding, Lin gave one more wave before closing the door.

Beth eased the car away from the curb and headed back in the direction of her apartment. She was glad there were hardly any cars on the road. Driving in the sleet was nerve-wracking, especially at night.

As she turned onto her street a couple minutes later, the car moved sideways on her slightly. Without even thinking about it, she turned the wheel into the skid. The tires gripped the road once more, and she regained control.

Taking a deep breath, then slowly letting it out, Beth pressed down on the gas pedal. She was alright. And she was almost home.

The row of streetlamps leading up to Beth's building were unlit, despite the late hour, and if not for the lights that she saw inside the windows of the houses she passed, Beth would have thought their street had lost power.

Without the streetlamps, the darkness was overwhelming and a bit disorienting. Beth had a hard time making out where the road ended and the sidewalk began. Oddly, despite the lack of light, the trees that lined the street on either side still seemed able to cast shadows onto her path, which was even more disconcerting.

Looking only a few feet ahead at the road directly in front of the car, her hands in a death grip on the steering wheel and her jaw clenched in concentration, Beth continued moving forward. Only three more frat houses to go until she reached the safety of her parking lot.

The loud chime of an incoming text broke through the icy silence of her focus like a sledgehammer, and her involuntary response was to glance at the cell phone that lay on the passenger seat beside her.

When her eyes returned to the road only a second later, Beth glimpsed a shadowy form by the driver's side headlight and slammed on her brakes, but it was too late. The thud as the car made impact caused her heart to stop for a moment, and her blood ran cold.

"Oh, dear God, no. Please God, no."

Though the hit wasn't forceful enough to set off her airbag, Beth knew it was enough to cause a pedestrian serious damage, or worse. With trembling hands, she put the car in park and cut the engine, then threw open the car door. Her knees nearly buckled as she stepped out; she was shaking uncontrollably.

"Oh God, please let it be an animal." Beth's voice was barely a whisper. She had left her scarf in the car, but she couldn't feel the biting chill of the cold, wet weather against the exposed skin of her face and neck. The thumping bass of the dueling frat parties on her street was drowned out by the deafening rush of blood past her ears.

Still standing behind her open car door, Beth gripped the top of the door frame to steady herself. She was on the verge of throwing up.

Afraid of what she would find mangled under her car, Beth made the sign of the cross and stepped out from behind the door to see what she had done.

Chapter Three

Thomas watched from behind a tree, still rubbing his leg just above the knee, as a girl in a bulky blue coat stepped out of the car that had hit him to look for his body. He grimaced as he heard her whisper a prayer, then make the sign of the cross.

The girl's head was turned away from him as she examined the driver's side front tire, moving slowly toward the front fender. Thomas smiled, amused, as she shook her head in disbelief upon seeing there was nothing there.

Bending his knee to test the leg that had been twisted unnaturally by the impact just a minute before, then putting his full weight on it, Thomas confirmed that he was fine. He had fully healed, of course.

Looking up at the girl once more, he saw her put a hand on the hood of her car as she bent down to look underneath.

He knew what she must have been thinking—how could it be that there was no sign of the man or creature she had hit? She knew she had hit something. She had felt the impact, and there was a fresh dent in her bumper.

Though the effects of the alcohol from the redhead were already wearing off, Thomas was sated, his thirst for blood quenched at least until the following evening. Still, he didn't quite feel like slinking off into the darkness just yet. He was in a playful sort of mood, and this girl, with her absolute horror of having hurt another living thing—well, she intrigued him.

Stepping out from behind the tree, Thomas approached the bewildered girl, his feet sure and soundless on the iced-over sidewalk.

"Miss, are you alright?"

Visibly startled, the girl spun around to face him and lost her balance, slipping on the slick road underfoot.

Thomas reached out and grabbed her arms just in time to keep her from falling backwards onto the hard ground.

"Thanks," she replied breathlessly, steadying herself.

She looked at him as she said this, and her wide, green-blue eyes took him by surprise. Her dark hair was parted in the middle and pulled back with metal clips, keeping the shorter hair in the front out of her face. The sleet that continued to fall was getting caught in her long, sweeping eyelashes, making her look like some mythical ice princess, and a dusting of small brown moles on the girl's cheeks made her face look alive and real, increasing her appeal.

By instinct, Thomas' gaze moved from the smooth curve of her cheek to the creamy skin of her neck, from her perfect ears to her delicate collarbone, and his smile grew wider. In short, the girl was unexpectedly exquisite, and he was curious what other treasures she could be hiding underneath that bulky coat.

She discreetly tried to wriggle free from his grasp, so Thomas released her arms. Clearing his throat, he considered how to proceed.

It was obvious from the way she looked at him that she was not some dumb, drunk party girl who could be won over with a well-placed complement or the flash of his devilishly handsome grin. In fact, he sensed fear in her as she took a step back and accidentally bumped into the side of her car. She was like a cornered rabbit, and he could hear her heart beating rapidly underneath all her layers of clothing. That, too, intrigued him, and his own pulse quickened in response.

"Are you having car trouble?" Thomas asked, trying to distract her from her fright.

"No," she replied slowly, as though willing herself not to be afraid of him. "I thought I hit something. You didn't see anything, did you?"

Thomas smiled reassuringly. "No, I don't think so. Perhaps you skidded a little and hit the curb. It's very slick out here tonight."

She nodded, still looking at him with a curious intensity, the lovely dark arches of her eyebrows coming together ever so slightly as she tried in vain to figure out how she should feel about him.

"I must have been mistaken," she said finally, taking another step away from him. "Everything is fine. I should get going now, but thank you for your help." She zipped her coat up as far as it would go, covering up that beautiful neck, as she side-stepped around him to get to the open car door.

"My name is Thomas," he called to her as the safety of her car was just within reach. "Thomas Callahan."

The girl stopped, her right hand clutching her keys, her left hand resting on the top of the door, then looked over her shoulder at him.

Encouraged by the momentary pause in her flight, Thomas smiled again and, getting around the obstacle of the open car door, extended his hand in greeting.

Her wide-eyed expression and parted lips were easy to read—should she abide societal norms and accept his outstretched hand, or should she listen instead to the voice inside her head that told her to get away from him as fast as she possibly could?

Societal norms won, and, putting the keys in her coat pocket, she took his hand in hers and shook it. "I'm Beth."

Of course, the girl was smart enough to keep her last name to herself.

Having just fed, his body radiated warmth, and Thomas enjoyed the cool feel of her skin on his. He held her hand for a moment longer than required and looked intently into her beautiful eyes, trying to gather as much as he could about her in those few seconds of study.

Beth.

The withdrawal of her hand from his was accompanied by a sudden sense of loss, and his temper rose. As a young vampire, Thomas would have pushed her into the car and taken what he wanted—held her, loved her, consumed her. And once he had satisfied himself, he would have killed her or left her, never to see her again, either way. It was that thought that stilled his hand now, because her wide eyes and trembling lips made him want something more.

He put on a pleasant expression as he watched her quickly shut herself in, lock the doors, then start the car. Within seconds, she was driving away. He raised his hand in a slow wave, just in case she was looking at him in her rearview mirror.

Still irritated by her sudden departure, it occurred to Thomas that the girl, Beth, likely lived nearby. The street they were on was residential and did not connect to any other main roads on campus, and when she had driven away, she had slowed down slightly, just ahead, before continuing down the street. It was as though she had been contemplating whether to stop or keep moving, away from him.

Testing his theory, Thomas stepped quickly to the other side of the street, where there were more trees, and took his place in the shadows. Only five minutes later, her little silver car came cautiously back around the curve. This time, she turned into the driveway of a three-story brick house, only two houses down from where he stood watching.

With his heightened senses, he could see that Beth was still trembling as she got out of her parked car and practically ran to the front door of the house, carrying a backpack. She fumbled with her keys before succeeding in letting herself in. Moments later, the lights came on in a unit on the second floor.

So that was where the pretty morsel lived.

Pleased with himself, Thomas moved silently through the trees, making his way back to the forgotten cellar of the Office of Admissions in the center of campus, where he made his home during his visits to the University. The frozen limbs of the beech, elm, and ash trees that lined East Avenue glistened under the streetlights, and he thought it odd that he found the sight of them quite beautiful.

Approaching the stately red brick building he called home, he looked right and left as he crossed the street. He had already been run over once that evening, and he doubted the next hapless driver would be quite as alluring as the last. Just as he stepped back up onto the sidewalk on the other side of the street, Thomas heard a young man coughing behind him. At that sound, the world around him stopped.

The sidewalk and the trees, the buildings and the lampposts, everything became strangely obscured, as though a dense fog had rolled in. His head was heavy; he could hardly keep his eyes open.

Thomas shook himself to clear his mind of its befuddlement and nearly lost his balance.

Seeing nothing now but the surreal fog all around him, Thomas reached blindly with both hands for something to hold on to. He searched in vain for several seconds before his fingers alighted on a surface of coarse fabric. The feeling was somehow familiar, though he could not imagine how or why.

Thomas closed his eyes, running his hands more boldly over the surface, and he suddenly realized that he was squeezing someone's shoulders.

His eyes flew open then, and he saw that he was no longer on East Avenue at Freeman University in the middle of the night. He was in a cramped room with a dirt encrusted window on the far wall that, despite its condition, still let in enough of the midday sun to make the room seem almost bright.

But there was no cheer in the room, only a palpable, heart-wrenching sadness.

Looking down, Thomas realized his hands were resting on the shoulders of a sobbing man in his early forties. The man was seated on a wooden stool at the bedside of a young woman—a girl, really, with tangled blond hair that had been matted down with sweat and pasty white skin that seemed to be acquiring a blueish hue even as he looked upon her. Her homespun brown dress had dark spots on what little of the bodice peeked out from under the blankets, with the pillow bearing similar stains.

It was blood, and from the overwhelming smell of body odor and ammonia, he knew the girl was dead.

"She is at peace now, Mr. Waverly. She suffers no more." It was Thomas who had spoken the words, and the grieving man shuddered, submitting to the inevitable truth that he had lost his daughter to the plague of consumption that had claimed so many.

His wife had succumbed to the disease only weeks before—Thomas knew this somehow. And now the man was left to care for his remaining son on his own, though for how long, it was unclear, as the man himself had begun to show signs of the ailment over the past few days.

Almost in response to his thoughts, the man put his hand to his mouth, overcome by a fit of coughing. Thomas tightened his grip on the man's shoulders, trying to give him some of his own strength, at least for a time.

Once the episode had passed, Thomas looked to his right and saw a wooden crate on the floor, which served as a table. A brown, leather-bound book had been placed on its surface, just within reach.

Thomas picked up the book and opened it, the motion as familiar to him as breathing. Without thinking, he turned to the Letter of Saint Paul to the Corinthians, Chapter 15, Verse 51. Then he began to read, his voice as clear and strong as the faith he carried in his heart.

"Brothers and sisters: behold, I tell you a mystery. We shall not all fall asleep, but we will all be changed, in an instant, in the blink of an eye, at the last trumpet. For the trumpet will sound, the dead will be raised incorruptible, and we shall be changed."

With one hand still on Mr. Waverly's shoulder, Thomas felt the man tremble, sobbing.

"For that which is corruptible must clothe itself with incorruptibility, and that which is mortal must clothe itself with immortality. And when this which is corruptible clothes itself with incorruptibility and this which is mortal clothes itself with immortality, then the word that is written shall come about:

"Death is swallowed up in victory. Where O death, is your victory? Where, O death, is your sting? The sting of death is sin, and the power of sin is the law. But thanks be to God who gives us the victory through our Lord Jesus Christ."

Thomas closed the book, breathing in deeply, his soul refreshed. Who, upon hearing these words, would not have their despair be replaced by hope?

The man looked up at him with mournful eyes. "Thank you, Thomas." He drew in a sharp breath, overcome with emotion once more, and Thomas thought he might start coughing again. "May I...may I still call you Thomas, now that you are in your studies?"

Thomas nodded, smiling. "Yes. I am still just Thomas for a little while longer."

The scene faded, and Thomas closed his eyes. When he opened them again, he was back in the present, leaning against a tree, the ground still shifting slightly beneath his feet.

What had just happened to him? What had he just seen?

He asked himself the questions only to avoid the answer. Somehow, Thomas knew that what he had experienced was no vision. He had actually been there, done those things, spoken those words.

His head was reeling. It could not have been him, holding a Bible, feeling sympathy, providing comfort. That was not who he was. And yet, it had seemed so familiar, so true.

Straightening up, Thomas resumed his self-assured stride toward the back door of the Office of Admissions. Inside his own mind, however, he was not as confident. Something had happened to him, something that had not happened since the day he had turned. He had recalled a human memory.

And he did not like that one bit.

****

As soon as she stepped into her apartment, Beth turned to lock the door. With trembling hands, she reached for the deadbolt and slid it noisily into place.

She could not stop shaking.

The worst thing was that she didn't know what she was afraid of. She had gotten out of her car, nauseous with the dread of having seriously injured or killed someone, but then found nothing. That fact alone was strange, because she would have bet her senior project that she had hit something. Then that man—that very, very attractive man—had appeared out of nowhere to ask if she was all right.

His voice had been silky smooth, with a low and sultry timbre, and his smile was equally warm and inviting. But when Beth had looked into his eyes, she had seen nothing. Felt nothing. It was a most disconcerting thing, as though she were in a dream, speaking with a figment of her imagination. At first, she was frozen, unable to move or think or speak. Then her alarms went off, and all she had wanted to do was get away.

When the man had called out, just as she was about to get into her car, and told her his name, that feeling of panic had dissipated. Suddenly, it seemed ridiculous running away from a handsome stranger who was only trying to help. Beth had taken his outstretched hand, and it had been warm to the touch. If she were being honest with herself, she would admit that she had enjoyed the brief contact. It had made her feel a pleasant lightness in her stomach. She was almost drawn to him, and in that moment, she looked into his eyes again. Once more, however, she had seen nothing. Only darkness.

And now here she was, contemplating how to barricade the door.

Beth turned toward the windows of her living room, which overlooked the street where those events had unfolded only minutes ago. Anything that wanted to harm her could easily do so—a set of stairs and locks would not stop it.

It?

Another tremor of fear coursed through her. Even as she told herself she was being irrational, Beth hurried into her bedroom and went straight to the nightstand. Opening the top drawer with hands that still shook, her eyes landed on a small glass vial, and she reached for it. The vial almost fit completely in her palm, and she wrapped her fingers around the smooth glass, pulling on the green plastic stopper at the same time to get to what was inside—holy water.

She sat on the edge of the bed, leaving the drawer open, and stared at the vial for a moment.

Her mother had given her the vial, along with a crucifix to hang above her bed, freshman year after having helped her move into the dorms with her dad. "Whenever you feel alone or scared," she had said to Beth, "just remember that God is with you, watching over you."

At the moment, Beth was both alone and scared out of her mind. She dipped her finger into the vial, wetting it, then crossed herself. "God, protect me."

She drew a deep, calming breath and let it out slowly, her eyes drifting shut. After a few more of the same slow breaths, she closed the vial and set it back in the drawer. It was then that she noticed a black velvet pouch that had been shoved in the corner of the drawer.

Picking up the bag, she pulled on the silver ribbon that cinched it closed and reached into the opening to pluck out a necklace. Her cousin Alex had given Beth the necklace the summer before sophomore year, when Beth had attended her cousin's engagement party. Alex—who was more like a sister than a cousin as Beth had grown up in a house with three older brothers—hadn't said much about the necklace, other than that it had belonged to her fiancé's family for almost two hundred years. The necklace certainly looked like an heirloom with its thick, almost clunky silver chain and a large turquoise-blue stone on a matching silver mount.

The only thing Alex had told Beth about the necklace was that it had the power to give its owner the thing the owner most desired and that it had brought Alex and her fiancé together. Although Beth believed in miracles, she hadn't taken her cousin's story about the necklace's "magical powers" seriously enough to consider making a wish on it herself. Sitting on her bed trying to process the absurd fear that had gripped her that night, however, Beth wondered why she had dismissed her cousin's story out of hand. Her cousin wasn't stupid—she was a lawyer at a well-respected law firm in Atlanta, and she had found the most wonderful man to marry. And besides that, if holy water had the power to keep her safe, why couldn't an amulet have the power to give her what she asked for? It wasn't blasphemy to allow for the possibility, was it? God worked in numerous and mysterious ways, didn't He?

Beth tucked the necklace back into the bag and put the bag under her pillow. She didn't know what she wanted to wish for, or even if she wanted to wish for anything. That is, she didn't have anything specific in mind. But it wouldn't hurt to have the amulet close by, at least until she calmed down and was thinking rationally again.

By the time Beth left Mass the next morning, she was feeling more at peace with the events of the previous night. The terrified feeling that had gripped her so fully was now only a periodic wave of uneasiness that grew less frequent and less intense as the day wore on. Whether it was the result of an additional dousing of holy water that morning—both at home and at church—or the amulet she now wore around her neck, or possibly just the passage of time since the incident the night before, she didn't know.

The important thing was that she was beginning to feel like herself again.

Sunday was typically a busy day, and this Sunday was no different. After church, Beth met Lin at the dining hall on West Campus for brunch. It would have been a good opportunity for Beth to offload some of her emotional baggage about the panic she experienced the night before, but for some reason she couldn't explain, she kept the event to herself, at least for now.

After brunch, Beth headed to the lab, where she spent the rest of the afternoon running experiments and working on a problem set for the Advanced Fluid Dynamics class she'd decided to take that semester despite her better judgment. Five hours went by with no real progress on her project, but at least the problem set was done.

Normally, she would have snuck a bagel from the dining hall to have for dinner so that she could work another hour or two in the lab before heading home to do laundry and get ready for the week, but Ryan was going to cook them dinner to celebrate the anniversary of their first date. So, at five o'clock, she called it quits.

Ryan lived in Collegetown, just a few blocks from the lab. He had often suggested that she spend the night at his place when she was working late. While it would have been convenient, Beth knew where that road would lead and politely declined each time the offer was made.

Feeling the need to dress up for their anniversary dinner, Beth had stuffed a pair of black knit stockings, a dark green skirt, and a soft V-neck black sweater in her backpack that morning so she could change out of her sweatshirt and jeans. Dressing quickly in the cramped bathroom at the back of the lab, she paused only briefly to examine the state of her appearance in the small mirror above the sink. Then, satisfied that she had done her best, she turned off the light and went to gather up her things.

The drive to the apartment Ryan shared with two of his law school classmates was exactly three minutes long. Beth parked the car across the street and noticed that his roommates' cars were not in their usual spots. They were going to have the place all to themselves. A flutter of anticipation that bordered on anxiety grew in the pit of her stomach.

Please God, she prayed silently, *don't let this be a repeat of our date two weeks ago.*

Telling herself that everything would be fine, she took a deep breath and got out of her car.

Ryan was standing in the open doorway grinning the same adorable smile he had used on her when he asked her why an engineering student was studying in the law library just over a year ago, the day they had first met.

She couldn't help smiling back—then and now.

"Hi, gorgeous," he said, leaning in to brush her lips with his. "Happy anniversary."

"You, too."

Ryan had only retreated a couple of inches from her mouth when he came back for another, more thorough kiss. Pulling away a second time with obvious reluctance, he tugged at the zipper of her coat and helped her out of the puffy layers. As Beth turned around to face him again, coat off, Ryan's eyes landed on the necklace she was wearing. "What's this?" he asked, reaching for the silver chain and pulling the amulet out from inside her shirt, where she had tucked it that morning to avoid drawing attention to it. "Don't tell me this is an anniversary present from your *other* boyfriend."

Laughing, Beth slapped his arm. "Don't be ridiculous. I'm having a hard enough time keeping one boyfriend happy." The truth of her response didn't hit her until after she had spoken the words, and their meaning lingered in the air between them. She hurried to say something else to displace the silent echo of her statement. "It's a necklace my cousin gave me my sophomore year. I've never worn it and just happened upon it last night, so I thought I'd give it a whirl."

Ryan stepped back from her and grinned. "I like it. It looks vintage."

Grabbing her hand, Ryan led her into the kitchen.

"Something smells delicious."

"Just some spaghetti and meatballs," he replied with a casual shrug. "I got the recipe from my very Italian grandmother, so what you're smelling is a whole pile of garlic that she insisted I put in the sauce."

"Well, I love garlic. It keeps the vampires away. And the boyfriends."

He laughed as he released her hand and moved over to the stove to check on the sauce. "Not this boyfriend. I made sure to have a large supply of breath mints on hand just for this occasion."

Beth watched as Ryan lifted the lid on the pot of sauce and meatballs bubbling on the gas burner and stirred it a little, then reached up to get two plates from the cupboard. He looked just like the future lawyer he was studying to become. His dirty blond hair, cropped short on the sides and just a little longer on top, made the perfect frame for his handsome, honest-looking face, and he always wore a preppy short-sleeved polo shirt and khaki pants, regardless of the weather. His baby blue eyes matched the color of the shirt he wore tonight, and his face was clean-shaven, making him look younger than his twenty-four years, especially when he smiled.

Beth's gaze moved from Ryan's face to his strong arms and broad shoulders. He certainly wasn't the body-builder type, but he did just enough to make those arms the envy of every male student in the School of Engineering. She loved how the muscles rippled subtly from underneath his sleeves as he served up the plates.

"When you're done checking me out, can you grab the salad out of the fridge." He flashed her a teasing smile.

"I am not checking you out," she replied, feigning indignation at his comment. "Why would I be checking you out? I already know what you look like."

"Yeah," he said, placing two meatballs and a generous portion of sauce on the heap of spaghetti he had just put on her plate. "But you haven't seen me in five days, and I've been working out."

Beth chuckled as she slipped the purse off her shoulder and put it on the counter so she could help him get things ready for dinner. Realizing her car keys were still in her hand, she dropped them into the front pocket of her purse.

Beth opened the fridge to find the salad on the top shelf, covered in plastic wrap, then moved the wooden bowl to the countertop near where Ryan had set out two plates and salad tongs.

When the food was served and placed on the small,

multi-purpose table in the "dining room" just outside the kitchen, Ryan appeared at her side with a bottle of red wine and two wine glasses.

"I'm okay," said Beth, holding up her hand to stop him from pouring some of the wine into her glass. "I've got an early class tomorrow morning, and you know I'm a lightweight when it comes to alcohol."

"I know," he sighed, beginning to fill her glass despite her protestations, "but it's our anniversary."

He leaned down to kiss her cheek, and she conceded with a smile. "Okay, maybe I'll have just a little."

As they ate, they made easy conversation about their day. Ryan playfully teased her about the endless problem sets she had to work on, and she in turn joked about how easy law school must be when the right answer to every question was "it depends."

"Where are Ricky and Madison?" she asked as they stood at the sink doing the dishes together some time later.

"Ricky is spending the night at Monica's, and Madison is watching the game with some of the guys. He'll probably crash there for the night."

Beth nodded quietly as she dried the dishes and put them back in the cupboard. She wondered if Ryan had asked them to find somewhere else to be that night. Even if he had, it was only to make sure they could have some time together, just the two of them. It didn't mean that he expected anything to happen. Did it?

"You're awfully quiet," said Ryan in a low voice. "You okay?" He was leaning back against the counter next to the sink, his arms folded casually in front of him. His brow was furrowed in a tender look of concern, and immediately Beth felt guilty for thinking he had any bad intentions.

She smiled and nodded, moving toward him and wrapping her arms around his waist as he opened his arms to receive her. He was warm and smelled faintly of soap, which she liked.

"Come on," he said, releasing Beth from his strong arms and leading her by the hand out of the kitchen. "Let's go sit on the couch and watch TV, like a lame old married couple on their anniversary."

Beth laughed. "That sounds wonderful, actually."

Ryan dropped down onto the drab brown leather couch with the remote control he had grabbed and raised his arm in invitation. Beth sat down beside him and, settling back against his arm, lifted her feet up onto the couch, folding her legs beneath her.

"This is the only way to watch television," he sighed, holding her closer and flipping the channels until he found a basketball game that had just started.

They sat in comfortable silence for the most part, with Ryan making comments about the players now and again and Beth adding what she could. Everything she knew about sports she had learned from Ryan, not having come from a family that followed any college or professional sports. But she was a quick study and had impressed her boyfriend more than once when she had anticipated what call the ref would make or cited some obscure rule that had been completely ignored by the officials.

At halftime, Ryan turned to kiss Beth's forehead. "I'm thirsty. I'll be right be back."

She nodded and sat up to let him get to his feet. A few minutes later, he came back with two more glasses of the wine that had accompanied dinner.

Beth laughed as she took the glass he offered her, fully intending not to drink it. "When you said you were thirsty, I thought you were going to get some water."

"Well," —he touched his glass to hers, then took a swallow— "it's not every day a guy gets to celebrate his incredible luck at being with the most beautiful, smartest, nicest girl on campus."

Beth took a small sip of her wine to be polite, then looked at him with a teasing smile. "I think that's the wine talking."

Ryan took two more rather large gulps of wine and set his glass down on the end table. Then he took the glass from her hand and put it down next to his.

The mood between them had changed, and Beth could see the shadow of desire in his eyes. Her stomach rose into her throat as he put his hands on either side of her face and gently tucked the loose hairs behind her ears. "You know I love you, don't you?"

The fluttering feeling inside her grew as she slowly nodded, and Ryan drew her face to his and kissed her.

His kiss was hungry and wanting, his lips pressing on hers and parting them, his soft, wet tongue tracing her upper lip just before entering.

She closed her eyes and kissed him back, tentatively enjoying the warm feeling that radiated from her core to her fingertips and toes.

As they kissed, Ryan leaned back into the couch, pulling Beth with him. His hands moved deftly from her face to her back, applying gentle strokes from her shoulders to her waist, his lips still locked onto hers.

Hands on her hips, he moved her carefully to lie

beside him with her head on the armrest next to his. Effortlessly, he rolled his body onto hers. "You are so beautiful," he mumbled between kisses.

The warm feeling elicited by his hands on her body and his mouth on hers caused her to forget certain cautions, and she wrapped her arms around him, holding him tightly to her.

Slowly, his hands slipped under her sweater as his fingers found her skin. A new feeling rose from deeper inside as her boyfriend's hands traced the short distance from her belly to the clasp of her skirt. Before she could register the action, the clasp was undone, and the zipper was pulled down. With the waistband of her stockings accessible now, Ryan nudged it down and dipped his fingers between her skin and her panties, his hand moving downward, ever so slightly.

Finally realizing what was about to happen, Beth turned her head, freeing her mouth from his kisses as she pressed her hand against his chest, putting distance between them. "No, Ryan."

Removing his hand, Ryan reached up to touch her cheek, guiding her lips to his once more. His kisses were sweet, and the weight of his body only added to the heady effect of his mouth claiming hers. Closing her eyes, she lost herself again in the feelings swirling inside her, and her arms reached around him of their own accord once more, as though she could possibly urge him closer than he already was.

As he continued to kiss her, his legs shifted, one of them finding a spot between her own. With one hand in her hair, the other hand traveled downward along the outer curve of her hip and thigh to the hem of her skirt. Changing course, the hand slowly went up, under her skirt, and moved inward, the destination becoming obvious to Beth, even under the spell of his relentless kisses.

Breaking contact with his mouth again and opening her eyes, she tried to shove him off her. "No!"

"Come on, Beth," Ryan pleaded, his one hand still resting on her inner thigh, rubbing seductively, though paused for the moment in its upward progress. "Don't you love me?"

"Yes, Ryan, I do. But I don't want to do this. I don't want to have sex. You know that." She pushed his chest, harder this time, and tried to sit up, but he shifted again so that his full weight was on her.

"Please, Beth. It's been a year. I'm not going anywhere. I'm yours, and I want you to be mine."

Though she knew Ryan would never hurt her in any way, the small voice of caution got louder inside her head, and she raised her own voice in response. "I said no, Ryan. Now get off me."

Visibly frustrated, Ryan moved off her and stood up. "I just don't get it, Beth. I love you, and you love me—this is what people who love each other do. It's not a bad thing. It's not a sin."

"I know sex is not a bad thing. It's special, and it's supposed to be between a husband and wife."

Ryan snorted and rolled his eyes. "Yeah, according to a bunch of crotchety old priests who've never had any. Not everything the Church says is true, you know, Beth. Sometimes you just gotta think for yourself."

The blood rushed to her face, the hurt, embarrassment, and anger hitting her all at the same time. "I'm sorry if you don't agree, but it's what I believe." She was having a hard time keeping her voice steady, and she certainly didn't want him to see her cry.

Ryan stopped pacing and sat down next to her again, taking her hands in his. "Can't you see how it makes me feel, you constantly saying no? It's like you don't really love me, even though you say you do."

She could feel her heart pounding faster and took a deep breath in a vain attempt to calm herself.

"If you don't want me to say no, Ryan, then stop asking me. You've known the answer all along, and it's not going to change. I don't want to have sex before I'm married." Hearing how harsh her words sounded, even to her own ears, she softened her tone. "Look, it's nothing against you. I love you, and if we ever get married, we'll have the rest of our lives to do those things."

"But I want you now. God, Beth, it's been a year. I'm about ready to burst waiting for you."

She stood up, her hands forming fists at her side as any sympathy she had for him was replaced with anger. "I'm sorry to cause you so much suffering, Ryan. Maybe you'd feel better if I just left."

She turned on her heel and managed to take a few steps toward the front door before Ryan caught hold of her arm. "Beth, wait, just wait."

Shaking off his grip, she turned to face him. She could feel pressure building behind her eyes. She knew the tears would come. No matter what her emotion— fear, anger, pain, happiness—her body's first reaction was to cry, and she hated that about herself. Beth's anger doubled, and she focused on that, willing the tears not to fall. At least not yet.

"I never hid my beliefs from you, Ryan. And it's just not fair of you to keep pushing me like this. It's not fair, and it's not right, and I'm tired of it. I don't want to worry every time I come over about how I'm going to say no to you. I just want to enjoy being with you, without being scared of you."

"Is that what this is about, Beth? Are you scared of it? It's nothing to be scared of. I'll take care of you, I promise. You mean so much to me—"

"No," she cut him off. "That's not what I meant. I just don't want to do it. I don't want to have sex. If I'm crazy, then I'm crazy. But I don't want to have sex with you or with anyone right now. And I'm sorry if your ego can't handle that."

Leaving him standing there slack-jawed, Beth grabbed her cell phone off the coffee table and stormed to the closet by the front door, where she hurriedly slipped into her coat and grabbed her scarf off the hanger.

"Thanks for dinner," she threw over her shoulder as she opened the door and escaped into the cold night.

As she dashed hastily down the stairs and to her car, trying not to slip on the ice, the hot tears she had been holding in started to fall. She inhaled the frigid air, wrapped the scarf around her neck, then brushed away the tears with the back of her hand.

Approaching her car, Beth dug both hands into her coat pockets, looking for her gloves and her keys. It was then that she realized what she had just done.

"Oh, crap." Standing in front of her car door, she remembered that the keys she was looking for were in her purse—the purse that was still sitting on the counter in Ryan's kitchen. And the last thing she wanted to do was to go back for them.

Taking a quick look at Ryan's front door and

seeing that it was still closed, she decided she would just walk home. Her upstairs neighbor had a spare key she could use to get into her place, and she could call Ryan tomorrow, after they had both cooled down, to get her purse back. Everything would work out in the end, she knew that. But she just didn't want to face him again tonight.

Adjusting her scarf so that it covered her ears and pulling on her gloves, Beth trudged up the slushy sidewalk toward campus. It would take her five minutes to get to the lab, then another thirty to go across campus to her apartment. And it was really freezing out tonight.

Thanks a lot, Ryan.

The sound of her boots crunching against the salt that was generously sprinkled on the sidewalk seemed loud against the quiet of the evening, even through the scarf. One block over, where the clubs and restaurants of College Avenue were located, she could hear the dull repetition of a bass keeping time to her footsteps. The sound of people having fun made her sadder, somehow.

Tears welled up behind her frozen eyelids again, and she told herself to stop. The way the evening had ended was not her fault. She had told Ryan on their first date that she was a virgin and did not believe in premarital sex. He had said that he admired her conviction, that her views were refreshing. Had he been lying to her then, or was he just tired of waiting around? What did he think, that she would change her mind?

Yes, that was exactly what Ryan thought, she realized. And that she couldn't think for herself. How could he have said that to her? Did he really believe that? Did he really think she didn't have a mind of her own? And if that was what he really thought, then why would he want to be with her in the first place?

Annoyed and emotionally exhausted, she swiped at the new tears rolling down her face as she left the revelry of Collegetown behind and turned right to continue walking toward the Engineering Quad. As she was about to turn again to get on East Avenue, she thought she heard footsteps coming up beside her. She turned to see who was in such a rush to get past her and nearly had a heart attack at the dark eyes looking back at her.

Chapter Four

"It's a bit chilly tonight, isn't it…Beth?"

Beth's head went numb for a moment and her heart raced as she stood there staring at the gorgeous specimen of a man she had met just the night before. His lips were curved in an enticing smile, but his gaze still sent shivers up her spine. The instinct to flee was not as strong seeing him tonight as it had been the night before and, taking a quick look around and seeing that they were on a well-lit street with students still wandering back and forth between the two ends of campus, Beth swallowed her fear and managed to speak.

"Thomas?"

"You remember me." His low voice was almost as irresistible as his smile.

"Of course, I remember you." There was nothing about the events of the previous night she would ever forget. "Where did you come from? I mean, I didn't realize you were right behind me."

Thomas started walking, and Beth found herself walking beside him.

"I saw you go by as I was coming out of Little Poe's, and I've been trying to catch up with you ever since. You're a fast walker."

Beth put her hands in her coat pockets and looked straight ahead. The cold remnant of a tear streaked down her cheek, but she didn't want to call attention to it by wiping it away. "I'm sorry, I didn't realize that. I guess I was a bit distracted."

"I can see that. More car problems?"

She heard the amusement in his voice, and when she looked over at him, he was indeed smiling. It was not a rude or sarcastic smile, by any means, but at the same time there was no kindness behind it. Rather, it was the proud smile of someone who knew a secret he would never tell.

"No," she answered, looking away again. "Something a little different."

"I see. Anything I can help you with?"

At that question, Beth stopped abruptly and turned to face him. "What do you mean?"

As she stood there, looking up at Thomas, his magnificent appearance struck her again. A bit taller than her five feet four inches, he was easily six feet tall. His dark hair was on the long side of clean-cut, and the cold wind had made it just messy enough to look incredibly sexy. His nose was straight and perfectly placed on his strong, masculine face, and his eyes were a beautiful dark brown. Perhaps it was his dark lashes and eyebrows, or perhaps something else, but Beth couldn't help feeling that there was something ominous behind those eyes. It was almost as if his eyes held a warning, even while his mouth invited her to draw closer.

Before Beth realized she was staring at Thomas' mouth, his lips parted and he spoke again. "Well, I don't mean to brag, but damsels in distress are my specialty."

Blinking free of her trance, she shook her head.

"Well, I'm not a damsel. In distress, I mean. I don't need your help."

He pressed his lips together and nodded slowly. "I understand. In that case, perhaps you can help me instead."

"Me help you? With what?"

He smiled smugly again. "I'm thirsty." He paused, almost long enough to allow her to speak, before continuing. "Come have a drink with me."

She could feel her eyes grow wide with shock even as she told herself to act casual.

"I'm not a big drinker." At least her voice sounded calm, even if her hands were fidgeting inside her coat pockets.

"Coffee then?"

"I don't drink coffee after four o'clock. It would keep me awake all night." She realized as the words left her mouth how much like an old lady she sounded. Lin was right—she may as well have told the guy that she had to get home to soak her dentures.

Though her responses should have completely put him off from pursuing any further interaction, Thomas simply replied, "Then how about some chamomile tea? I've read that'll help calm your nerves and get you in the right mindset for bed."

The way the man said "bed" sent Beth's heart racing, and she couldn't help but wonder if the innuendo was intentional.

"Maybe some other time," she managed to utter.

He took a step closer to her, and her breath caught.

"I will remember you said that." His voice was seductively low, his face deliciously close to hers. She swallowed hard.

"I take it you're on your way home," he continued, seemingly unaffected by her multiple rejections as he resumed walking. Without a conscious decision to do so, Beth fell into step with him again.

"Do you live on North Campus?" he asked, tilting his head in her direction.

"Yes." It was all she could manage to say.

Suddenly feeling too warm, Beth tugged at her scarf to loosen it. The cold air on her neck calmed her, and she focused for a moment on just breathing in and out to the rhythm of their footsteps.

Feeling more collected, Beth looked over at Thomas and found a thoughtful smile lingering on his lips.

Unable to formulate a coherent thought while looking at his handsome face, she shifted her gaze to the path ahead once more. "Do you also live on North Campus?"

"No," he replied, without elaborating.

"Are you going to visit someone you know up there?"

"Not unless she invites me in." She could hear the grin in his voice.

"Rest assured, she is not going to invite you in," Beth countered.

"What a pity."

She couldn't resist looking at him then and chuckled as his lips came together in a feigned pout.

"I have a boyfriend." Beth tried to sound nonchalant with her statement. After all, she did not want to seem presumptuous, and she certainly didn't think a guy as good-looking as Thomas would be on the market for an overly-conservative wet blanket like her.

But at the same time, she wanted Thomas to know that she was not interested, or at least that she knew she shouldn't be.

"That doesn't surprise me," he answered, his voice betraying no disappointment or, for that matter, any other feeling whatsoever. "Pretty girls usually have boyfriends. And their boyfriends are usually assholes. Present company excluded, I'm sure."

Wanting to change the subject, Beth asked, "Are you a student here at Freeman?"

"Not in the traditional sense. I'm more of a…visiting researcher."

Beth raised her eyebrows in interest.

"A researcher? What are you studying?"

He gave a long sigh in response, as though trying to assess how to dumb down his field of research so that she could understand it. "You can think of it as a mixture of hematology and human psychology."

"Really? That sounds interesting. Is that through the School of Medicine?"

"Well, it's somewhat of an independent study kind of set-up."

If he was trying to be mysterious, he was doing a pretty good job of it.

"Where are you from?" She looked up to see how he would react to her question, but again, the handsome face betrayed no emotion.

"Boston originally. But my…research has taken me to many places. Though I confess I consider the Northeast my home. I always find myself back here, sooner or later."

"It's this beautiful weather that keeps you coming back for more, I'm sure."

Thomas recognized her sarcasm and smiled. "Yes, something like that."

"Do you have family still in Boston? Do you get back there often?"

The smile evaporated, and his voice took on a more serious tone. "No and no."

She hadn't meant to hit a nerve, and the only thing she could think of to do in the few seconds of awkward silence that ensued was to apologize. Before she could say the words, though, he spoke again, more gently this time.

"I only mean that I have no family left in Boston, and though I enjoy being in this part of the country, I have never gone back to Boston, and I don't believe I ever will."

Beth nodded, searching for the right words. "I think it's like that sometimes with the places we grew up. They are wonderful to think about, but when we experience them again as adults, the reality of those places dims the fondness of the memories somewhat."

"Yes, I suppose that's it exactly." Thomas took a deep breath, almost as though he were relaxing back into his former state of effortless confidence. "But what about you? What brings you to this fine institution of higher learning?"

She could feel him looking at her intently, and she kept her eyes glued to the sidewalk as a result.

"I'm in the Engineering School, majoring in Mechanical Engineering. It's my last semester, actually."

"An engineer. I wouldn't have guessed that."

Beth rolled her eyes at the typical male response, even though she knew he couldn't see her do so. "Why do you say that? Because I'm a girl?"

Thomas laughed. "No. Because you are a feelings person. You have empathy, sympathy, kindness. You make decisions with your heart, not your mind. And I've always thought of engineers as pretty, well, logical and thought-centered people."

They had come to a crosswalk, beyond which lay the bridge to North Campus. Thomas' arm brushed her shoulder innocently as they stopped to wait for the light to turn, and even through her puffy coat, the contact sent an excited shiver up Beth's spine. Instead of giving back her personal space, however, Thomas continued to stand close to her. His nearness conveyed a familiarity they did not share, but she could not bring herself to rebuke him or to step away. In fact, she found herself craving more of the closeness.

"You don't know me," she replied, willing herself to continue the conversation so that she could focus on something other than the man's physical presence. "How can you say that I am any of those things? I could be a cold, self-centered, heartless person, for all you know."

"You are none of those things. I've been studying humans for a long time." Thomas gestured toward the pedestrian signal, which had just turned to Walk. "And it only takes a few minutes to figure out what type of person someone is."

"Tell me then." They stepped up onto the sidewalk on the other side and began walking across the bridge that stretched over the gorge between Central Campus and North Campus. "Tell me how you know me."

The salt sprinkled on the sidewalk crunched underfoot as they took a few steps in silence. "First," he said, holding up a gloved hand for emphasis, "there is your behavior last night. You were under the impression that you had struck something, possibly someone, and you were trembling in fear at the notion that you might have caused another living being to suffer."

"That's hardly an indication of anything other than human nature," she countered. "No one really wants to hurt anyone else."

"The fact that you think so only proves my point. You have a kind heart."

Beth raised her eyebrows in protest, then allowed herself to smile slightly. "All right, go on."

"Second, you had tears in your eyes when I came upon you this evening. You have been thinking about something, something that has been troubling you, and you are struggling with what to do about it. You know how you feel, what you ought to do—that isn't the problem. The problem is that if you do what it is you know you must, another person's feelings will be deeply hurt. Empathy and sympathy—the two worst enemies of decisive action."

Beth shot him a defensive glare, which she then immediately regretted because it only proved that he was right in his assessment of her. She took a moment to regroup. "Shouldn't we consider how our actions will make others feel?"

His lips curled in self-satisfaction. "What is this problem that weighs on your mind?"

Beth had not told her best friend about what had been going on with Ryan. She hadn't told her mother or her brothers or her closest cousin. She hadn't really wanted to. Why then did she suddenly feel the urge to tell this stranger how she dreaded seeing her boyfriend because she knew what would happen when they kissed? She wanted to tell him how stressful it had been, that she didn't know how she could continue this way, and that she knew it would only get worse.

She turned away from Thomas and looked ahead at the silhouette of the bare tree branches against the moonlit sky. "It's personal."

He did not press and seemed content to walk in silence as they turned down her street, where they had met just the night before. In a few minutes, Thomas would know where she lived. Beth tried to remember how scared of him she had been then, and even earlier that night. But now, relishing in his closeness and his seeming concern for her wellbeing, she wondered what she had found so threatening.

"I know one other thing about you from our brief time together," he said without warning, his silky-smooth voice causing her to turn and look at him as they stood at the foot of her driveway under a streetlamp. His brown eyes shone warm with a compassion she had not seen there before, and as he opened his mouth to speak, she thought of how soft his lips looked and her cheeks grew warm, despite the cold breeze.

"You like to do the right thing, and you usually do."

With that, he bowed his head slightly to her, then turned to walk back the way they had come.

****

Thomas knew she was watching him walk away, and he smiled to himself. Beth was no longer afraid of him, and he would even go so far as to say that she had enjoyed their little walk. She had felt safe with him, and she had wanted to tell him about her troubles. At one point, he had thought she would, but she had held back.

Hours later, after a little snack behind the all-girls' dormitory, Thomas lay on his makeshift bed in the basement of the Admissions building awaiting the sunrise and thinking of the pretty, brown-haired Beth. He remembered the glistening cheeks, wet with tears that she proudly refused to wipe in his presence as they walked back to her apartment from Central Campus. He recalled her innocent stare when he had so correctly assessed her personality, those full lips parted as she tried to discern whether the tingly exhilaration she experienced in his presence was fear or something else entirely.

Everything Thomas had surmised about the girl had been spot on. Beth was pure and good. Uncorrupted and incorruptible. Well, perhaps not incorruptible. Thomas would see to that.

He stretched out and turned over to one side, trying to relax despite the restless excitement that was building inside him. She would be a challenge, Beth. He could have her whenever he chose, of course, but that would be no fun. He wanted her to come to him, and she would. It would take time, but the reward would be well worth the wait.

And in the meantime, he would have the pleasure of pursuing her, wooing her into his arms and into his bed, where he would first have her flesh, then her blood.

Yes, there was nothing quite as thrilling as the anticipation of a hunt and the feast that came afterwards. He had not felt such excitement in a long while. And it felt good.

Chapter Five

Thomas knew he was dreaming. He was back in his mortal body, and his surroundings seemed vaguely familiar. He had been in this small sitting room before. The midday sun shone bright through the window to his right, making the room stiflingly warm, and as Thomas looked around, he remembered the cream-colored walls that contrasted with the dark walnut chairs and the red velvet cushions. Mesmerized for a moment, he stared at the brass lighting fixture suspended from the high ceiling in the middle of the room and followed each arm that extended gracefully upwards from the unlit petaled glass center.

The tentative brush of a hand on his arm caused him to turn toward a young woman who was sitting beside him, smiling encouragingly.

"Thomas?" She had a sweet smile, and her dress, though plain blue in color, had a tightly-fitted bodice with buttons that trailed down from the high collar between her ample endowments.

"Yes, Edith?" he heard himself reply.

"You were about to tell me something. Mother will be back in a moment with Father. Please, tell me?"

Her blue eyes were wide and expectant now, but Thomas knew that what he was about to tell her would fill them with bitter tears.

Edith leaned in closer, her flaxen curls catching the

sunlight coming in through the window and reflecting it in the most becoming way, and Thomas breathed in the scent of lavender.

She wanted Thomas to kiss her—he knew that. But he could not allow himself to satisfy her wish now, only to break her heart with his next breath. It would be a cruel deception.

Even as he was about to tell Edith of his decision, the sight of her, her nearness, caused Thomas to hesitate. He had wanted to be the man she thought he was. He had tried. Day and night, Thomas had prayed that he was mistaken about his calling, that he could find contentment in being a husband and father, like most of the men he knew. But with each step he took in her direction, he sensed the Lord pulling him in another. To ignore it would be to deny who he was, who he was meant to be. Yet even as he sat there, the words about to leave his lips, Thomas prayed again.

At the sound of approaching footsteps, Edith pulled away to create a more proper distance between them, and his mouth grew dry. The time had come.

"Thomas, how good of you to come see us in the middle of the day. We did not expect you until the dinner hour. Your parents are well, I hope?"

Edith's father was short and round, with a ridiculously full head of dark, curly hair that was only just starting to gray around his ears. He was a jovial man who found humor in every situation, and Thomas wondered how the man would manage to find mirth in the message he was about to deliver.

"My parents are well, thank you, Mr. Winthrop. They send their regards."

"I hope you conveyed our thanks to your mother

for the beautiful flowers she sent over the other day from your garden," added Mrs. Winthrop, taking a seat next to her husband, adjacent to where Thomas and Edith sat. The matron was built like Edith, with a narrow waist that looked even narrower in comparison to her chest. "I simply cannot understand how she can grow such beautiful roses when I have the same soil in my garden but can't coax my rose bushes to bloom as large or with as rich a color."

"Thank you, Mrs. Winthrop. You are too kind."

With the pleasantries behind them, three sets of eyes looked expectantly in his direction, and Thomas now prayed for the strength to say what he must.

"Mr. and Mrs. Winthrop, Edith," he began, taking in a deep breath, "I have come here to share some news that I do not believe you are expecting to hear."

Edith's growing smile made him regret his choice of words, but he forged ahead.

"I have been thinking deeply about my future, not just recently, but for the past few years, and as much as I have tried to deny it, I can only come to one conclusion. I am called by God to be a priest to His people, and I will be joining the brothers at St. John's when the new semester starts next month."

The color immediately left Edith's face, making it paler than her hair, and for a moment Thomas thought she might faint. Her mother put a hand to her mouth and gasped, but then remembered her manners and smiled blankly at him, unable to do much else.

"You are joining the seminary, then? You have decided?" Mr. Winthrop, for the first time that Thomas could remember, wore a serious expression.

"Yes, sir, I will be a seminarian, with the hope of

59

one day receiving Holy Orders. I am so sorry this was not what you expected to hear from me today," Thomas continued, turning slightly to address Edith, whose eyes were starting to glisten. "If you only knew how much I've prayed that I was mistaken about my call…"

"Young man," Mr. Winthrop spoke again, "it is a blessing to be called to the priesthood. Do not apologize for it. It is true that this was not what we were expecting. But," —at this he stood, extending his hand— "it is likewise a blessing for us to know such a man."

Thomas rose slowly and shook the hand of the Edith's father, thankful for his gracious response.

"Please give our congratulations to your family," Mr. Winthrop continued, still shaking Thomas' hand. "They must be very proud to have raised a son who is worthy to be called to this vocation. Please remember to keep us in your prayers, young man, and be assured that you will be in ours."

"Thank you, Mr. Winthrop. Thank you." Thomas could think of nothing else to say.

Looking over at Edith one last time, he saw a tear streak her cheek as she stared at the ceiling. His heart broke for her.

Taking her hand in his and raising it to his lips, he kissed it reverently, then, nodding his farewell to the still-seated Mrs. Winthrop, quickly left the room. As he made it to the end of the hall and reached for the door handle to let himself out, he could hear Edith sobbing as her father told her to take heart.

Sighing deeply, Thomas opened the door and stepped out into the bright sunshine.

****

Thomas awoke to the falling of night, as he did every evening, but on this occasion his whole body buzzed with an instinctive awareness.

Jumping to his feet, his lips curled back in a defensive posture to bare perfectly white teeth as he listened for an intruder. Even with his heightened sense of hearing, however, the only sounds passing through the brick walls around him were the hum of a car and the dull voices of two male students who were passing by outside.

He was alone.

As his body relaxed, Thomas remembered having had this sensation before. It had been so long ago, he doubted his own memory of it, but even as he paced the cement floor in the dark, dank basement, shaking off the last of it, he knew he was not mistaken. This prickly sensation in his limbs was his body's reaction to waking from a nightmare. It was a feeling from his mortal life.

Suddenly longing to be outside without a ceiling and four walls to confine him, Thomas pushed through the hidden door he used to get into and out of his lair and, emerging on the other side, breathed in the cold night air. Physiologically, breathing was a pointless exercise—he needed no oxygen to fill his lungs. But still, the rhythmic nature of the act gave him peace of mind.

That was twice now that he had been assaulted with memories of his past life. No, he corrected himself—they were more than memories, more than dreams. They were lucid visions, vivid reenactments in which sight, smell, sound, taste, and touch were intact. Not only did Thomas experience those scenes with his senses, but he'd also relived the emotions. He had *felt* as he had when he'd been a mortal man. With Edith, he had been torn between his calling and his nature. He regretted disappointing her, mourned the loss of the life he could have had as her husband, but at the same time he'd known in the core of his being that he had no choice but to follow his heart. Even now, fully awake and walking briskly in the direction of the bars, the sounds of the poor girl's sobbing filled his ears, and his heart ached with sympathy for her.

Thomas stopped dead in his tracks. Since when had his cold, dead heart ached with anything, let alone *sympathy*?

He shook his head, trying to clear his thoughts, and then began walking again. There was nothing wrong with him; he was fine. Just a little out of sorts. It had started when he had met that girl, Beth, hadn't it? Yes, that was it. In all his efforts to appeal to the innocent engineering student's good nature, Thomas had awakened something in himself that he neither needed nor wanted. It hardly qualified as a concern. He would simply push it back inside himself, where it belonged, and he would be fine.

For now, Thomas needed to feed. A good lay probably wouldn't hurt, either.

****

Between Beth's afternoon lab and Ryan's law review meeting, it wasn't until after dinner on Monday that Beth could meet up with him to get her purse. They had exchanged a number of texts throughout the day to arrange their meeting, all of which were very ordinary in tone and avoided any mention of what had transpired the night before.

Still, as the day wore on, Beth grew more and more anxious at the thought of having to face her boyfriend. She had spent all night lying awake thinking about their relationship and where it was going, only to come to one conclusion. Beth had to break up with him. It was impossible for her to continue going out with him when the thought of being alone together filled her with dread. Did she love Ryan? Yes. Was Ryan the right person for her? Did he bring out the best in her? No.

As Beth walked briskly from the dining hall across the street from the Engineering quad toward Ryan's apartment, wrapped up like a mummy against the biting cold, however, she started having second thoughts about the decision.

She had never had to break up with anyone before. The only other boyfriend she'd had, sophomore year, had broken up with her because "she wasn't fun." Though she had hated the feeling of being rejected then, she hated the prospect of doing that to someone—someone she cared a lot about—a hundred times more.

Part of her thought maybe Ryan had avoided mentioning their fight over text because he didn't think he had behaved wrongly. Perhaps he was planning on breaking up with her. As she walked up to his front door, Beth fervently hoped that was the case.

Ryan opened the door before Beth's finger reached the doorbell.

"I'm sorry you had to walk all the way here," said Ryan, pulling her inside and shutting the door quickly behind her. "I would have brought your purse to the lab, but I figured you had to come get your car, anyway."

"Don't worry about it, it's fine."

They stood there in the small foyer looking at each

other for a few seconds before Ryan spoke again.

"Do you have time to stay and talk, or do you need to get going?"

Beth spotted her purse on the edge of the dining room table, just a few steps away, and considered grabbing it and escaping with the excuse that she had some problem sets left to work on, which was true. She could always break up with him tomorrow.

As she looked into Ryan's big, innocent-looking eyes, Beth's resolve began to fade even more, and she realized that if she didn't break up with him now, she would have no will to do it the next day or the day after that.

"I can stay for a few minutes," she replied, unzipping her coat. "We should probably talk."

Ryan nodded and took the coat from her, throwing it on the back of a chair, near her purse.

He took Beth's hand and led her to the couch where they had watched the basketball game just the night before, and she remembered the look in his eyes as he had kissed and touched her.

Slowly, she sat down, leaving some distance between them, and placed her hands in her lap. She had come up with a way to ease into the break-up as she stood in line at the dining hall an hour ago, but she could not for the life of her now remember what she had wanted to say.

Taking a deep breath, she was about to recite the speech she had composed when Ryan spoke instead.

"Beth, I know what you must be thinking."

Beth blinked in surprise. "You do?"

"Yes." Ryan inched closer to her and took her hands in his own. "You're thinking I'm a horny, selfish bastard who only cares about himself and has no regard for your feelings."

He looked down at her hands and rubbed them nervously with his thumbs before looking back into her eyes. "To some extent, you're right. I'm not good like you. When I'm with you, kissing you, holding you, I just want more, and all rational thought leaves me. I want you more than I've ever wanted anything. You know me, once I know what I want, I do everything I can to get it. I might have to work hard, but I'm willing to do that because it always pays off. With you, though no matter what I do, no matter how hard I work, I can't have you. And it frustrates me. It's like I'm not good enough, and I tell myself that it's just because of how you were raised and what you believe, and sitting here I know that's true. If you were anyone else, this problem wouldn't exist. We would be a real couple. I wouldn't be frustrated all the time, and you wouldn't be mad at me. We would just be together, really together. But you're not anyone else—you're you, and it's you, your goodness, that's a big part of what makes you so attractive to me."

Beth wasn't sure how to feel about her boyfriend's confession. Part of her was flattered, charmed even. But another part of her was annoyed. Did he see her as a challenge, then? Was sex with her something he could have if he only worked hard enough?

She reminded herself to open her mind and try to listen to what Ryan was saying, how he was feeling. In the end, maybe he was just hurt by what he perceived to be rejection. Feeling hurt led to people doing and saying all sorts of stupid things. She needed to give him the benefit of the doubt. And there certainly was a lot of doubt from which he could benefit.

"So, what does all that mean?" she finally asked. "What are you saying?"

Ryan sighed and looked down again. "I'm saying I'm sorry for how I've treated you. I will try to do better."

His words echoed in her head. He would *try* to do better.

Beth supposed she should have been placated by Ryan's honesty. After all, who could really know that they would *actually* do better at something? Wasn't "trying" the best anyone could reasonably do? But something about the way he said it, or maybe the way he didn't look at her when he spoke those words, made Beth shake her head slowly as she realized that *nothing was going to change*. Ryan wasn't sorry for trying to get her skirt off. He was only sorry that he hadn't succeeded—yet—and that she was mad at him for it. And not so deep down inside, Ryan still hoped she would change her mind about sleeping with him because, despite the allure of her "goodness," he resented her for making him wait.

Gently, Beth took her hands back into her own lap and looked at Ryan until his eyes raised to meet hers. Then she said what she knew had to be said. "I don't think we should see each other anymore."

Ryan stared at her, his eyes wide with shock. "What? You're breaking up with me?"

She nodded once. "I think it's for the best."

Her heart swelled with a mixture of grief, sympathy, and relief at having said the words, but at the same time, it hurt to look at him. Ryan's brow was furrowed, as though Beth had just spoken in a foreign language and he was concentrating very hard to understand what she had just said. Then he shook his head.

"I can't believe it. I can't believe you're breaking up with me. For what? Because I love you? Because I love you so much that I want to be with you?"

When he put it that way, it did seem awfully ridiculous.

Beth stood up but tried not to pace. "It's just too stressful for me, Ryan. Every time I'm with you, I'm afraid of what's going to happen. I want to kiss you, I want to hold you, but at the same time I dread it because of what might happen next, because I know you're going to want to go further and I'm going to have to say no. It's this huge thing that's always hanging over our heads. I know I'm always going to disappoint you. And I don't like that feeling!"

Her explanation sounded terrible out loud, like she was selfish and emotionless, caring more about her own peace of mind than working on their relationship, but she was just being honest. This was how she felt, and she didn't want to it to be that way anymore.

"So, you're just going to run away from it? From us?" Ryan was surprisingly calm, and, almost in response to that calmness, Beth became more agitated.

She didn't want to listen to his logical analysis. She didn't want to think about how odd she was, how out of place her beliefs were, and how old-fashioned.

Despite the fact that it would be proving him right, she turned away and took a step toward the door, but Ryan reached for her arm and stopped her progress.

"Beth." He spoke her name with such tender supplication that she could no longer hold back the tears that had begun to fill her eyes.

As she heaved a quiet sob, he turned her to face him and drew her in close, pressing her head against his shoulder and wrapping his arms around her.

"I'm sorry I can't be like everyone else," she muttered into his shirt. "I just can't do it."

He held her closer and kissed the hair on the top of her head. "You could never be like everyone else. I don't want you to be."

She relaxed into his arms and tried to quiet her sobs. The stress of their relationship had been building inside of her for too long. All the same, she wished she could have held in her tears a bit longer, just until she had gotten to her car.

When her breathing had returned to its normal rhythm, Ryan loosened his embrace, and Beth took a step back. She had no choice but to look at Ryan's handsome face, smooth and flawless except for the wrinkles that persisted between his eyebrows as he no doubt considered what he should say next.

"I'm not changing my mind," she said softly, making herself speak before he could say something that would make her take back what she'd said.

After a moment, he nodded, his hands resting on her shoulders. "Okay, Beth. If that's what you want. If that's what will make you happy. But can you promise me two things?"

"It depends on what those two things are." Beth had learned as a child never to commit to the unknown.

He chuckled quietly before answering. "First, if you feel like you've made a mistake, that we shouldn't have broken up, will you come back to me and tell me?"

It didn't seem like an unreasonable request, so she nodded. "Yes."

Ryan smiled before continuing. "Second, will you still come with me to the Barrister's Ball in three weeks? I already bought the tickets, and I don't want to take anyone except you. Even if we go as friends, that's okay with me. No pressure, no expectations. I promise."

That one she had to think about for a minute. The Barrister's Ball was a formal dance the Law School held every year at the end of February to raise money to support the local Legal Aid office. She had bought a new dress for the event when she had been home for Christmas break. It felt like such a long time ago, back when she was looking forward to the dance, before things had gotten so messed up.

"I don't know…"

Ryan raised his eyebrows ever so slightly. "Please, Beth?"

How would any jury ever decide against Ryan's client when he could look so vulnerable, so irresistible?

She let out the breath she hadn't realized she was holding in and relented.

"Okay, but we'll go as friends."

Ryan grinned as he moved in for a hug. "Thank you, Beth."

She hugged him back, confused and irritated and sad. What was she doing? Why couldn't this thing with Ryan have just worked out the way she had wanted it to? Why did it have to be so difficult, and why did neither outcome—staying together or being apart—seem right?

"I should go," she mumbled against his shoulder. He released her immediately but brought his hand to her cheek in a tender gesture.

"Okay. I'll walk you to your car."

As she drove away from Ryan's house a few minutes later, her eyes flooded with tears once more. It was over. Beth had done what she had set out to do. There was nothing to worry about now; she was alone.

She cast a quick glance outside her window as she passed by Little Poe's, and, oddly, her thoughts turned to Thomas. Was he in there tonight? Was he watching her drive by?

No, that was ridiculous.

Still, she looked in her rearview mirror and, seeing no one she recognized, wondered absurdly if she would have run into him again tonight had she been walking home instead of driving. She had to admit, it was nice talking to him the night before. The guy was incredibly handsome and charming, and he was a researcher, so he had to be smart. Talking to him had seemed easy—so much so that she had almost told him about her problem with Ryan. And now she wished she could tell him what had just happened, that she had ended her relationship.

"I have completely lost my mind," she said out loud, wiping the tears off her face with the back of her hand. She had just broken up with her boyfriend, and less than a minute later she was thinking about another guy. It was at that moment that Beth had an even crazier thought.

Had she never met Thomas, would she have just broken up with Ryan?

Chapter Six

When Beth told Lin the next day at lunch that she had broken up with Ryan, Lin seemed to take the news a lot harder than Ryan had.

"You dumped him? Why in the world would you dump a guy like that? Are you out of your mind?"

Beth took a bite of her turkey sandwich, looking down to avoid Lin's glare. Chewing thoroughly, she followed up with a couple swallows of water, knowing full well she was just stalling.

"I didn't see it going anywhere," Beth finally replied, setting down her glass. "It just wasn't going the way I had expected it to. I wasn't happy anymore."

"The guy's in love with you. Where else did you want it to go? Did you want him to propose to you or something?"

"No," Beth answered quickly. "He just isn't the right guy for me, that's all."

"Not the right guy?"

It was as though Lin's idea of moral support was to repeat the last thing Beth said in the form of a question.

"If Ryan's not the right guy for you," continued Lin, "then who the hell is?"

Without intending to, Beth recalled the way Thomas Callahan's shoulder had brushed hers as they stood waiting for the light to turn on the edge of North Campus. She thought of the warm brown eyes that seemed to see right through to who she really was, the dark, windblown hair that glistened under the streetlight, and the soft, perfect lips that were just as sexy as the silky, low voice that passed through them.

"I don't know," Beth managed to answer, her throat a little dry. She put the glass to her lips and drained the last of the water from it.

Lin shook her head. "Well, whatever. It's done now. So did you do the stupid 'we can still be friends' thing, or are you never going to see him again?"

With a sigh, Beth pressed her fingers to her temple, attempting to ease the headache that was just beginning to throb.

"I didn't say anything like that, but I did agree to go to the Barrister's Ball with him."

Lin slapped her hand down on the table, drawing glances from the three girls at the table closest to them. "That guy is so smart. He's going to make a hell of a lawyer."

Beth frowned, puzzled. "What do you mean?"

"When is the dance?" asked Lin, ignoring her question.

"Two weeks from Saturday."

Lin laughed, dimpling her round cheeks. "That's just enough time for you to miss him. He'll come pick you up, looking dashing in his tux. He'll sweep you off your feet with his compliments and his dancing. And by the end of the night, you'll be in his arms, at his mercy, begging him to take you back. Brilliant."

Beth shook her head, still frowning. "No, it's not going to be like that at all. He had already bought the tickets. I agreed to go with him so they wouldn't go to waste. I told him we would go as friends."

"Friends my ass. You'll be his girlfriend again by the time the clock strikes midnight, or I'll turn into a pumpkin."

"No," Beth repeated, her face getting warmer. "I'm not getting back together with him. Haven't you heard anything I've said? He's not the right person for me, and I'm not the right person for him."

Lin was quiet for a moment. With her head tilted to the side and her chin raised slightly, she leaned back in her chair and studied Beth, making Beth's cheeks grow even hotter.

"Why are you looking at me like that?"

"Because, now I understand what's going on here." Lin's lips curled into a matronly smile, and she folded her arms across her chest. "You've got someone else on your mind. Someone other than Ryan. Who is it?"

Looking down and seeing that the sandwich was gone and the water glass was empty, Beth panicked for a moment, at a loss for what to do to avoid answering the question outright. She hated lying—how could she say that there was no one else on her mind when clearly there was?

She decided to answer a different question instead.

"I am not interested in dating anyone else at the moment." That much was true. She wasn't about to jump into another relationship, even if the opportunity presented itself. Which it hadn't.

"Uh-huh." The grin on Lin's face was a clear indication that she wasn't buying what Beth was selling.

"Listen, you can fantasize all you want about me having a relationship with a mysterious stranger, but the only guy I'll be seeing this afternoon is my unfortunate research assistant, Adam. And if I don't leave right now to trek up to the lab, I'm going to be late for our completely unromantic rendezvous."

Beth pushed her chair away from the table and stood, picking up her tray with more clatter and clumsiness than the action warranted. "See you for breakfast tomorrow?"

Lin nodded, obviously amused at how flustered she had made her friend. "See you later, playgirl."

Smacking Lin on the arm as punishment for her insinuations, Beth made her way to the tray return area, then headed for the lab, almost at a jog after glancing at her phone and realizing how late she actually was.

Adam was waiting outside the lab when Beth arrived, simultaneously frozen, sweating, and out of breath.

"You didn't have to run on my account," said Adam in his typical nonchalant fashion as Beth dug around in her pockets for the keys to the lab. "I get credit just for being here, even if I'm not doing anything."

"I know," replied Beth, finally having found the keys and unlocking the door. "But I still feel bad making you wait."

Adam was a strange sort of guy, even by Beth's standards. Although he was a freshman, assigned to work with her as part of a program that matched freshman engineering students with seniors to allow the newbies to see if engineering was really what they wanted to do, Adam looked more like a grad student. He had unruly dark brown hair that appeared almost black and was too long for how thick and curly it was, not to mention a full-on mountain man beard. His nose was on the large side, and his eyebrows seemed to have a life of their own, moving this way and that when he talked.

Despite his awkward looks, though, Adam carried himself with grace and confidence. He was always calm and collected. He never worried about exams, as far as Beth could tell; he never worked on problem sets in between experiments; and he never asked Beth for advice on what classes to take or which professors were the most approachable. Adam just did his own thing and made life look easy, which made Beth feel like a complete mess in comparison.

That afternoon was no exception—while Beth flipped through her notebooks, trying to find the calculations she had scribbled down the night before for adjusting the experimental housing, Adam sat quietly in front of one of the computers with a clean notepad off to one side, a pencil tucked behind his ear, and his right hand on the mouse, already clicking through the previous day's results.

"It doesn't look like we're getting any closer," he announced once Beth had taken a seat at the computer next to him and logged on.

"I know." She sighed. "It doesn't matter how tight we make the stupid thing, it always moves."

Adam grunted in response.

Beth went through her half-legible calculations again. "What do you think about setting the housing to drop from only halfway up and seeing how much it moves at that height? Do you think that might help us figure out what's causing the misalignment?"

Adam pulled the pencil out from behind his ear and scratched his head with it, causing half of the writing implement to disappear into his mass of curls. "It's worth a shot, I guess."

They walked together to the experimental lab next door, which was a room with a platform set up around an opening in the floor. The opening extended down three floors, and a ladder on the edge of the platform allowed them to go down those three floors to the landing area each time they released the experimental housing, so they could upload the data, check on the components, and then reset the experiment to do the whole thing over again. As tedious as it was, Beth comforted herself each time she labored up and down the ladder by thinking of the wonders it was doing toning her glutes.

After spending a couple of hours running the experiment numerous times at different heights, they made their way back to the lab to pore over the disappointing results.

It wasn't long before Beth threw her pencil down in frustration and buried her face in her hands. "This is never going to work. I may as well just start making up numbers for my report."

"Don't worry," replied Adam, eating a granola bar and leaning back in his swivel chair. "You won't need to resort to fraud. You'll figure it out."

Beth slumped forward even more, laying her arms flat on the desk so she could rest her head on them. Maybe if she napped for the next two hours, she would receive the answer in a dream.

"Hey, Beth, I need to leave early today to pick my mom up from the airport. She's going to stay with me through the weekend. Maybe longer."

Beth lifted her head and smiled at Adam, distracted

for a moment from her experimental woes.

"That's nice that she can come for a visit."

Adam nodded. "Yeah, I guess. She's been pretty torn up about her grandmother passing away. They were very close."

Beth frowned in reproach. "Your mother's grandmother died? Your great-grandmother? When? You never told me."

He shrugged it off. "It happened just after the New Year. She was really old, just a month shy of a hundred. We knew it was coming."

"Mmmm." Beth nodded thoughtfully. "It's still hard to lose someone you love, no matter how old they are."

A few seconds of silence passed between them before Beth spoke again. "Anyway, yeah, go get your mom and don't worry about this stuff. It'll be waiting for you on Thursday, and I will most likely not have made any progress between now and then."

Adam grinned. "That's the spirit. Keep up with the positive thinking."

She punched his arm gently as punishment for his sarcasm. "Have fun with your mom."

"Oh yeah," he replied in the same sarcastic tone, putting his notepad in his backpack and heading to the door. "It's gonna be one hell of a good time."

Chapter Seven

By Friday, Beth was starting to panic. It wasn't a full-fledged "I'm doomed" feeling, but rather just a queasiness that hit her every time she thought about her experiment, how little progress she had made, and how quickly the project deadline would be upon her.

She was glad to have a distraction that night. Lin's "online friend" Tyler had come up to see her, as he said he would, and Lin had asked Beth to meet them for dessert at eight o'clock at the Bon Goût Café in Collegetown.

Beth had seen pictures of Tyler online. He was average-looking, in Beth's opinion, with straight, sandy brown hair that had been obviously highlighted falling across his forehead and over his left eye in long bangs. He wore wire-rimmed glasses in the picture and had a smirk on his face, which Beth wasn't sure how to interpret. On the one hand, Beth was predisposed to think the smile looked creepy, but Lin thought it showed an impish charm.

In a way, Lin was right—the guy did know how to turn on the charm, in his writing at least. Beth had read some of the messages he had sent to Lin, and she could definitely see why Lin was falling for him. His messages were sweet, self-deprecating, and made him seem like a good "listener." Beth was interested to see how the real Tyler compared.

She still had her doubts about the guy's intentions and half expected Lin to call her that afternoon, when he was supposed to arrive, to report that he was actually a balding forty-five-year-old man, but Lin hadn't called. She hadn't texted, either, for that matter. Beth had sent her friend a message as she sat alone in her apartment eating dinner to confirm that they were still on for dessert, but still nothing.

Nevertheless, at the appointed time Beth stood just inside the door of the cozy café, passing the minutes by looking at the floor-to-ceiling drawings of different cakes and pastries that were set against the lavender walls as she waited for Lin and Tyler to show up. Lin was never on time for anything, and tonight was no exception.

At eight-twenty, however, Beth's self-consciousness kicked in. The man behind the counter, who looked one hundred and fifty percent French, kept eyeing her suspiciously, and she wondered if the guy would call the cops and report her for loitering if she didn't buy something soon.

Ten minutes later, just as Beth was giving up on Lin, her phone buzzed. She pulled it out of her back pocket and read the message.

—*Sorry Beth. Not gonna make it. We'll all go out together tomorrow night. U can't say no.*—

Three seconds later, another message came in.

—*Tyler is amazing.*—

At least she wasn't being stood up for someone who was just mediocre.

She was about to sneak out of the place while Frenchie was busy with a customer when she heard her name.

"Beth?"

Her heart was beating recklessly fast even before she turned around to see the breathtakingly handsome Thomas come up to her.

He smiled beautifully and moved to hug her in greeting. She desperately hoped he couldn't feel her heart about to beat out of her chest as she returned the hug as briefly and platonically as humanly possible. Even still, his cheek seemed to brush hers in an innocently seductive manner.

"Hi," she managed, feeling and sounding as wooden as a marionette.

"Now I know you're not here for coffee as it is well past four o'clock. Are you waiting for someone?" His tone was innocent and interested, but there was something in the shimmer of his eyes that told her he already knew the answer to his own question.

"Yes. I mean, I *was* waiting for someone—my friend and her boyfriend—but she just texted me that they aren't coming. I was about to leave."

"How lucky for me," he said, charmingly. "Now I can swoop in and rescue you from a night of sheer boredom."

"Please, you don't have to mess up your plans for me," replied Beth too quickly. "I mean, I'm fine. Part of me is relieved I can go home and do some laundry, maybe work on some problem sets."

She could hear how lame she sounded, and yet she couldn't stop the words from coming out of her mouth.

Thomas curled his lips in an understated smile, as though to say he thought her nervous chattering was adorable.

Pushing a few stray locks of hair out of her face,

Beth tried to think of a way to extricate herself from the situation without embarrassing herself further.

"I should get going." It was the best she could come up with.

"No, you shouldn't," he replied, taking her gently by the arm and guiding her away from the door and toward the array of sweets behind the glass display where the French proprietor stood, silent and watchful. Looking up at the mustached man, Beth thought she saw his eyebrows lift in admiration of Thomas' confidence. He may have even been smiling at them, though it was hard to tell with all the hair on the man's upper lip.

Beth's gaze moved to the cheesecakes, strawberry tarts, and chocolate ganache cakes behind the glass. They were like Thomas—deliciously enticing, and most likely regrettable after the fact.

"Go ahead, pick something. I'll share it with you so you don't have to feel bad that you ate the whole thing."

"I don't know," she replied, unable to look at him, her pulse quickening even more at the thought of the two of them eating off the same plate.

"Come on," he crooned, his body moving just a little closer to hers as he shifted his weight from his right foot to his left. "It's the perfect opportunity for you to make good on your promise."

"My promise? What promise?" Beth looked up to see Thomas grinning at her suspicious tone.

"The promise you made to me when I walked you home—that you would have chamomile tea with me. You don't remember?"

He cast her a look of feigned disappointment, and

she couldn't help smiling. "I remember I said 'maybe.'"

Thomas waved off her defense. "Funny, that's not how I remember it. Now, which will it be? Cheesecake or chocolate cake?"

She looked back at the display, though she didn't need to. "Chocolate. Don't get me wrong—I like cheesecake, too. But I just can't resist chocolate."

Thomas smiled, as though he were taking a mental note of her weakness for future reference, then ordered a slice of the chocolate ganache cake and two chamomile teas. When he took out his wallet to pay, Beth put out her hand to stop him.

"No, please, you don't have to pay for mine."

He gently skirted her reach and handed a twenty to the cashier. "You can get it next time. Maybe."

Not wanting to cause a scene, Beth lowered her hand and thanked him.

Carrying her tea and the slice of cake, she followed Thomas to a two-person table by a painting of an eclair near the back wall of the café. She sat down, her whole body tight with stress and nervous excitement. Despite the high ceilings in the place and the echo of pleasant conversation around them, all Beth could hear was the sound of her heart about to beat out of her chest.

There was no reason for her to have ordered cake and tea, she thought as her fork sank into the decadent dessert in the center of the table. She put it in her mouth and couldn't help letting a sound of pure happiness escape her lips.

"Oh, this is so good," she said, forgetting her anxiety at the taste. Whether it was because of the sugar from the frosting or the caffeine from the cocoa beans, she dared to look across the table at her cool and confident companion.

Her gaze traveled from Thomas' casually perfect hair to his big brown eyes and velvety lips, and she suddenly found that she couldn't look away. It was the first time Beth had seen him in a well-lit setting, and it almost stole her breath. Part of her had been hoping to find some flaws that had been hidden by the darkness and shadows outside—a mole, pock marks from adolescent acne, stray hairs around his eyebrows— anything to ease the tightness in her stomach. Instead, she found him to be more handsome, more alluring than she remembered. And the half-smile on his face as he reviewed her features in return was enough to bring her close to a faint.

"You look very uncomfortable," he said finally, breaking the silence. "Lovely, but uncomfortable."

If the cake were not one of the most delicious desserts she had ever tasted, Beth would have put her fork down given the amount of fluttering going on in her stomach.

She was fully aware that Thomas was continuing to study her as she shoveled more cake into her mouth to avoid replying. After a few long moments, he brought his elbows to rest on the table and clasped his hands together under his chin. "So, where's your boyfriend?"

Beth almost spit out the bite she was chewing.

He unclasped his hands and picked up his cup of tea, peering over the rim at her as he brought the cup to his lips, his eyes smiling slyly as he drank.

Of all the questions he could have asked, this was by far the worst. By telling the incredibly attractive man opposite her that she was newly single, she would be opening a door she didn't even want to acknowledge was there. Still, she hated dishonesty and couldn't bring herself to tell a lie, even a little white lie.

"I don't have a boyfriend anymore. We broke up this week."

"Oh, really? What happened?"

He casually took another bite of cake.

Drawing a long sip of tea with the fervent hope that it would calm her down, Beth considered how much of the story she would need to tell Thomas to satisfy his curiosity, if indeed it was curiosity she saw in his big brown eyes and the subtle curve of his lips.

She decided to take the Freudian approach.

"Why do couples break up?"

Thomas arched his eyebrows in contemplation. "Well, I suppose usually, at your stage in life, that is, couples break up because they realize they have less in common than they thought or were willing to admit when they first started dating. Different goals, different philosophies, different outlooks. Sometimes it's intellectual incompatibility, or possibly sexual incompatibility."

Again, Beth nearly spit on Thomas. "No, no, nothing like that. I mean, we never slept together."

Thomas' smile grew victorious. "Perhaps that was the problem, then."

"What? No. It had nothing to do with sex because I don't believe in sex outside of marriage. He knew that and he respected it." *Well*, she added silently, *for the most part.*

"So, you're a virgin?"

How had it come to this so quickly?

She slowly exhaled. "Yes."

"Interesting."

Crossing her arms and leaning forward in her seat, irritation overcame her nervous anxiety. "What do you mean 'interesting'?"

He laughed. "You don't need to be defensive about it. It's just different, that's all. I like different."

Her heart pounding in her chest again, she contemplated eating the last bite of cake, just to have something to do. And because it was delicious.

"It's all yours," Thomas said, pushing the plate toward her. He seemed to have a talent for reading her mind.

Beth sighed. "Well, you seem to know all about me now. Why don't you tell me about yourself?"

He ran his fingers through his perfect hair, then put his hands on the table in front of him, palms down. "I'm really not that interesting. I'm far from a virgin."

Beth laughed out loud, the tension in her back and shoulders finally dissipating a bit. "You've been dying to tell me that, haven't you?"

Thomas laughed along with her. "You have a good sense of humor," he said, once they had both recovered.

"I like to laugh."

"You like to make people happy." He wasn't laughing now, just looking intently at her, as though he were trying to figure something out.

"I'm happiest when the people around me are happy. Isn't everyone?"

He shook his head slowly. "I could usually care less what the people around me are feeling. Does that bother you?"

"No," she replied, without a pause.

"Why not?"

"Because I don't believe you."

Her answer seemed to take him by surprise, and he drew his eyebrows together. He looked…confused. "Do you think I am a nice person?"

Beth tried to recall what she had seen in his eyes that first night they met, or, rather, what she hadn't seen. But now, looking at Thomas, the warmth in his eyes and the curve of his lips, she wasn't scared at all. Rather, she sensed—no, she knew—that he had good in him. He was by no means an open book, but that much she knew.

"I believe that you are, yes. You haven't given me any reason to think otherwise. At least, not yet."

The muscles around his mouth relaxed and his lips parted slightly, as though he didn't know what to say in response, and suddenly he seemed not as confident as he was five minutes ago.

"I hope I never give you reason to think otherwise," he said finally, looking her directly in the eyes, without a hint of teasing or laughter in his low voice.

Beth swallowed hard and looked down. The honesty in his expression was so clear, it rattled her. After all, he hardly knew her, and she hardly knew him. As she looked up at him again and found him gazing at her with that same openness, she wondered what actually unnerved her more—his desire not to disappoint her, or her complete willingness to believe him.

"The cake's all gone, and so is the tea," she said, just loud enough to break the awkward silence.

"Does that mean you have to go?"

It wasn't just the words he spoke or the way he said them. There was something about Thomas, his whole presence, which she found overwhelmingly captivating. It was the tilt of his head, the lines of his eyebrows, the way he leaned forward, just slightly, as though he wanted to be closer to her. It was more than any mere mortal woman could be expected to handle.

"Yes," she replied, somewhat reluctantly. Then she chuckled softly as she pushed her chair away from the table and stood. "I'll need to get a good dose of sleep tonight since I probably won't be so lucky come tomorrow night."

"Oh? Why is that?" Thomas picked her coat up off the chair and held it open for her as she put her scarf around her neck.

"Thanks," she said shyly, not used to such chivalry and trying not to think about how close he was as she stepped into her coat.

Remembering what he had just asked, she replied, "My friend, the one who stood me up tonight, she wants to me to go out with her and the guy who's visiting her from out of town, so I'll probably end up going."

"That's the boyfriend you mentioned earlier?"

Thomas pushed the door open and held it for her to pass through. She nodded and smiled at him in thanks. "Yes. His name is Tyler, and he's visiting from NYU. I've never met him before. Lin met him online, and I was worried about her meeting him in person for the first time this weekend, but I guess she likes him, so it must be going okay."

"I would say so. They were busy getting to know each other that they missed their date with you."

Beth laughed. "You make it sound so seedy. I'm sure they just lost track of time."

"I'm sure that's what it was," he replied in the

same suggestive voice, making her laugh again. "In any case, I hope I meet your friend Lin soon."

Beth looked up at him as they continued walking, a little puzzled. "Why do you want to meet her?"

He grinned, one side of his perfect mouth raising just a little more than the other. "Because I want to thank her for not showing up tonight."

****

It was almost midnight, and Adam was cold.

"You're sure you saw him go in there?" his mother asked, breaking the silence that had hung over them since she had arrived with the car to meet him ten minutes ago. They were sitting in the parked car across the street from a bar about a mile east of Collegetown. It was a place the locals frequented, as there weren't many college students who wandered this far from campus for a drink, even on the weekends. "You know you woke me up when you called," she added, throwing in a little maternal guilt trip.

Adam let out a measured breath and rubbed his hands together for warmth. "Yes, I'm sure, and yes, I know I woke you up. It was the first thing you told me when you picked up the phone and the first thing you said when I got into the car."

"Okay, just checking." She put her hands on the steering wheel, still looking toward the neon red "Open" sign that hung in the window of the seamy-looking bar. "How do you know he's in there?"

Irritated, Adam ran his fingers through his hair, then scratched his scalp through the unruly mop on his head. "Because I followed him from Collegetown and I've been staring at that door ever since."

"But how do you know it's *him*?"

"I told you," Adam replied, not trying to hide his frustration, "*he*'s the one who was talking to the redhead at the frat party and took her upstairs. I didn't actually see the marks on her neck, but she described them to me the next day, and she told me she woke up hours after her encounter with *him* in that same frat house not knowing what had happened to her or where *he* had gone—it's what you told me to look for. It's got to be him. In any case, we'll know one way or another tonight, won't we, Mom?"

"Yes, I suppose we will."

It was only a few minutes later that the dark-haired man he had followed earlier that night pushed open the door of the bar with some force and exited the establishment. He stopped briefly just outside the door to put on his black leather gloves, then turned to walk up the sidewalk toward Collegetown, away from their parked car.

"That was him," whispered Adam, just in case the gloved stranger could hear him. "Did you get a good look at him?"

"Yes," his mother replied, her tone cold and clipped.

"He looked pissed. I wonder what happened. Should I follow him?"

"No." She turned slowly to face him. "He is just as my grandmother described, just as my grandmother's mother had described to her. He hasn't changed. He can't change."

"Then what are we waiting for? Let's kill him." His mother stopped him, grabbing his wrist just as he reached behind him to the crossbow that was propped up against the back of his seat.

"I said no, Adam. We need to go in there and make sure. We need to see for ourselves. If he is what my grandmother said he is, then we will find him and eliminate him, and my grandmother's soul will rest easy, along with the soul of her mother and her mother's family. They will all find peace if we succeed."

Adam gave an impatient sigh. "Then let's go."

She nodded, and they opened their car doors almost simultaneously.

Nothing immediately struck Adam as odd upon entering the local watering hole. The place was well-packed with men and women, mostly in their thirties and up, chattering away, drinks in hand. The two bartenders behind the counter were busy making drinks for the patrons, at the same time trying to entertain the loners sitting there with no one else to talk to. Nothing strange there. The one flustered-looking server in a tight white V-neck tee shirt and even tighter black jeans was running from one table to the next to collect orders and distribute drinks, but nothing about her appeared out of the ordinary, either.

"I'm going to check the ladies' room," said his mother, tapping Adam on the shoulder to get his attention. "Why don't you check the men's room?"

He nodded, and they made their way through the crowded area to the other side, where signs with arrows indicating "Guys" and "Gals" pointed down a narrow hallway to two doors.

An older man with a long graying beard and hair tied back in a low ponytail was standing at the pisser when Adam entered the restroom. The man looked up at him, then back down to finish his business. As the man zipped himself him up and moved over to the sink to rinse his hands in a disgustingly cursory fashion, Adam pushed open each stall door and looked inside. They were all empty.

He was about to leave when the door to the restroom cracked open and he heard his mother's voice calling. "Adam, get over here. You need to see this."

Adam stepped out of the men's room and was pulled quickly into the women's room next door before any of the staff could see him.

"What are you dragging me in here fo—"

The question hung in the cold air, unfinished, as Adam's gaze landed on a woman's crumpled body propped up against the wall under the half-open window in the corner, hidden by the stalls. Rushing to her side, Adam lifted her head and pushed the bleached-blond hair away from her face to reveal the creases and early wrinkles of a woman in her mid-forties.

Her eyes rolled around beneath closed lids for a few moments as he tried to wake her, then slowly she opened them. Raising her hand to the back of her head, the woman groaned aloud.

"What happened?" she croaked, her voice thick and ragged. "Where is he?"

"Where is who?" asked Adam, already knowing the answer.

"My tall, dark, and handsome stranger," she mumbled dreamily, blinking slowly as her head dropped back against the painted white wall.

His mother took a step closer and crouched beside the woman, taking her hand. "Check her," she said to Adam, without looking away from the woman's face.

Adam brought the woman's head forward to rest

against his chest and ran his hand under the woman's hair, along the back of her neck. When he withdrew it, his fingers were covered in blood.

"So, it is true." His mother's expression revealed no emotion, but her eyes gleamed triumphantly.

The woman lifted her head off Adam's chest and looked at him. "He left without even a kiss."

Adam brushed the hair away from her face again, more tenderly this time. "You're okay. You're going to be fine."

Then, turning to his mother, he added in a quieter tone, "What should we do with her? Do you think we should take her to the hospital?"

His mother shook her head unsympathetically. "No. We can't risk alerting the authorities. Besides, she's more drunk than anything else. Her pulse is fine. I don't think she's lost much blood. Leave her there and let's go. We've got work to do."

Adam gently moved the woman off himself and leaned her up against the wall once more. "You have to take better care of yourself, ma'am. You can't trust every pretty face you see."

It wasn't clear from the blank stare and unblinking eyes whether she had heard Adam, let alone understood, but there was nothing more he could do for her. He stood up and followed his mother out of the bathroom and back outside to the car. She tossed him the keys.

"Don't you think it's strange that he didn't hardly drink from her?" asked his mother as Adam pulled away from the curb. "It's not like him—not from what my grandmother told me, and not from what that girl told you."

"That's not my main concern right now."

Adam could see her turn to look at him out of the corner of his eye as he made a quick right to take the road that led to his apartment building.

"What is your main concern, then?"

He took a deep breath. "When I spotted him, earlier tonight in Collegetown, he was with the senior I help out at the lab, Beth."

"Did he hurt her?"

Adam shook his head. "No. He walked her to the bus stop and waited with her for the bus to arrive. Then, when she had gotten on, he left and headed to the bar we were just at."

"So, he didn't do anything to her?" His mother sounded just as baffled as he was.

"Nothing. They were just talking."

"That bastard is up to something. Something bad. We have to find him and destroy him. He's had his way for too long."

"Mom?" They had just turned into the parking lot for his apartment complex, and he pulled into the first empty spot and shut off the engine.

"What is it?"

Adam looked at her. "We can't let him hurt Beth. She's a good person, a genuinely kind, good person. He can't have her."

With a reassuring maternal affection Adam wasn't used to, his mother put her hand on his shoulder and gave it a squeeze. "Don't worry, Hon. We know what this evil looks like now, seen it with our own eyes. We have the advantage. His time has finally run out."

Chapter Eight

Sleep had done nothing to improve Thomas' mood. He rose the next evening just as agitated and annoyed as he when he went to sleep that morning, possibly more so. In addition to being painfully thirsty as a result of the previous evening's unexpected hesitation, he'd had another memory—a memory of his first day at the seminary.

Damn these visions. He dressed for the evening in the dim light of a single bulb that hung from the low ceiling of the basement he slept in. It wasn't just the people who lingered in his mind long after he had awakened—Brother Simon with his hearty laugh, Brother Ian ever ready with a word of encouragement, and even Father Joshua, whose long-winded and circuitous sermon at their first Mass foretold of countless similar sermons to come. No, it was the *feelings*, the real emotions that he had not felt in his cold, dead heart since the day he had turned. The anxiety of meeting new people as the students gathered for Mass that first morning. The excitement of starting something new mingled with the sadness of realizing that nothing would be the same for him again.

At least when he was in the midst of one of these visions, he could handle the emotions. He was human then, after all. But in the evening, when he woke, he did not have the capacity to deal with the sentiments that were stirring within him. He was simply not equipped for it.

Thomas was, after all, a vampire, not a human being—a selfish creature, made for one thing and one thing only. He was driven by thirst and designed solely for the purpose of quenching that thirst. He was attractive to lure his prey; strong to secure his victim and take the blood he needed; quick and graceful to make a clean escape; immortal, more or less, to avoid the fires of hell that otherwise awaited him. That was it. That was all there was to him. All the rest—the playful banter, the seduction, the sex—it was merely recreation, crafted purely for his own enjoyment to distract him from the realization of his soulless depravity.

Feelings were quite contrary to Thomas' very nature, and yet here he was, Brother Simon's laughter still ringing in his ears, nervous energy coursing through his body.

Thomas set out into the night to find the one thing that could calm him, the one person whose company made him just a little more able to manage the havoc of the now daily reminders of his human life. It mattered not that he had just seen her last night or that they had not made plans for this evening. Thomas didn't care what Beth would think when he found her again tonight. All that mattered was being with her until he could figure out what the hell was happening to him.

She had told him she was going out tonight with her friend and her friend's boyfriend, who was visiting from out of town. That meant that Thomas would most likely find them at one of two places: Little Poe's or the Good Vibes Lounge. The Lounge was a bit more up-scale, with three large rooms playing different types of music, more attractive servers, and more expensive drinks. It would have been his choice for entertaining someone who was visiting for the weekend. That's where he would start, but first he needed to feed.

As he walked, he remembered with disgust his attempt to drink from the woman he took into the restroom at Sal's, just outside Collegetown. She had been drunk, of course, and had approached him from across the room with no pretense as to what she wanted from him. She hadn't even checked to see if the restroom was empty before pushing him up against the wall and attempting to unzip his pants.

Unable to play along for even a minute or two, Thomas had swiftly turned, his hands gripping her upper arms so that her back was against the wall. Her lips had curved upward in a lustful grin, and she had begun to undo the buttons of her shirt so that he could see the swell of her breasts framed in silk and lace.

Objectively, despite her forty-some years, every one of which showed in the lines of her painted face, she was an attractive woman, and she had a fine figure that should have easily tempted his senses. But he could not bring himself to touch her. With some effort, he had moved her head sideways and bitten the back of her neck. The blood was good, and he could have lost himself in the feeding after a moment or two, but then the woman grabbed him between the legs in an attempt to arouse him, and the blood spell was broken. Repulsed and angry, he had stepped back abruptly from her after only two mouthfuls and, with her sad and longing eyes watching him, he had made his retreat.

That could not happen tonight. Thomas had to have blood. He could not risk seeing Beth in this state, or it would end very badly for them both.

It was too early in the evening to find an intoxicated college student to meet his needs, so he decided to go downtown to the bus station, where the homeless population tended to gather to pass the night. His concern due to the previous night's inability to drink properly from his victim quickly evaporated when he found a man talking to himself in a dark alley behind the station. Thomas was almost unable to stop himself from sucking the man dry. But just as the man passed out in his arms, Thomas reluctantly pulled his blood-stained lips from the man's neck and set him down, pulling a nearby sleeping bag over him.

Licking his lips, Thomas smiled. There was nothing like a full belly to right the mind.

The Good Vibes Lounge was about two blocks from where Thomas had shared dessert with Beth the previous night. As he approached, he noticed a line was forming outside the door to the establishment. At least twenty eager-looking young men and women waited to get inside. More importantly, a brown-haired beauty donning that same bulky blue coat he had grown quite fond of, with a blue and gray striped scarf wound about her pretty neck, bobbed up and down to keep warm.

Next to her, a cute Asian girl, who Thomas assumed was Lin, hung onto the bent arm of her dour-looking boyfriend chattering away, not at all perturbed by the cold. In stark contrast to Beth's coat, scarf, jeans, and suede booties, Lin wore a half-zipped dark brown leather jacket that revealed a black sequined top underneath, and her legs were bare from just above the knee, where her tight black skirt ended, all the way down to her sandaled feet. It was as though one girl were standing in line to party at a nightclub in Miami and the other to volunteer at a soup kitchen in Detroit.

And there was no question in his mind that he would rather be the hungry man in Detroit than the partygoer in Miami.

Turning his eyes to the boyfriend, with his dark, artificially highlighted hair slicked back and over to one side, Thomas' lips curled in a sneer. It was obvious the guy was only listening to every third word his bubbly girlfriend was saying, at best, and from the way he kept his hands in his pockets with one knee bent and one hip cocked, Thomas could tell the guy was scanning the crowd for a pretty face to distract him.

Asshole.

"Thomas?"

He was still across the street when Beth called out to him, surprise clearly written on her face, but punctuated with an upturned smile that indicated his arrival was welcome.

"It's so weird to see you here, after running into you last night," she added as he stepped up onto the curb and came to stand beside her.

He smiled and for a moment forgot how to speak. Beth's eyes looked bigger and more gorgeous than he remembered, with dark blue eyeshadow on her lids, black eyeliner, and mascara accentuating her natural beauty. Her cheeks were rosy from the cold breeze that kept gusting past, and her inviting lips were pink and shiny from the lip gloss she wore.

"Hi," said Thomas, finally, trying not to grin too widely. He resisted the urge to kiss her cheek, remembering how embarrassed she had been the previous evening when he had hugged her.

"This is my friend Lin who I was telling you about." The Asian girl, beaming and bouncing her head from side to side, waved at him in greeting. "And this is her friend Tyler who's visiting from NYU."

He noticed that she didn't introduce him as Lin's boyfriend tonight and wondered whether she had developed the same distaste for the guy that he had.

Tyler took his hand out of his pocket and leaned in to shake hands with Thomas. "How's it going, man?"

Thomas had no choice but to meet him in the gesture, as unpleasant as it was.

Beth smiled as she looked at Thomas, rewarding him for his sacrifice.

"This is perfect," Lin chimed in, releasing Tyler's arm for a moment so she could grab hold of Beth's. "Thomas, why don't you come inside with us and hang out for a while? That way, I don't have to keep a constant watch on this one as she tries to escape."

Although he wouldn't have thought it possible, considering how pink her cheeks already were, Beth blushed.

"Are you on your way somewhere? I mean, do you have somewhere you have to be?" continued Lin, determinedly.

"No, not particularly." Thomas was torn by the desire to move the windblown hair off Beth's flushed cheek and the urge to pull her into a long, torrid kiss. Unfortunately, he could do neither. Yet. Instead, he looked directly into Beth's eyes and asked in a softer voice, "Do you mind if I crash your party?"

"No, of course not," she uttered, her voice almost a whisper. Clearing her throat, she turned to Lin. "Now you don't have to worry about me being the third wheel."

Lin laughed as the line finally began to move, and in a few minutes they had stepped into the warm foyer just inside the front doors, where the electronic sound of techno music coming from the dance floor hit their ears at an almost deafening level. Following Lin and her boyfriend, they approached the counter, and Thomas smiled politely at the scantily-clad woman who waited with an impatient glare to check their IDs and take the cover charge.

"Please," said Beth, fumbling to pull out her wallet and ID as Thomas placed a twenty on the counter, along with his ID. "I'm getting this. Last night you promised that I could pay next time."

Thomas looked up at her with what he knew was a cocky smile. "I did not promise. I said maybe."

She sighed and shook her head as she handed only her ID to the woman behind the counter, but the curve of her lips told him she appreciated it.

"Beth," said Lin, motioning to her from a few feet away, "give me your coat so I can give it to the coat check guy."

Thomas watched as Beth froze, still standing by the front counter, her hand on her back pocket where she had just put away her ID.

"I'm still a little cold," she said finally, the jostling from the people in line behind her trying to get to the counter moving her reluctantly in Lin's direction. "I think I'll keep it with me."

Lin rolled her eyes as she stepped toward Beth and tugged at the scarf around her neck.

"What are you doing?" Beth tried to turn away, but Lin caught her arm.

"Beth, you're going to look ridiculous going in there with your Arctic attire. Just let me take your coat."

"No, I'm going to look ridiculous going in there wearing the getup you made me wear," Beth returned through gritted teeth.

Interested, Thomas moved in to get a better view of the skirmish.

Lin looked over at him in a silent request for assistance. He chuckled quietly at Lin's dilemma.

"Beth, come on. There are people behind you trying to get in. Just take off the damn coat!"

"Fine!" Pushing Lin's hands away, Beth unzipped her coat, then shoved it in Lin's direction. "There, happy? Now let's get inside where it's dark and no one can see me."

Thomas couldn't help staring at Beth, who stood with her arms crossed protectively in front of her. Although her jeans fit her curves perfectly, Thomas saw nothing particularly scandalous about them. The "getup" Beth was protesting must have been the tight-fitting sleeveless blouse she wore on top. It was burgundy in color and had a subtle lace pattern, with little golden clasps down the front that were there for no functional purpose but gave the top the look of a corset. The neck was scalloped and dipped deliciously low, showing off the beautiful curves of Beth's breasts.

Instinctually casting a glance in Tyler's direction and catching him openly gawking at Beth's chest, Thomas contemplated breaking the NYU student's neck.

"I agree," said Thomas, reluctantly deciding against harming Tyler for the time being. He took a step closer to Beth and put his hand at the small of her back to guide her. "Let's get inside."

Stepping through the black fabric curtains that separated the front entrance from the techno room on the other side, he could feel Beth's body tense up as they found themselves in a sea of people, some dancing, some talking, many just pushing their way from one side of the room to the other.

He could tell that Beth was a little overwhelmed by the whole scene—the loud "music," if you could call it that, the wall-to-wall bodies, the drinking, the strobing lights. Lin and Tyler had already been swallowed up by the crowd, and Thomas was trying hard not to bare his teeth each time a hapless dancer bumped into him and momentarily caused his hand to lose contact with Beth's back.

Deciding to take more active measures to avoid losing her in the mess of people, he found her hand and grasped it, then started leading her through the flailing bodies all around them to the other side of the room where he hoped there would be more space. He was pleasantly surprised when Beth curled her fingers around his, and an unfamiliar warmth traveled up that arm and into his chest.

Finding a spot by the wall where they could stand without fear of being trampled, Thomas released her. She stood close to him, her bare shoulder touching his through the white dress shirt he wore.

"This isn't really my thing," she said finally, holding her hands at her waist, the fingers of one hand playing nervously with those of the other.

"You're kidding me," he said, and she broke out into a laugh at his sarcasm.

Smiling teasingly, he pointed to her corset top. "And I suppose the next thing you're going to tell me is that you don't usually wear tops like that."

Beth looked down at her chest, then, realizing how much of her bosom was exposed, attempted to adjust the neckline.

"I'm sorry to be the one to break this to you, Beth, but that neckline's not going anywhere."

"I suppose you're right." She laughed nervously, letting her hands drop. "I'm just going to have to accept that I look like an eighteenth century prostitute tonight."

Her eyes met his, and her laugh receded into a thoughtful smile.

"I think you look beautiful," he said, his gaze never leaving her face.

Shaking his head to ward off the spell he was in danger of falling under, Thomas added, "Do I have Lin to thank for that?"

Beth nodded, looking down again. "Yes. I went over to her place so we could all walk to the bus stop together, and she took one look at the turtleneck sweater I was wearing and dragged me upstairs to her room. You should have seen the other shirts I turned down, and the black leather pants."

"Mmmm, I wish I had."

She laughed again, and the warm feeling inside him grew.

The crowd on the dance floor was steadily growing and encroached on their space. Thomas looked at the staircase to their right. "I think the room upstairs has Latin dancing tonight. Samba and rumba and whatnot. Do you want to see if the crowd's a little thinner up there? I'm feeling a bit claustrophobic here. Plus, I'm not sure how much more of this techno I can take."

"Sure," she grinned. "Let's go."

The back of her hand brushed his as he took a step in the direction of the stairs, and, encouraged, he took her hand once more. The sounds of techno faded into a salsa beat as they moved up the stairs and entered a thankfully less-crowded room. Looking around, it was obvious the clientele who chose to come up here were more serious about their dancing than the crowd downstairs. The women wore short, full skirts that twirled nicely when they turned, and the men invariably had on dress pants that fit tightly in the seat and partially unbuttoned dress shirts in various bright colors.

Thomas led Beth to the bar area and stepped up to the counter. A moment later, the bartender approached and gave them a friendly smile.

"What can I get for you two tonight?"

Thomas turned to glance at Beth and was amused to see a deer-in-the-headlights look as she contemplated how to answer.

"I'm guessing drinking is not really your thing, either."

Her lips lifted into a shy smile. "No, it isn't."

"Well, how about a margarita? That's a pretty safe drink, and it goes with the atmosphere up here."

She nodded, and Thomas looked back at the bartender to place their order.

A few minutes later, drinks in hand, they spotted a couple vacating a high-top table and quickly went to claim it.

Thomas watched as Beth took a cautious sip from

her drink, then set it down. "It's good," she said, her blue eyes sparkling.

Pleased, Thomas nodded. "I'm glad you like it." He took a sip from his own glass, still looking at her.

"What are you drinking? I didn't hear what you ordered."

"It's just whisky." Aside from the feel of it sliding down his throat, he wouldn't have the benefit of even the slightest buzz from consuming the drink. "Would you like to try it?"

She raised her delicate eyebrows in a dubious look. "It sounds like the kind of drink that burns on the way down to your stomach."

He laughed as he nudged the glass toward her. "It is. But that doesn't mean you shouldn't try it."

With what could have been a mischievous grin, she picked up his glass and took a small sip. He repressed the urge to laugh as she put it down, grimacing. "Wow," she said in a coarse voice, as though several layers of her throat tissue actually had been eroded. "That really does burn."

"Now you know firsthand. That's worth something, I think."

"Yes," she replied, her tone once again smooth and melodious. "That is worth something."

She went back to sipping her margarita, and he went back to his whisky. Without a conscious thought, Thomas touched the rim of the glass where Beth had placed her lips.

After a hundred and forty years of existence as a vampire, this was a new experience for him. He was not seeking to feed on the bright-eyed girl in front of him. He just wanted to be with her, near her. And as much as he hated to admit it, he wanted Beth to care for him. He told himself that this was all part of the challenge he had both made and accepted—to corrupt the incorruptible innocence of a kind, sweet soul. But Thomas was beginning to realize that nothing could be farther from the truth.

Just then, a young man distracted by talking to a girl over his shoulder bumped into Beth's arm, causing her to spill a little of her drink. Instantly, Thomas gripped the edge of the table, half a breath away from flinging it aside and tearing the boy's throat out. The guy quickly muttered an apology, pausing briefly to glance at Beth's cleavage in the process, then went on his way.

Looking up at her kind eyes and soft mouth, Thomas realized something else. Not only did he not want to harm Beth, but he found that he would do anything to protect her—from the world, as well as from himself. It was a startling epiphany, and one that Thomas didn't know what to do with.

Beth must have seen a change in his expression because she reached across the table and touched his hand tentatively. "Everything okay?"

Thomas looked up from her hand to her face and was taken aback by the genuine kindness and concern in her expression.

"Yes, more than okay."

Her fingers rubbed the back of his hand briefly as she withdrew. Her eyes, however, continued to study him.

"What were you thinking just now?"

What was he thinking? How could he possibly answer that question? How could he tell her that she had done strange things to him, that from the moment she had run him over with her car, he had been having glimpses of a life he had long since forgotten? That he had been *feeling* things with a heart that was no longer beating? That, for the first time since he'd been turned, he wanted something more than blood?

"I was thinking we should dance."

The music changed to a mambo, and the urge to touch Beth compelled Thomas to step around the table and get closer to her.

At his approach, Beth laughed. "I don't know how to dance like that." She pointed to the center of the dance floor, where several couples were moving their feet and hips enthusiastically to the Latin beat.

"We don't have to dance like that." Thomas extended his hand, palm up. She looked at it for a moment, unmoving, before exhaling softly and slipping her hand into his.

"I'm warning you now, this isn't going to be pretty."

He closed his hand around hers.

"I'm certain that's impossible."

Beth looked nervous, but he knew it was the prospect of dancing that caused her anxiety, not him. Or, if he was the cause, it wasn't that she was *afraid* of him as she had been the night they'd met. Rather, it was because she found him attractive. Because she *liked* him.

The idea that Beth might like him on a personal level—that she might enjoy spending time with him—was thrilling in a new and unusual way. Not the thrill of the hunt that Thomas was used to. No, this was something completely different.

He felt…honored.

Thomas led Beth to a spot along the edge of the dance floor, where they wouldn't be the center of attention, then turned to face her. The song that had been playing was ending, and a new one started up. Swallowing hard, Thomas stepped toward Beth and placed his right hand on her waist, holding her arm up with his other hand in a classic ballroom position. The feel of her body under his hands made him close his eyes for a moment as he tried to collect his thoughts.

"So, how are we supposed to dance to this, exactly?"

Regaining his senses, Thomas replied, "This is a merengue. It's easy. Just step with your feet—right, left, right, left. Bend your knees as you step, and your hips will move just like theirs." He motioned with his head to the couple closest to them. "I'll help you. Just follow me."

She nodded, and they began. Despite her apparent nervousness and lack of experience, he found they moved well together. She undulated her hips to the rhythm with an innocence that was incredibly sexy. She had no idea what each sway was doing to his insides. But her gaze was fixed shyly on his feet, and with their bodies moving in synchrony with the dance, he couldn't help craving a more thorough connection.

"You know, you're supposed to look at your dance partner every once in a while. Just as a courtesy, mind you."

Beth smiled, looking up into his eyes. "I don't mean to be discourteous," she replied, more steadily than he had expected. "I would just hate to break your toes with my big, clunky feet."

"Nothing about you is clunky, Beth."

At that, she lowered her eyes again, making him regret what he had just said.

As the song ended, Beth pulled away from him.

"Do you want to take a break?" he asked, disappointed to lose contact.

She nodded silently, and he led her off the dance floor to a vacant spot near the back wall of the room. Their drinks had been picked up, and another group had taken over their table.

"You did well for your first merengue," said Thomas, feeling the need to say something as they both stared awkwardly out at the dance floor.

"Only because you know what you're doing," she replied, surprising him by turning her face toward him. "You like to dance?"

"It depends on the partner." He flashed an impish grin, eliciting a chuckle from her.

Beth gazed out onto the dancefloor again, and Thomas took the opportunity to study her lovely profile. Her hair was up in a twist, which was a change from her usual ponytail and gave her appearance a more classical elegance. He followed the soft lines from her heart-shaped jaw to her delicate collarbone, then quickly reversed course to avoid staring at her lovely breasts.

"I'm glad we ran into you tonight," said Beth, continuing to look out into the crowd. "It was nice of you to change your plans to come in with us."

"It wasn't a change in plans. I thought you might be here, so I came to find you."

Slowly, she turned to look at him. "You wanted to see me tonight?"

"I want to see you every night."

There was no reason for Thomas to be so honest. Such truths would not necessarily endear him to Beth. In fact, they could scare her away. They *should* scare her away—his words and everything about him.

But from the way she looked at him now, the way her chest rose and fell with each breath and the way her eyes brightened just a little, Thomas knew she wasn't afraid of him anymore.

The back of his hand brushed hers tentatively, testing the waters. When she didn't pull away, he moved so that his palm was against her open hand. Miraculously, her fingers curled, securing his hand in hers.

"Do you think Lin would be very upset if we went next door and got something to eat?" he said, suddenly despising the noise and lights and bodies all around them.

"I can text her so she doesn't worry."

As they made their way to the stairs, hand-in-hand, Thomas wondered how it was that she had agreed to leave the club with him. And how long it would take for her to realize she had made a grave mistake.

Chapter Nine

The only thing Beth was aware of as she left the club with Thomas and walked into the pub next door was the feel of his hand in hers. It was warm and firm, holding her with just enough pressure to be both purposeful and tender at the same time.

Her stomach was fluttering fiercely with a giddy excitement that bordered on nausea. Thomas was interested in her romantically. That much was pretty clear, and she wasn't doing anything to dissuade him. She had been staring at him all night, enjoying every minute of their brief contact as they danced, and savoring the feel of his hand in hers. She had even conveniently broken up with her boyfriend to pave the way for him.

The realization of that truth hit her hard. Though she had tried to deny that Thomas had anything to do with her breaking up with Ryan, she knew deep down that had she not met Thomas, she wouldn't have found the will to do it, at least not yet. Even if it was on a subconscious level, the possibility of being with Thomas, real or imagined, had been more appealing to her than the thought of continuing to be with Ryan, and that had been the push she needed.

Lin had been right all along.

Though it was well past eleven, there was a fair-sized crowd gathered under the dark wooden beams and dim lights of the Viking-themed drinking establishment they had entered, aptly named Valhalla. The tables consisted of tall barrels with round wooden tabletops affixed to them, and the walls displayed faux Viking artifacts circa 1000 AD.

The waiter seated them at a table near the windows and put a couple of menus in front of them before leaving them alone again. Unconsciously, Beth put her hand on the table, palm up, and looked at it, still contemplating the feel of Thomas' hand against her skin and how, if she had really loved Ryan, she wouldn't have enjoyed it so much. Then, realizing they had both been silent for several minutes, she glanced up to find Thomas' gaze fixed on her. His eyes were almost sad, though his lips held the trace of a smile, and she watched as he reached across the small table. Without thinking, she extended her own hand to meet him halfway, and her stomach floated up into her throat as they made contact again.

Embarrassed by her reaction to such a simple gesture, she lowered her eyes shyly, and his hand tightened around hers in response.

"I've never been in this kind of situation before," he said finally, and she let out a slow breath, trying to force her body to relax.

He turned her hand over and traced each finger with the index finger of his other hand, from the knuckle to the nail, studying them, and she had serious concerns that she would not be able to maintain consciousness if he continued to do so.

"What situation?" she prompted, breathlessly.

He didn't answer right away, but mercifully stopped his tracing and simply held her hand in both of his. Just as he was about to speak, the waiter came by to see if they had made any decisions. Thomas' eyes darkened for a moment, but then the shadow passed and he turned to Beth. "What would you like?"

Beth had given no thought to eating or drinking and had little desire to do anything other than hear what Thomas had to say. "Uh…I don't know. I guess maybe just something to drink. I'm not really hungry." *And I might throw up all over you if I eat in my current state.*

Apparently requiring no further input, Thomas looked back at the waiter. "A White Russian for her, and whisky for me, please."

"What's a White Russian?" she asked once the waiter was out of earshot.

He flashed his naughty-boy grin at her. "It's a drink that I think you'll like. It's vodka, Kahlua, and cream. It tastes like chocolate."

"Oh my, you're going to turn me into a lush."

They both laughed, and the mood between them grew a little more relaxed.

When their drinks came a few minutes later, Thomas let go of her hand, and she heard him let out a breath as they broke contact.

Beth picked up her glass and moved it toward the glass he held in his own hand. "Cheers," he said, as their glasses touched with a quiet clink.

"Cheers," she replied, still staring into his somber brown eyes. They looked so deep to her now, like bottomless pools of dark honey. His eyebrows knit together in concentration, and she found herself wrinkling her own brow in concern. "Tell me what's bothering you," she prompted gently. "Please."

Thomas looked up from his whisky and raised one

corner of his mouth in a weak attempt to smile.

"I believe I'm in what you might call a conflict of sorts."

"A conflict? With who?"

He shook his head quickly. "No, no. It's more of an internal conflict."

"Oh? Why?"

Thomas didn't answer at first, but just gazed at her from across the table, still wearing that half smile, and she almost forgot to breathe. Then he took another sip of whisky, as though to fortify himself.

"I've always known what I've wanted, and I've always taken it. I don't ask permission. I don't consider anyone other than myself. My entire existence is one of self-satisfaction, regardless of cost. It is the very definition of selfishness. That is who I am. It is my nature, and I've embraced it."

As she opened her mouth to protest his self-analysis, he raised his hand to cut her short. "You don't know me."

Thomas was right. She didn't know him. She had only spoken to him a few times, and just because holding his hand gave her a thrill didn't mean he was a good person.

Meeting his eyes as he pondered his next words, though, Beth could see right to the core of him. And she was drawn to him, the essence of him, for a reason she couldn't explain. It was not his outward beauty, nor his confidence, nor his attentions that attracted her. It was him, and it was a feeling so strong that it needed no other justification.

"I may not know your history," said Beth, her voice low and impassioned, "but I know you. Just as you know me."

Thomas closed his eyes for a moment, as though her words caused him physical pain, then opened them again. His breathing was purposeful, his chest rising and falling in sync with her own.

By the slight furrow of his brow, the tilt of his head, and the pursing of his lips, she knew Thomas was searching for the words he needed to give voice to his thoughts. He took another sip from his drink, his eyes leaving hers for only a second.

"You don't remember, then? You don't remember what you felt the first time we met?"

His question surprised her—she hadn't known that she had been so obvious in her reaction to their first meeting.

"I do remember. But I don't feel it now. I was wrong."

"No—you were not wrong. You were absolutely right to be fearful of me. You should fear me now."

She wondered what was going on in his head, why he was saying these things. Where was the confident man who had taken her by the arm last night in the café and wouldn't let her retreat to her apartment without sharing dessert with him first? Where was the bold dance partner of just a little while ago, who had put his hands firmly on her body as he led her through the sexiest dance she had ever experienced?

Her confusion must have shown on her face, because Thomas sighed and shook his head slowly. "This isn't me," he said finally, still shaking his head. "I'm not like this. You've done something to me, and I can't understand why or how, and at first it was terrible—I couldn't bear having those feelings again.

I'm not equipped for it anymore. But now, especially when I'm with you—I don't know. It's disconcerting and uncomfortable, but I can't imagine being without it again."

Beth's heart swelled with some strange mixture of sympathy, concern, and affection for the beautiful, troubled soul who sat opposite her. This time, it was she who reached across the table, her fingers lightly grazing the top of his hand as it stroked the side of his whisky glass.

He stopped, looking up at her as though seeing her for the first time, and turned his hand over to firmly grasp hers again.

She reciprocated the pressure, wanting him to know that she was there for him, that he could tell her anything and she would understand.

"It's not fair what I'm doing to you," he said finally, looking down as though defeated. "You're too kind, too good. You should tell me to leave you the hell alone."

"No, I shouldn't." It was like he was a different person, even from the man who had crossed the street to stand next to her outside the club. What had happened? "I don't want you to leave me alone," she continued, squeezing his hand. "I like you—I like being with you. I can't say that I understand most of what you've been saying, but if I've caused you to be upset, I'm sorr—"

"Don't apologize. You don't ever have to apologize to me."

They were both quiet for a moment. Beth examined his face, the soulful brown eyes, the carelessly perfect hair framing the worry-creased forehead, and the velvet lips that pressed together with a depth of feeling that she desperately wanted to understand.

"You can tell me anything, Thomas," she said, breaking the silence. "I know we just met, and I may not understand, but I will listen, and I will do whatever I can to help."

He didn't respond right away but brought her hand to his lips and kissed it. Her face warmed at the feel of his lips on her skin, and she hoped she wasn't blushing.

Letting go of her hand, he clasped his own together, laying them on the table, as though he were about to negotiate the price of a car.

"I want to see you again," he said abruptly.

"I want to see you again, too," she replied, holding his gaze while tamping down the prickles of excitement chasing up from her chest into her neck and face.

"But you have to promise me something."

Beth nodded, forgetting her rule about not making promises until she had heard what she was agreeing to.

"If you don't want me with you anymore, if you want me to leave, you will tell me immediately. You will not worry about my feelings or what I will do. You will just tell me to leave you the hell alone. And in return, I promise that if you ever say those words, I will leave, no questions asked, and you will never see me again. Do you promise?"

Beth didn't even need a moment to consider her response.

"Yes, I promise."

Chapter Ten

From the time Thomas said goodbye to her when they had met back up with Lin and Tyler outside Valhalla, all through Sunday morning Mass and brunch with Lin and Tyler in the dining hall, and even throughout five unproductive hours of work in the lab, Beth wore a contented smile on her face. More than once she caught herself humming along with the movie soundtracks she had been playing in the background in the lab, and she wasn't even the slightest bit annoyed when she opened up the images from each run of her experiment to find no improvement whatsoever.

Adam had taken the day off to entertain his mother, so she was alone. With no one to talk to and only the show tunes to fill the silence, her thoughts kept turning to Thomas. He had squeezed her hands tenderly as he said goodnight to her the night before. Had she leaned in, even just a fraction of an inch, he would have kissed her. She could see it in his eyes, and the thought of that look now made her cheeks warm.

When the bus to North Campus had pulled up to the curb and Lin and Tyler were busy searching for the bus passes they had purchased earlier that evening, Thomas had inclined his head to Beth's ear. "Will you have dinner with me tomorrow?" he had asked in a low voice.

She had immediately said yes, which resulted in a

grin that stretched from one of Thomas' perfect ears to the other.

"Meet me at Luciano's at seven."

She had nodded, smiling, trying hard not to turn her head to kiss his cheek.

Now, her eyes kept darting to the decades-old schoolhouse clock on the wall, willing both hands to move closer to the six.

At five-thirty, she became convinced that time had in fact stopped progressing all together, having looked at the clock repeatedly only to see that the hands were in the same position. She was about to pull out her phone for another data point when there was a rapid succession of knocks at the door to the lab.

Startled away from her contemplation of temporal matters, Beth jumped up and rushed to the door. She half-expected—or, more accurately, fervently hoped—to see Thomas as she unlocked the door and pulled it open, but instead, it was Lin's tear-streaked face that greeted her.

"Oh my gosh, Lin, are you okay?"

Lin's face was red with emotion, and she breathed in sobs as she shook her head wordlessly.

"Oh, Lin, what happened? What's wrong?"

She pulled her friend inside and hugged her as the door swung closed with a squeak and a click. Lin's chest rose and fell in random spurts as she continued to cry against Beth's shoulder. Beth just held her, saying nothing, rubbing her back soothingly as she waited for her friend to calm down enough to tell her what had happened, although she had a pretty good guess as to what, or rather who, had caused Lin's current state.

After several long minutes, Lin drew in a deep

breath and pulled away. More deep breaths followed as Beth reached behind her to grab a few tissues, then handed them to her friend.

"Oh, Lin," Beth whispered, her hands on her friend's shoulders. "Did he break up with you?"

That released a new flood of tears, and Lin was back in Beth's arms, sobbing uncontrollably.

After several more minutes, Lin had settled herself enough for Beth to lead her to the swivel chairs in front of the row of computers where photos of Beth's experiment were still up on the screen, and they sat down. Beth grabbed another box of tissues off the shelf above the monitors and put it beside Lin, who pulled one out and wiped her nose half-heartedly.

"I thought everything was going fine," she began, looking at Beth through watery eyes, her voice unsteady. "We had such a great weekend. We talked about everything, from our families to our dreams to our fears. Everything. I felt so comfortable with him. It was so right."

"What happened?" Beth prompted, afraid Lin would start sobbing again if she paused for too long.

"He put his bag in the car, getting ready to leave after we had brunch today, then he came over to me, smiling. He hugged me, and I thought he was going to tell me he loved me, Beth…"

Her voice trailed off, and Beth reached over and grabbed her hand. "What did he say?"

More tears slid down her face as she looked up at Beth. "He said he had a great weekend with me, but that this 'thing' wasn't going to go anywhere, so I shouldn't try to talk to him anymore."

She heaved a breath and shook her head, as though

she couldn't believe he'd actually said that. "He didn't even pretend he was sorry, Beth," she said, still shaking her head. "I think he had been planning to do it all along."

Beth's heart broke for her friend, and at the same time, she was furious with that selfish bastard. She knew there was a reason she didn't like that blond-streaked head of hair and that lop-sided grin of his. If she ever saw him again, she would knock that grin right off his face, and hopefully a few teeth along with it.

"You didn't sleep with him, did you?" Beth couldn't help asking the question, thinking of Thomas' insinuations over dessert about the reason Lin had stood her up.

Lin breathed in and out, closing her eyes for just a moment before answering. "We…we were naked together in bed, but we didn't have sex."

Beth let out a sigh of relief. "Oh, Lin, aren't you glad you didn't have sex with him? Think of how much worse it would have been if you had."

Her friend didn't say anything, but just nodded quietly, the tears still falling.

"I'm so sorry you're going through this, but at least now you know he's a jerk. People like that have empty, meaningless lives. He will never have love. But you will. I know you will."

Lin's shoulders shook as she drew in an unsteady breath, and Beth hugged her again.

"I'm such an idiot," said Lin once she had calmed down again. "How could I be so stupid? How could I fall for that? For him?"

"Good people don't expect others to behave so cruelly," replied Beth, still thinking of ways she could inflict pain on that sorry excuse for a human being if he ever had the misfortune of crossing her path. "You don't expect that someone is going to lie to your face, pretend that they care for you, then turn around and tell you to just—"

"...to just fuck off," Lin finished the sentence for her, sensing her hesitation, and Beth pressed her lips together in concern. "I know how you hate to say bad words," added Lin, the faint trace of a smile fighting to break through her mournful expression.

"Yes, but sometimes the situation calls for it."

The two of them sat in their swivel chairs, side-by-side, wordlessly swaying their legs back and forth. Beth wanted to say or do something to make Lin's hurt go away, but she knew she couldn't undo the damage that jerk had caused. He had abused her friend's kindness, betrayed her trust, and Lin would never be the same again. She would be okay eventually, Beth knew that, but she was forever changed now.

Finally, Lin sighed and looked over at Beth. "So, what's the story with you and the hot visiting researcher? Are you going to see him again?"

Beth's cheeks immediately caught fire at Lin's question, and Lin noticed.

"You are, aren't you!" Distracted for a moment from her own woes, Lin's face brightened.

"Don't look at me like that," Beth countered, busying herself with logging off the multiple computers she had been using. "He's just a nice guy who doesn't know anybody else on campus, that's all."

"He's nice, all right. The tall, dark, and handsome kind of nice. So, when are you going to see him again?"

Beth could feel Lin's eyes boring a hole through

the back of her head as she shoved her notebooks, pencils, and laptop into her backpack, ignoring the question. When she turned around to put the backpack down, Lin was still looking at her, expectantly.

Letting out an exasperated sigh, Beth gave up. "I'm having dinner with him tonight. But it's not a date."

"Ha! I knew it. That's awesome, Beth."

Noticing that her friend had gotten quiet again, Beth paused to look at her. Lin's eyes were downcast, and her hair had fallen forward to cover part of her face, as though she were deep in thought. Beth knew the fresh wound of being dumped by Tyler had stung her anew and hoped that the memory would start to fade before too long.

"You okay, Lin?"

Lin looked up and forced a smile. "Yeah. Just thinking. You should be careful with this guy. You don't really know him. He could turn out to be a creep, a real monster, like Tyler."

Beth nodded politely. But in her heart, Beth didn't think such a thing was possible.

****

Thomas arrived at the restaurant twenty minutes early, so it was no surprise that Beth was not yet there. After he had finished scanning the room for her, he told the hostess he would wait outside and quickly stepped out the door into the frigid night air, ignoring the young woman's dreamy gaze as she followed him with her eyes.

Once outside, Thomas paced, walking from one end of the block to the other, his hands shoved into his pants pockets, his head down. It wasn't the cold that bothered him—he hardly sensed it. Rather, he kept wondering what he would say to Beth when she arrived. More importantly, he wondered what she would say to him. Would she find him as endearing as she had the night before? Or would she see him for what he truly was? Would she take one look at him and remember the fear that had shaken her to the core the first night they met?

Worse yet, what if she had already changed her mind about him? What if she wasn't coming at all?

The more Thomas thought about it, the more irritated he became. Why was it so important that he be with her? He didn't need her. She was merely an amusement, something different. Something to look at, play with, use up, then discard. Yet even as he recited those thoughts to himself and understood that, logically, they should be true, he knew they were not. He was not the same vampire he was before. The visions he kept having, they were changing him, whether he liked it or not. And there was nothing he could do to stop them from coming.

He had awakened from another one merely an hour ago. It had been just as real and disconcerting as the others, and it, too, had changed him, reminded him of things he didn't know he had forgotten.

Like his mother.

He was a child this time, lying in bed, trembling. Ironically, in this vision, he had just awakened from a dream, one he'd had often as a child. As he relived the scene, he could recall his childhood dream vividly—the dark, winding passages, the cold, damp air that pressed itself into his lungs, the whispers all around him. He'd lain still in his small bed, eyes wide open and a blanket pulled up past his chin, trying to discern whether the whispers had followed him. He was torn between the desire to call for help and the fear that he might be heard by the evil he had just escaped in his dream.

Finally, he gathered up the courage to utter a quiet plea.

"Momma?"

Only a few seconds later, his mother was at his side, stroking his hair lovingly and murmuring soothing words in a honey-sweet voice.

"*A pheata*, my darling. Did you have a dream, Tommy?"

She spoke with an Irish lilt that was as comforting as the warm kiss she placed on his forehead.

"Yes, Momma. It was the bad one."

His mother kissed him again and put her hands on his cheeks.

"You've nothing to worry about, my love. Your momma is here, and nothing dare harm you in my presence."

He nodded, absolutely convinced, and almost immediately his eyes grew too heavy to keep open. His mother pushed the hair away from his face as he turned onto his side and let the peace imparted by his mother's touch carry him away to a more restful sleep.

There was nothing to fear with his mother beside him—not shadows nor whispers nor illness nor death. He was completely safe.

"Hi, Thomas."

On instinct, he spun around to face the speaker, having briefly forgotten where he was and why. One glimpse at the beautiful, smiling eyes looking up at him was all he needed to remember.

"Hi, Beth."

She giggled shyly. "Hi," she said again.

He fought the urge to dip his head for a kiss and instead straightened his back and cleared his throat. "Should we go inside?"

She nodded, still smiling, and he couldn't help smiling in return.

Before he could succumb to his desire to touch her, he took a few steps to the door of the restaurant and opened it, motioning gallantly for Beth to enter before him.

"Who says chivalry is dead?" she quipped, just loud enough for him to hear her.

"Certainly not I," he replied, following her inside.

They were seated at a table for two near the front of the restaurant, and Thomas waited until Beth had lowered herself into the chair the waiter pulled out for her before taking a seat himself.

Despite the fact that, biologically, he didn't need to eat, Thomas had dined at Luciano's several times before. There was something about the place—the dim lighting, the wood paneling on the walls, the dark reds and golds in the fabric of the chairs—that calmed him.

"I've never been here," said Beth, as though in answer to his thoughts. "It's weird, isn't it? I've been going to school here for almost four years and yet I've never eaten at this restaurant."

"It's a little out of the way," he replied, "and a bit fancier than necessary. But it's good. I hope you like it."

"I'm sure I will."

Her hair was gathered into a low ponytail at the base of her neck, and already the shorter strands were coming loose, falling haphazardly about her lovely face.

They made small talk as they looked over the menus and placed their orders. The whole time, he wished they weren't sitting with a table between them. He wanted to be near her, to touch her soft skin, to feel the warmth radiating from it, and having a physical obstacle between them made him want her all the more.

But it wasn't just the table between them tonight. There was something else. It was as though Beth was making an effort to keep her distance. True, she wasn't exactly giving him the cold shoulder, but he could sense her reserve. She was careful not to let his fingers touch hers when she handed him her menu to pass to the server. She kept her hands folded in front of her when the menu was no longer there to protect her, looking down at them each time there was a break in the conversation. Even her ankles were crossed demurely under her chair.

Beth did not want him near her tonight.

Perhaps she was having second thoughts after all, Thomas mused, half bitter, half resigned. She was just too polite to stand him up.

"Are you okay?"

Beth's question caught Thomas off-guard, and he looked up from the water glass he had apparently been staring at. Then he chuckled, sitting back in his chair a little, allowing his shoulders and his back to relax. "Funny, I was actually just wondering the same thing about you."

Her lips curved upward as she lowered her gaze to her folded hands. "I'm sorry if I made you think anything is wrong," she said softly. "I guess I'm just feeling a little guilty."

Thomas wasn't sure what that meant exactly, but it made the hairs on the back of his neck stand on end. "I'm afraid to ask what you feel guilty about," he replied, with an honesty he was not aware he possessed.

She smiled apologetically and shook her head. "I'm very happy to be here, having dinner with you," she said, effortlessly finding her way to the heart of the matter. "I've been thinking about seeing you again since the moment I got on the bus last night."

He couldn't help grinning at her admission.

"That's why I feel guilty—because here I am, happy, with nowhere else I'd rather be, when my best friend is probably sitting alone in her room, crying her eyes out."

Thomas felt his smile fade and almost bared his teeth. "What did that asshole do to her?"

Beth's face glowed even warmer as she raised one corner of her mouth. "I could tell you didn't like Tyler, even in the brief time we were with him last night. Maybe you really can figure people out like you said you could."

"He wasn't hard to figure out. The way he stared at you while Lin was hanging on his arm talking to him was a dead giveaway."

Beth's face immediately turned crimson. "He was not staring at me."

"Well," replied Thomas, casually, "he may not have been looking at your face…"

He promptly received a rather painful punch in the arm from across the table, and the two of them laughed. She had the most pleasant laugh—it started off high, then cascaded into a waterfall of soft, low chuckles. Her eyes were wide and bright, hiding nothing, and Thomas felt as though he, in turn, would be unable to hide anything from her.

It was a sobering thought.

"I presume he broke up with her?" he asked as the waiter appeared and placed a basket of warm bread in front of them, along with a small plate of olive oil for dipping. He missed the taste of bread, he realized suddenly. He could still smell it, and, smelling it, he could almost remember the taste, but as soon as he broke off a piece and put it in his mouth, it held nothing more pleasant than the flavor of wet cardboard for his taste buds to enjoy. He forced himself to swallow it down, watching the expression on Beth's face as she tasted and experienced what he could not. Oddly enough, he found some measure of joy in that.

"Yes," she replied, breaking off another piece and dipping it in the oil. "He very casually broke up with her just before he got in his car to leave. It seems Tyler had no intention of dating Lin after this weekend." Beth sighed, still holding the bread between her fingers. "I guess I don't get it. Why would he drive over five hours to be here if he didn't want to have a relationship with her?"

"He wanted something from her," said Thomas, emphasizing the word "something." "It just wasn't a relationship."

"She said she didn't have sex with him."

"You asked her?" Thomas looked thoughtfully at Beth, intrigued that she would be so bold as to ask her friend such a question.

The color rose in her cheeks again as she nodded quietly. "Sometimes I have a hard time keeping my mouth shut," she added after a moment. "I asked before even considering how it would make Lin feel. But she answered, and she said she didn't. I believe her."

Thomas nodded, despite the fact he didn't believe Lin had been honest with Beth. The way Lin had been hanging all over her then-boyfriend, smiling at him even when he wasn't looking—no, that ship had already sailed before they went out that night.

"She'll be all right," said Thomas, noticing the concerned furrow forming in Beth's brow. "It's good she has someone like you to talk to."

"I try to help," Beth broke off another piece of bread and moved it in slow circles in the oil, her mind somewhere else, "but I don't always say the right things. I have a different philosophy on, well, most things when it comes to relationships."

"You mean sex?"

Beth nodded, keeping her eyes on the bread that was now saturated with oil. "I feel, sometimes, that I'm the only one who thinks the way I do. Sometimes I'm proud of that. Sometimes it just makes me tired, and I wish it didn't always have to be an issue."

Thomas picked up the glass of wine they had ordered and raised it to his lips. The wine was tasteless to him, too, but still he enjoyed the feel of the liquid on his tongue as he swallowed.

"Why is it an issue?" he asked, setting down his glass.

Beth shrugged. "I don't know. It just always ends up being this huge thing. I mean, it's everywhere—on TV, in advertising, in everyday conversation. It's expected, and it's common, and there's nothing special about it anymore. It's like eating and drinking. And if you don't have a boyfriend or you're not sleeping with the boyfriend you've got, then there's something wrong with you. That's what people think, anyway."

"I don't believe everyone thinks that way," offered Thomas, meeting her eyes as she finally looked up at him.

"A lot of people do."

Her eyes sparkled, even in the dim light of the restaurant, and he marveled at how expressive the subtle arching of her eyebrows could be.

"Is that why you broke up with your boyfriend, then? Did you differ in your opinions on this issue?"

"Yes," said Beth softly. "I suppose, in the end, that's what it was. He was always pushing for more. It was too stressful. I just couldn't deal with it anymore. It sounds terrible, I know. A lazy way out. But I wasn't enjoying being with him because of it, so there was no point in continuing the relationship, you know?"

"Sounds like the real issue was that he was an asshole. If you don't mind my saying."

Beth chuckled. "He's a good guy. We just didn't agree on this one thing. He blamed it on my religious upbringing, and I'm sure that's a big part of why I believe what I believe. But it's not the only reason, and I know plenty of people who have sex on Saturday night and then go to Mass on Sunday morning."

Thomas smiled. "That is one way to do it. Sin today, ask forgiveness tomorrow. Everybody wins."

She laughed outright, tossing her head back, the loose strands of hair bouncing happily around her face.

He drew in a sharp breath, then released it slowly. There was no use denying it—she was doing something to him. He was changing, softening. He didn't even want to fight it anymore.

The server was clearing away their plates when Thomas finally spoke the thoughts he had been holding in throughout the meal.

"I was afraid you wouldn't come tonight. I've never worried about…things like that before."

A grin slowly spread across Beth's face, and her cheeks took on a rosy glow even as her eyes dropped shyly to the dessert menu in front of her. "When we first talked, on the walk to North Campus, I didn't believe you when you said you could figure someone out after only a few minutes with them. But when I'm with you I feel like you know everything about me. It makes it easy, in a way. But hard, too." Her voice was low, but clear, and he wanted more than anything for her to raise her eyes to his once more.

Almost in answer to his silent plea, her wide blue eyes, which looked even bigger in that moment, met his. It was all he could do to keep from dashing the table against the wall and reaching for her. Instead, he merely smiled back, trying his best to hide the longing that gnawed at him, just beneath the surface.

Unable to think of anything witty or amusing to say, he asked, "What are your thoughts on dessert?"

She cast another glance at the menu before answering. "It all looks so good, but I think if I have any more carbs tonight, I might go into a diabetic coma."

He nodded, trying to maintain the pleasant look on his face despite the growing knot in his stomach at having to say goodbye to her so soon. Dessert would have at least kept her with him for another twenty minutes or so.

The server brought him the check, and Thomas

looked up to see Beth scowling as he put down four twenty-dollar bills.

"I thought we lived in the twenty-first century. Why is it that the waiter assumed you would be paying?" The slight curve of her lips assured him that she wasn't truly angry.

"He didn't assume anything. I asked him to bring me the check earlier, when you were in the restroom. I wasn't about to have you emasculate me on our first real date."

Beth laughed, conceding defeat, and they both got up to leave.

As they walked out, ready to face the bitter cold, Beth slipped her arm through his, and his heart swelled to an unreasonable degree. He placed his other hand on the arm entwined with his and squeezed it gently. Though she kept looking ahead at the icy sidewalk they were walking, he saw her smile.

They were both quiet as they stepped carefully away from the restaurant and toward the Engineering building, where he knew she had left her car. As they were about to turn up the path that led to the parking lot, Thomas stopped abruptly. Beth turned to look at him, her warm breath against the cold air forming a magical cloud of water vapor around them.

"I don't want to say goodnight just yet," he said softly, holding her hand against his arm in an effort to keep her near.

She nodded, smiling, and he breathed a sigh of relief because he knew she felt the same.

"Neither do I. I know where we can go."

Chapter Eleven

"This is my favorite place on campus."

They were standing side-by-side in the empty gallery of the Lorin Art Museum in front of the floor-to-ceiling windows that overlooked the lights of West Campus below. No part of her body was touching his, and yet every inch of her could sense him standing there beside her.

Thomas was watching her closely—Beth could feel that, too. Her whole body tingled with the intensity of his gaze. It was paralyzing. She racked her brain for something else to say, just to break the spell, but could think of nothing. Instead, Beth fixed her eyes on the dots of light from the cluster of dorms below. They were perfectly scattered against the darkness of the night outside, creating a scene that would have been peaceful had it not been for the clattering of her heart.

"Beautiful." It was unclear if Thomas was talking about the view outside, and her pulse quickened at the thought that he may not be. In stark contrast to her current state, his voice was calm and composed, betraying nothing of his thoughts or intentions. "I didn't realize the museum was open this late," he added.

"Not many people do." She did her best to keep her voice steady, continuing to stare outside. "I brought my parents here when they were visiting during my first semester of college. My dad asked the lady at the desk how late they opened, and she said midnight, every day except holidays, when they're closed. So, I come here sometimes when I'm feeling stressed out or sad or just need some time alone to think. I'll spend a few minutes looking at the paintings and exhibits, but most of the time I just look out there."

He moved slightly closer, and she shut her eyes reflexively, breathing in the faint scent of sandalwood that floated off his body and seemed to surround her. His hand touched hers tentatively, and she grasped it, like a lifeline, opening her eyes again but still staring outward. She was too afraid to look at him.

"You've done something to me," he said, rubbing the top of her hand with his thumb.

She laughed, then quickly looked at him, worried that he might mistake her laughter for derision, forgetting that looking at him was unwise. "I think you have that backwards." Her voice sounded small and weak. Why had she brought him here, to a grand room overlooking a beautiful nighttime scene, with no one around except for the half-asleep grad student manning the desk downstairs?

Thomas took a long breath, then exhaled slowly, and she was pulled out of her introspection as she considered what might have motivated his sigh. His dark eyebrows were pulled together to form a line bordering on a frown, and his eyes were downcast as he seemed to be studying the hand he held in his.

"Tell me what you're thinking." Though she spoke softly, Beth was in control once again. Something was troubling him, and she would find out what. She would help him, if he would let her.

Thomas breathed deeply again, turning her so they

faced each other, with the large windows framing them to one side. "It's not easy for me to explain," he answered after a long pause, his eyes finding hers.

She looked into his warm brown eyes. Through those portals she could see something stirring within him. She could see into his soul.

A few moments passed before he spoke. "You've awakened something inside me," he said finally, studying her face in a way that made her cheeks warm. "It's something I forgot I had, something it has served me well to forget. I have no desire to have that part of me back, you see. But the more I am with you, the stronger that part of me becomes and, well, I'm just not sure that part of me can coexist—can survive—with what I have become. It is incompatible with what I truly am."

She nodded, though she had no idea what he was saying. Still, she thought of what her mother often said to her when she was feeling sad or confused, and it seemed an appropriate response to the present situation.

"I can't say that I understand what you're feeling, Thomas. But what I do know is that everything happens for a reason, even if we don't know what the reason is. It's like hearing the answer to a question you haven't thought to ask yet. Sometimes we just have to wait and see what happens to understand the why. We just have to let it be and trust that, if our intentions are pure, it will be for the best."

Her words seemed to strike a chord within him, and his fingers tightened around her hand. His eyes wandered down to her mouth, and she knew what he was thinking. She was thinking it—wanting it—too.

Her face moved closer to his even as she told

herself it was too soon, as though by some force beyond her own volition. It happened so slowly, the anticipation was almost painful. His warm breath brushed across her lips as he closed the distance between them. Her eyes drifted shut as he tilted her chin with one hand and pressed his lips gently to hers.

He wasn't asking for more, but as his velvet lips brushed hers in the most innocent of kisses, her lips parted. She could not hold back. Her tongue darted into his mouth, confirming the softness of his lips and what lay just past them, and he answered in kind. His arms moved to wrap around her waist and pull her closer to his chest, and she reached up to bury her fingers in his hair.

The sound of footsteps in the hall outside the gallery moments later brought an abrupt end to their kiss, and she turned guiltily from him to stare out the window, as though that would keep anyone who walked in on them from knowing what had just happened. As though the kiss did not linger, warm and palpable, in the air between them.

The footsteps echoed down the hallway and passed the open doorway of the gallery without slowing down.

"I'll walk you back to your car."

She nodded, smiling ever so slightly at the realization that he sounded just as breathless as she felt.

Despite the lingering warmth of the kiss, Beth shuddered as they stepped out the glass doors to walk back toward the Engineering Quad, where her car was hopefully still parked. The museum was a seven-minute walk from the Engineering buildings, but it took only seconds for the biting cold to seep into her fingers and begin working its way through her.

Still, she did not put her hands in her pockets to keep them warm or to fish out the gloves she knew were in there. Stealing a quick glance at Thomas, she noticed he had not put on the black leather gloves he always wore outside. As they stepped around a frozen puddle, Beth wondered if Thomas was thinking the same thing she was thinking.

He was.

Without a word, his hand reached for hers.

"Your hands are cold," he said, looking over at her with a mischievous grin.

Pulling her closer as they crossed the street, he put his hand, still holding hers, into his pocket, rubbing the top of her hand with his thumb. "Better?"

"Yes," she whispered, trying to swallow down the fluttering in her chest. She wondered how it could be that their hands could fit so perfectly together.

A few minutes later, they were standing in front of her car. Turning to face her, he took her other hand in his free hand and put that one in his other pocket. As a result, she couldn't help standing close to him, their bodies inches apart, his breath falling warm on her face. Not that she minded one bit.

Looking up at him, she saw the corners of his mouth rise in the subtlest of smiles, just as he lowered his lips to hers. With her eyes closed, the softness of his mouth, the careful touch of his lips on hers, was the only thing she could feel. The frigid breeze on her cheeks, the hard pavement under her feet, the sounds of college kids laughing in the distance—they did not exist.

A low rumble, almost a growl, escaped from him as he reluctantly pulled away. "Can I see you again?"

he asked softly in her ear, kissing her cheek along the way, then lingering deliciously close.

Her hands still in his pockets, she pulled him closer. "That may well be the stupidest question anyone has ever asked me."

He laughed, taking his hands out of his pockets to cup her face.

"When?" she managed to utter, her skin tingling as he brushed her cheeks with his thumbs.

"How about in five minutes?"

She chuckled, but the sound was almost sad. Did she really have to wait until tomorrow to see him again?

"Don't worry." He sighed, creating some distance between them to make the parting easier. "I know you have things to do. How about tomorrow night?"

She nodded. "I have a meeting with a study group at six-thirty, and it'll probably last an hour. But after that?"

"Yes. After that. Shall I meet you here?"

She thought for a moment. "Sure. We can meet here, then do you want to see a movie, maybe? They have second-run movies showing on Mondays at the student center. I haven't been to the movies in forever, so anything they're showing would be new to me."

"To me as well. Tomorrow night then, seven-thirty, or as soon as your meeting is over."

"Sounds like a plan." She fished her keys out of her coat pocket, hesitated for a brief second before unlocking the car door, then turned around to look at him again. "Are you sure I can't drive you home?"

She knew she was prolonging the inevitable—he had to go home, and so did she. But she didn't want the night to end. Not yet. Even if it was just a few more minutes in the car with him, it would be better than nothing.

He smiled warmly as he came closer and placed his hand behind her neck, his fingers gently rubbing and sending explosions of feeling all the way down to her toes.

"I think it would be wiser for me to take a brisk walk than to be in a car alone with you."

As the butterflies in her stomach awoke for the hundredth time at the meaning of his words, he dipped his head to kiss her mouth, slowly and with purpose. Then, releasing her, he brushed the hair away from her face and smiled again. "I'll see you tomorrow."

"Yes," she replied, breathless. "Tomorrow."

****

As soon as Beth's car had turned the corner and was out of sight, Thomas spun around toward the woods, his eyes focused, his ears honed, his teeth bared. Something was watching him. The hairs on the back of his neck told him as much.

He scanned the edge of the woods for any sign of movement, trying to pinpoint the source of his alarm. At that moment, a group of four noisy college students came up from the road and crossed into the parking lot, no doubt taking a shortcut between Collegetown and Central Campus. Rather than stand there like a sentinel as they approached, he quickly moved away from the woods to an alley between the engineering buildings fifty feet away. There, he waited in the shadows while the drunk kids passed, with no view of the tree line.

As the laughter and chatter subsided into the night once more, he scaled the four-story academic building in the blink of a human eye and, lying flat on the roof not to be seen, turned his focus to the woods. It took him only a couple of minutes to realize that whatever had been watching him was gone. He was alone.

A cloud passed across the face of the half-moon in the sky, darkening the earth just enough for Thomas to leap back down to the ground unseen. Irritated, he hurried toward North Campus. He would check to make sure Beth had gotten home safely. Whatever it was that had been watching him was watching her, as well. He doubted that she was the target of the surveillance, but still, he would feel better knowing she was okay.

How long had they been watching? There was no telling. His instincts had only kicked in when Beth had driven away, but that meant nothing. He simply wasn't himself when he was with her. He didn't function as he knew he should. With Beth at his side, Thomas could tolerate the sights and smells of inane humans all around him; he could constrain the urge to take whatever it was that would have otherwise brought him pleasure. She was his pleasure. She was his balm. When he was with her, he felt less like a vampire and more— more like a man.

Seeing Beth's car parked in its usual spot, Thomas relaxed somewhat. He found the tree that had hidden him the first night they met and crouched behind it. From the shadows playing on the wall inside her apartment, he knew she was changing out of her clothes.

He wondered what she wore to sleep. Probably sweatpants and a sweatshirt, he thought, the corner of his mouth raising in a subconscious smile. She was unlike anyone else he had ever known. She was unlike anyone he would ever know.

Thomas' Repressing the urge to knock on her door, he turned to walk into the wooded area across from the apartment building. He knew from previous exploration that this patch of woods defined the border of North Campus and extended into the hills farther north. A walk in the forest would do him some good. After all, it was a long time until sunrise, and he wasn't in the mood for the bar scene tonight. He wasn't in the mood for anything.

The sound of his shoes on the layers of frozen snow as he moved deeper into the woods was hollow in his ears, the crackle of iced blades of grass breaking underfoot echoing the emptiness inside him. The events of the evening replayed themselves in his mind with each step. Her smile, her laughter, the scent of her, the taste of her mouth—all were imprinted in his memory. He had been foolish to see her again. There was no point.

What was he doing? He had no logical basis for pursuing her. He could no longer lie and say it was for the sake of vanity, for corrupting the incorruptible.

Away from the lights and sounds and smells of the dorms and college students still milling about, Thomas ran through the trees, uncluttering his thoughts. And as shadow and ice blurred together before his eyes, only one thing was clear.

Tomorrow night could not come soon enough.

Chapter Twelve

Thomas didn't remember falling asleep, but he must have. Because he was having another vision.

He had visited many who were suffering and dying—he was not a stranger to anguish and despair. The staleness of the air laden with the stench of urine and sweat was no longer so offensive to his senses. He did not cringe at the sound of weeping and wailing that echoed through the halls of the hospital, nor did he find the pleading touch of the dying men and women he ministered to in any way repelling. This was his vocation. It was his purpose, and he embraced it.

He was on his daily rounds at the hospital, praying with those who requested it, as well as for those who didn't, when he spotted out of the corner of his eye a familiar head of flaxen curls.

"No," he whispered, his muscles instantly tightening, his hands clenching into fists at his sides.

Drawing in a breath, and then slowly releasing it, he walked with a forced calmness to the young woman's bedside. She was facing the wall, away from him, and at first all Thomas could see were soft, yellow-gray ringlets haphazardly strewn across the pillow and down her back. Then, in what seemed like a fitful motion, the woman turned to lie on her back, and her hand flew out to catch his wrist.

"Thomas!" she croaked, looking straight into his

eyes.

Thomas fell to his knees, gathering her hands and kissing them. "Edith, not you too?"

At this, she laughed. It was an absurd sound, here in a room full of sickness and grief. It was the sound of fever and madness, and it made Thomas' hair stand on end.

"It's going to be all right," he said, realizing at the same time that his words were just as absurd as her laughter. It was not going to be all right. She was sick; she would die. It was all wrong.

When she had stopped laughing, she cocked her head to one side and looked at him again. Her eyes fell on the wooden cross he wore around his neck, and a wry smile played on her cracked lips.

"Are you a priest now, Thomas? Have you come to hear my confession? Or shall I perhaps hear yours?"

He knew it was the sickness that spoke to him. This was not his sweet, kind Edith, the woman he almost took to be his wife.

"I am not yet a priest," he replied softly.

She looked at his cross again. "He won't like that."

Thomas looked down. "What, my cross? Who won't like it?"

"Him." She held the sound of the "m" for several seconds, humming it like an incantation. Beads of sweat were forming at her temples, and her hands were unnaturally warm.

Rubbing her hands tenderly, he asked, "Can you tell me who 'he' is?"

Edith's eyebrows knotted together in a puzzled expression before relaxing once again. "The creature who lives in the woods," she replied, matter-of-factly.

"He can save us, you know. He can save us."

She was feverish, and Thomas' heart was filled with pity for her. He reached out to push the damp hair away from her face but was stopped by the wide-eyed look of horror on her face.

"No! Don't touch me! He will come back, I know he will come back for me. He couldn't take me with him, you see, because of the cross I wore about my neck. But it's gone now. He will come back, and this time he will take me. I will be his, not yours, and he will take away my fever and the coughing. I will live with him forever."

Thomas smiled, finally understanding. "You speak of our Lord, Jesus Christ. You are right, He will take away all that ails us. He will hold us and protect us from all harm."

She tossed her head back, almost violently, and shook the bed with her laughter. "No, I am not speaking of your Lord. I'm speaking of the one who lives forever in the woods. He will drink my blood and I his, and I shall live forever."

Chills ran down Thomas' arms as he watched Edith's eyes grow dark. She labored to pull herself up onto her elbows, leaning in closer to Thomas so that her face was only an inch from his. "And the first thing I shall do when I am in my new form is to take you, as you should have taken me."

She fell back, away from him, and began laughing again. Her laughter brought on a fit of coughing, and a nurse came rushing over to tend to her.

Getting up on his feet, Thomas hastily crossed himself, then, mumbling a blessing, made the sign of the cross in her direction. Turning to leave, he made the sign of the cross again and did his best not to run as he headed for the door.

****

Thomas woke in the basement of the Admissions Building in a cold sweat, the perspiration dripping down the sides of his face into his hair. He wiped the beaded skin with his hand, then stared at his damp fingers. When had he ever sweat? He had outrun angry mobs, bounded up the sides of buildings, jumped down from the tops of the highest trees only to leap up into the branches of others, and still he had never broken a sweat. He was a vampire, and vampires did not sweat.

Edith. The memory of the vision hit him again. That day and those that followed were so fresh in his mind, now that he had relived just those few minutes with her. He had visited Edith every day for a week after finding her lying in that bed in the public hospital. Each day, she had told him more about the creature. Each day, she had believed the creature would come to her in the middle of the night and make her immortal. She had died at the end of the week, still clinging to that hope, no matter how hard Thomas had tried to bring her back from the feverish precipice of insanity.

But it had not been insanity. He had discovered that for himself not long afterwards.

As Thomas got ready for the evening, he pushed away the memories of those terrible days by filling his mind with thoughts of the hours to come. What would Beth be wearing tonight? Would she have her hair up in a ponytail? Would she hold his hand during the movie? Would she let him kiss her as she had the night before, and would she kiss him back with the same fervor?

There was only one thing he had left to do before

146

he could go meet her. He had to feed. And for the first time in his life, he dreaded it.

****

Beth normally enjoyed her study group meetings. The group had been together since the first semester of her sophomore year, and she would never have been able to learn the material as well as she had without it.

Tonight's session, however, was testing the limits of her patience.

No one was in the mood to work. When the conversation devolved into an inane debate about whether cats could be taught to use a toilet to do their business, Beth decided enough was enough.

Despite her resolution to leave, it was seven-thirty-five by the time Beth had finally extricated herself, leaving her friends to continue their debate. In her haste to exit the student lounge of the Mechanics building, she didn't see Adam standing just outside and managed to run right into him.

"I'm so sorry, Adam!" She bent down to pick up the physics book she had knocked out of his arms. "Are you okay?"

"Yeah, no permanent damage done." Rubbing his injured limb briefly, Adam looked her up and down. "You in a hurry to go somewhere?"

The question caught Beth off guard.

"Uh, well…" She fiddled with the straps on her backpack. "I told someone I'd meet them at seven-thirty, so I'm trying not to be too late."

He nodded, crossing his arms. "So how are things going with you and Ryan?"

Beth couldn't stop herself from frowning. What business was it of his how things were going with

Ryan? She took a moment before responding. "Why are you asking?"

"It's just that I thought I saw you with someone the other night in Collegetown, but it didn't look like Ryan."

Beth didn't have to explain herself to Adam. Why did he care who she was going out with?

She took a deep breath to calm herself down. "Listen, Adam, I've gotta go. I'll see you Thursday night in the lab."

As she turned to leave, he gripped her upper arm, stopping her. Shocked, she swung back around to face him, ready to give him a piece of her mind.

The look of genuine concern in his eyes diffused her anger, though, and Beth held her tongue. Sighing, he let go of her arm.

"Look, Beth. I know it's none of my business, and I know you're not some dumb airhead who likes to party or anything like that, but there are a lot of creeps out there. And not just creeps—dangerous, psychotic weirdos who get off on hurting sweet, kind young women like you. So just…" Adam paused, as though trying to find the right words. "Just be careful. Okay?"

Beth stared at him, her mouth hanging slightly open. "Okay," she said, finally.

He reached over to pat her arm, then, sighing again, walked away from the student lounge.

As Beth quickly made her way through the building to the doors that led out to the parking lot, she wondered what that whole exchange with Adam was about. What had he been doing lingering outside the lounge in the first place? And why was he so concerned about who she was or wasn't spending time with?

Although Beth's initial reaction had been anger at his intrusiveness, seeing the expression on Adam's face as he told her to be careful made her think there was no bad intent on his part. He was actually worried about her.

Did Adam *like* her, maybe? In the romantic sense? Beth didn't think so, but she had been wrong about stuff like that before.

She was still going through the different possibilities in her mind when she pushed open the back door to the parking lot and found handsome, dark-haired Thomas standing beside her car, as comfortable and carefree as though it were seventy degrees outside, rather than seven below.

Beth couldn't help smiling.

She closed the gap between them as quickly as possible without running, then stopped about a foot away from him. Suddenly, she didn't know how to greet him. Should she just say hi? That didn't seem to convey how happy Beth was to see him. Should she hug him? Or kiss him, even?

The longer she stood there, lips parted, staring at him, the more awkward she felt until she was so embarrassed that she considered turning around and going back into the building.

Without thinking, she took a step back, but Thomas reached out to grab her hand and pulled her into his embrace, wrapping his arms around her. Even through her heavy winter coat, Beth melted into him, putting her own arms around him and holding on tightly.

Moving his hands to her arms, Thomas pushed her gently away from him, enough to look at her face as he spoke. "If you're having trouble deciding how to greet me, how about we agree right now that I get a hug when you see me…" He dipped his head and kissed her deliciously. "And a kiss."

She smiled, savoring the warmth his lips left on hers. "Am I that easy to figure out?"

He laughed. "If it makes you feel any better, just consider it a special talent I have, a talent that only works on you."

"Yes, actually, that does make me feel better." She stared into his eyes for a moment before collecting herself mentally. "Are you still up for a movie?"

Thomas brushed the hair that hung loose from her ponytail away from her face, making her cheek tingle where his fingers touched. "Yes, if you still want to. Did you eat dinner, or do you want to get something first?"

"I had a snack before the meeting, so I can wait until after the movie. What about you, though? Did you eat?"

His face darkened, but only for a second. "I'm good."

"Okay, great. I'm sorry the meeting ran over. The movie starts at eight, so we can still make it. I can drive."

Beth drew out her keys and unlocked the car. Reaching for the door handle, she noticed Thomas was still standing next to her.

"Do you want to drive?" she asked.

His lips curled. "I'm more than happy to be driven to the movies by the most beautiful girl on campus."

She knew she was blushing—he seemed to have a talent for doing that, too. "Okay. Well, it's unlocked. You can get in."

He looked almost relieved as he walked around to the other side of the car and opened the passenger side door.

"So," said Beth as she pulled out of the parking lot, "what did you do today?" She looked over at him and smiled.

"I thought about you. And I kept checking what time it was."

Beth chuckled, her cheeks warming. "I did the same thing."

When they stopped at a red light, Beth glanced in Thomas' direction. He was looking at her, his forehead marred by a slight frown, as though he were trying to solve a puzzle.

"What are you thinking?" she asked softly as the light turned green.

"I…" Thomas seemed at a loss for words, which was strange considering how confident he seemed a few minutes ago, when he had pulled her into his arms and kissed her. His vulnerability made her heart pinch, and she took her right hand off the steering wheel to place it, palm up, between them.

He grasped it immediately, their fingers intertwining.

"I missed you," she whispered when he said nothing more. "I don't know why—I just saw you last night, and we don't even really know each other very well. But I did. I missed you."

Thomas gave her hand a squeeze, and she squeezed back before letting go to grab onto the steering wheel with both hands again.

"I really have to get better at driving with one hand," said Beth glumly as she pulled into a parking spot at the student center, where the movie was showing.

Thomas laughed, and as Beth put the car in park and turned off the ignition, he reached for her face. Tenderly tucking the loose hair behind her ear, he rubbed his knuckles against her cheek.

"I'm happy," he said, his fingers still setting her cheek on fire. "That's what I was going to say before. That's what I was thinking. I'm happy, and I haven't been happy in a very, very long time."

Beth turned her head slightly to kiss the palm of his hand. "Come on," she rallied, undoing her seat belt. "Let's go watch a ridiculously unrealistic romantic comedy."

****

The auditorium at the student center was packed, especially considering it was a Monday night. Thomas wondered if college kids even bothered to study anymore. Beth had managed to pay for his movie ticket, claiming she got a discount as she wedged herself between him and the ticket counter, and Thomas let her have the small victory. It was worth it to see her smile.

As soon as they were seated, the lights in the auditorium dimmed and the movie started playing. Thomas pulled on the armrest that was irritatingly located between him and Beth, but the thing wouldn't budge. So, he leaned toward Beth as much as he could and dropped his arm on her side of the barrier. She wrapped her arm around his immediately, her fingers twining with his.

"Have you seen this movie before?" she whispered softly, turning her head to him.

"No." He didn't expect he would be watching

much of it tonight, either, as distracted as his senses were by the fact of Beth's presence beside him. He brought her hand to his lips and kissed it. "Have you?"

"No," she replied, sounding breathless, "but I've heard it's good."

It may well have been the best movie ever made, but Thomas would never be able to say one way or the other. Though his eyes were fixed on the large screen in front of them, his mind was on Beth and all the human feelings she had evoked since they'd first met.

Thomas was convinced that Beth was the reason he started having memories of his human life. He hadn't spared a thought on his former life since the moment he had turned, but over the last week, it seemed everything was coming back to him. With each dream-like memory, a new facet of his emotions was opened, and once opened, he couldn't close it off.

After the night he'd danced with Beth at the club, Thomas began writing down his episodes and the feelings he had experienced. He thought it would help him see a pattern, that somehow, if it was written on paper, he would be able to manage it, even when he was away from Beth. Although he seemed to need Beth more each evening, cataloging his memories had at least helped him define what was happening to him.

In his first memory, over a week ago, he was confident in his role as a seminarian, a man who could bring some measure of comfort and hope to those in despair. Being with Mr. Waverly as the man mourned the loss of his daughter had made Thomas feel a sense of purpose. He was doing God's work.

The next memory had been a little harder to get through. Thomas remembered the dread that had been building in the pit of his stomach as he worked up the courage to tell Edith he would not be marrying her, that he would be devoting his life to God, instead of her. He had known Edith's anguish and disappointment, and being the cause of those feelings had left him miserable with guilt despite his certainty that he was doing the right thing.

He'd experienced anxiety and excitement during those first days as a seminarian, and although the memory of that time was brief, just a flash in his mind, Thomas had remembered the relationships he had forged with the other men. He recalled each bond, each joke, each kindness, each aggravation—what it was like to be part of a community.

It was only after he had remembered that he'd had such people in his life that Thomas recalled the love of his mother. He'd been a child in that memory, and his world had revolved around the tenderness and compassion his mother bestowed upon him each and every day. He could almost feel her arms around him, imparting an indescribable sense of safety and warmth. His mother was his protection. His strength. Hers was a love like no one else's.

And once Thomas had recalled that feeling of love that conquered all fear and pain, his memories had seen fit to remind him that death and darkness still existed. He had experienced those emotions as he looked into the eyes of the woman he had almost asked to marry. He'd felt suffering and pain and hopelessness through Edith's eyes, and had he not remembered what it was to bask in the light, he would never have appreciated how devoid of light the darkness truly was. It was as though each memory had prepared him for the next. And with each memory, each feeling that awakened within him, he became less of a vampire and more of a man.

"Thomas, are you alright?"

Beth's question, along with the subtle squeeze of her hand, caused Thomas to notice that the credits were rolling and students were getting up all around them. The movie was already over.

"I don't think you enjoyed that movie," said Beth, pulling him to his feet. "You didn't laugh once."

Beth looked at him with tender concern, as though his enjoyment of the movie was essential to hers. His heart rose into his throat.

"I must admit, I don't think I noticed a moment of it. I was...thinking."

Beth stiffened at his side as they shuffled out of the auditorium. She kept her eyes forward as she led him out the doors and into the lobby. "What's on your mind?" she asked.

Her voice trembled, almost imperceptibly, and at once Thomas realized what had caused the reaction. Despite his declaration only two hours ago that she made him happy, Beth was afraid he was having second thoughts about her.

Thomas drew her away from the crowds that were funneling out the double doors into the frigid night and pulled her into a dimly lit corridor to the right. She made no protest, and when he turned to face her, he saw only trust in her eyes. It was so different from how she had looked at him the first night they'd met. Perhaps she, too, sensed on some level how much he had changed since then.

He took her other hand, enclosing both of hers in his grasp, and smiled. "I'm trying not to scare you with talk about how much I've grown to care for you in only a few days."

Beth looked down at their clasped hands, one side of her mouth curving. "So that's what you were thinking about during the movie?"

"Yes. That, and how much I've changed since I first met you. *Because* I met you."

Her smile grew, and her eyes found his once more. "That's not what I was expecting you to say."

"I know."

Thomas tugged her into his chest and, dropping her hands, wrapped his arms around her. Bowing his head, he whispered close to her ear. "I care about you very, very much, Beth. It's incomprehensible, actually. And a bit frightening."

As he lowered his mouth from her ear to her neck, unable to stop himself from planting kisses on the soft skin between her earlobe and her collarbone, he sensed someone approaching. His head snapped up to survey the intruder just as the man's words reached him.

"Get the hell away from her!"

Faster than a human heartbeat, Thomas pushed Beth behind him and sneered at the bearded man, almost showing his fangs. He wouldn't have thought twice about ripping the head off the man's body had it not been for Beth standing there, watching. Even still, killing the guy was not out of the question, depending on how the next thirty seconds unfolded.

"What do you want?" Thomas growled as Beth wriggled behind him, trying to see what was going on.

"Adam?"

At the sound of recognition in Beth's voice, Thomas's hands fell to his sides, and Beth stepped forward, smiling in a way the dark-haired, disheveled man didn't deserve.

"Thomas," she said, taking Thomas' hand, "this is Adam Keplar. He has the misfortune of having been assigned to help me on my senior project." Turning to the man, Beth continued. "Adam, this is my friend, Thomas."

Thomas tried not to react to the platonic definition Beth gave for their relationship, choosing instead to focus his energy on studying the grizzly-looking man in front of him. He was familiar, this large-nosed man with narrow-set eyes and an unkept beard, and yet Thomas knew he had never seen him before.

"Are you okay?"

The man addressed Beth, and Thomas didn't like that one bit.

"What are you talking about? Of course I'm fine." Beth looked at Thomas, as though he had any idea what was going on, before turning back to Adam. "It's weird to see you here. Twice in one night. Are you here with your mom?"

"Yes. She's in the bathroom, but she'll be here in a minute, I'm sure."

Adam didn't take his little eyes off Thomas, and Thomas reciprocated with his fiercest glare.

Beth must have sensed the tension between the two men, as she threaded her arm with Thomas' and gave a weak laugh.

"Well, I'd love to meet her, but Thomas and I are actually heading out. Maybe you can bring her by the lab later this week, if she's still around?"

She didn't wait for a response, but instead dragged Thomas by the arm in the direction of the lobby.

"Beth, don't."

The shithead's forceful tone caused her to stop and look back at him. "Don't what?"

She sounded annoyed, and Thomas almost smiled.

"Don't go with him. I'll take you home."

"I don't need you to take me home, Adam." Beth took a deep breath. "Look, I don't know why you seem to have an issue with Thomas, and I don't really care. I'm just going to assume you're having a bad day and let it go. I'll see you in the lab, okay?"

She pulled Thomas the rest of the way into the lobby and through the doors to the outside.

They were both silent until they had reached Beth's car.

"I'm so sorry about that," said Beth, digging in her purse for the car keys. The streetlamp they had parked under illuminated her face in a mystical way, and Thomas could see the distress of their encounter etched into her otherwise flawless face. It was almost enough to make Thomas go back and find the man again so he could act on all those vampire urges he had so valiantly suppressed.

"I really don't know what's wrong with Adam today," she continued. "He was acting weird when I saw him right after my study group meeting, asking me about Ryan—my ex-boyfriend—and telling me to be careful. It's just so strange. You two don't know each other, do you?"

She looked up from the purse, searching his face for an answer.

"I've never seen him before in my life. And I'm quite certain I never want to see him again."

Beth nodded, then, turning her attention back to her

purse, exhaled loudly. "Finally," she announced, pulling out a set of keys.

Before she could use them, they dropped with a jingle to the pavement. An irritated sigh escaped her lips as she crouched to retrieve them. She had just begun to say something else when she stood up quickly and half-closed her eyes, her body swaying.

Faster than he knew he should with people around, Thomas leaned in to grab Beth's arms and pull her body into his chest. Fear—an emotion he had no business feeling—surged through him, and he held her more tightly in his arms.

"Beth, are you okay? Beth?"

Her eyes were already fluttering open, and Thomas could feel her body stiffen as she regained consciousness.

"Beth?"

Thomas pushed the hair away from her face, then rubbed two fingers across her cheek, relief flooding his body as she looked at him lucidly and attempted a smile.

"I'm sorry, I'm fine. I just felt light-headed for a second when I stood up." Her eyes locked with his, and again Thomas could see that her thoughts were only for his well-being. "I didn't mean to scare you. This just happens to me once in a while, when I have low blood sugar or am stressed out. I got up too quickly, I guess."

"Please, don't apologize," he replied, keeping one arm around her waist. "For fainting or for your friend or for anything, ever. Okay?"

Beth didn't say a word but nodded her agreement.

"Let's walk over to the food truck we passed at the corner before we turned in here. Would that help?"

She nodded again. "Yes, I think so."

It would also keep her with him for a little while longer. And Thomas would take every minute he could get.

Chapter Thirteen

"I can't believe you approached him alone. All you had to do was wait two more minutes for me to come back from the bathroom."

Adam sucked in an angry breath as he slammed the car door and waited for his mother to go around to the passenger side. He heard her get in and didn't even have to turn his head to know she was still glaring at him in disapproval.

"What the fuck is wrong with you?" she started up again when he didn't respond. "Don't you know how dangerous the creature is?"

"Yes, I know how dangerous he is," Adam replied, his hands gripping the steering wheel so tightly his knuckles were turning white. "That's exactly why I couldn't wait for you. I saw him take Beth into the dark hallway and I thought he was going to hurt her."

"Fuck her if she's stupid enough to go somewhere with it willingly. You can't jeopardize your safety or our success because of your sentimental feelings for this girl. You know how close we are. We can't make any mistakes."

Adam started the car and cranked the heat up as he pulled out of the parking lot of the student center. Beth's car was gone now. Her car was still parked in the lot when he and his mother had come out of the building, and Adam had hoped to find them. He and his mother had walked around the parking lot and down the street, then gone back into the student center looking for Beth and the vampire, but to no avail. And when they had circled back to the parking lot, the car was gone. The creature had gotten away.

Adam prayed Beth was unharmed, but he wouldn't know for sure until he saw her. He wasn't scheduled to be at the lab again until Thursday, though. Maybe he could just drop by tomorrow, after dinner, when he knew Beth would be there, with an "idea" for her experiment. Or maybe he could run into her outside one of her classes. In any case, he just couldn't wait three more days to make sure she was okay.

"What's got you all wound up, anyway?" asked his mother, sounding a bit calmer now. "There's no harm done. The creature's not onto us. It has no idea we're hunting it."

"I know."

It was true—the evening had been successful. Adam had gotten closer to the creature than he ever had before. He had talked to him, for God's sake. Adam knew they would find him again.

No, that wasn't what bothered him. It was how the creature had acted that didn't make sense.

When he had first seen the creature pull Beth off to the side and into the darkened hallway, Adam had nearly panicked. Then, when he followed them and found the thing with his head bent close to Beth's face, he nearly lost his shit.

But as soon as the vampire saw Adam, it pushed Beth behind itself. It was almost as though the thing was protecting Beth from danger.

"Do you think the vampire cares about Beth?"

The question popped out of Adam's mouth before he could consider the effect it might have on his mother. A quick glance in her direction confirmed that it was a stupid thing for him to say, regardless of whether he was thinking it.

"Care? You think that killer has a heart—has a soul? Do you think that cold-blooded, murderous creature can feel anything other than hunger and lust and the pleasure of inflicting pain upon others? Have you forgotten what happened to your great-grandmother's family?"

"No," he replied, hearing the hard edge in his own voice. "I remember the story."

His great-grandmother had spoken of the massacre only once in his presence, but once had been enough. Adam could still remember the cold look in his great-grandmother's eyes when she'd recounted, likely word-for-word, the history her mother had passed on to her. It had been her mother's story, after all—her mother had witnessed the killing spree that had occurred in her neighborhood, an impoverished encampment northwest of Boston settled by Italian immigrants. The woman, Isabella Rossi, had only been four when she had watched the creature slaughter her whole family before her eyes.

Hiding in an overturned basket of laundry, the unfortunate girl had seen her father, mother, two brothers and a sister die a gruesome death. The creature had sucked the blood out of the first of its victims, but then, when its hunger had presumably been sated, it had continued to kill in the most brutal manner, killing for the sole purpose of extinguishing life. Deaf to the screaming and pleading, insensitive to the buffets and blows its victims threw out in a last, desperate attempt to live, the creature had ripped through their human flesh with glee. Watching them gurgle their last breaths, the monster held its victims' convulsing bodies as their souls departed and their blood turned cold, then calmly left the scene of the carnage when it believed there was no one left.

It was a wonder that Isabella Rossi, as the sole survivor of the Rossi family massacre, had not gone insane with the memories of what she had witnessed. How she could have carried on with her life after what she had seen was a mystery to him. But carry on she had, marrying a good man from another Italian family and raising four children of her own, his great-grandmother being one of them. She'd passed her story on to his great-grandmother, along with her hatred for the creature who had destroyed her family and the families of so many others.

Though Isabella Rossi had died when his great-grandmother was in her thirties, his great-grandmother had been blessed, or possibly cursed, with a long life. She'd lived almost a century carrying the weight of her ancestors' murders on her back, and though she had never spoken to Adam of the massacre again, the old woman's last words to Adam's mother had been "Avenge them."

There was no question as to her meaning.

Still, the behavior Adam had witnessed in the hallway of the student center had not been that of a crazed and bloodthirsty killer. Rather, the creature had acted almost like an overprotective boyfriend.

It didn't make sense at all.

****

Beth couldn't help noticing how quiet Thomas had been since the encounter with Adam. He had ordered nothing from the food truck but had insisted on paying for her meatball sub.

Now, parked outside her apartment building with the engine turned off, Thomas just stared at her in that thoughtful, sensitive way of his.

She crumpled up the empty sandwich wrapper and put it to the side, then reached for another napkin to make sure there was no sauce on her face.

"Feeling better?" he asked, almost startling her.

"Yes," she nodded, smiling in his direction. "I told you, it's just low blood sugar or something. Nothing serious."

He reached over and grabbed her hand.

"It's almost eleven." The disappointment in his tone matched her own feelings at the fact that the night was already over. "You have an early class tomorrow morning, right?"

"I do." Beth sighed and gave his hand a squeeze. "What about you? What are you up to tomorrow?"

His eyes widened, then he looked down and smiled. "My schedule is not as structured as yours. I just have some reading to catch up on. But my evenings are yours. That is, if you're free tomorrow night?"

Beth wished she could say yes. She wished she could see him between classes, have lunch with him, and spend her afternoons doing problem sets while he read his papers beside her. It was odd, but she wanted to spend every waking moment with him. He was so different than she had thought him to be the first time she'd met him, and even the second time. Looking at him now, waiting for her to answer, the smile on his face slowly fading as he realized what that answer would be—he was nothing like the sly, arrogant man she had come upon almost in the very spot where they sat now in her car. Now, when she looked into his eyes, she saw something vulnerable, something kind. Something wonderful.

"I wish I could," she finally said, "but I have a test on Wednesday that I really need to study for. And I know that if I see you, I'll want to spend more than just a half hour with you."

His gaze drifted down to her hand, still in his, and he nodded. "That's okay, I understand. I've been lucky to spend as much time as I have with you in the short while we've known each other."

"I want to know more about you, Thomas," said Beth, making his eyes snap back to hers. "I want to know everything. You were right the other day, at Valhalla, when you said I didn't know you. I want to change that."

"I want to tell you everything about me," he replied softly. "I've never felt that way before, about anyone. I'm—" Thomas paused, as though searching for the right phrase. "—I'm a very private person. And suddenly I find that I don't like myself as much as I once did. But even still, I want to tell you, even if it means you won't…"

He let go of her hand and looked out the window. Beth had never heard such an honest declaration of feelings before, and it tugged almost painfully at her heart.

She put her hand gently on his shoulder, wanting him to know how much she cared for him, how much she loved what little she did know about him.

"We have time, Thomas. Whatever it is that worries you, you'll tell me when you're ready. And it won't make me think any less of you. I promise."

He let out a small laugh as he turned his head toward her, his lips planting a chivalrous kiss on the back of the hand she still had on his shoulder. "I hope you're right."

Beth waited a moment, in case he wanted to say more, but he didn't, and that was okay. She lifted her hand to brush his cheek, eliciting a smile. "Wednesday night, then? Around seven, where we met tonight behind the Engineering building?"

His smile grew wider. "Wednesday night it is."

Later, as she lay in bed in the darkness, thinking about the evening she had spent with Thomas, Beth touched the chain around her neck and ran her fingers down the links until she reached the stone that hung from it. Grasping the amulet in the palm of her hand, she thought about why she had put the necklace on in the first place, and why she hadn't taken it off since the night she found it in her drawer. The vial of holy water was in her purse, always with her, too. Fear had made her turn to these objects, seeking some superstitious sense of protection from having them with her. But she was no longer afraid. Was it because she was being protected? Or had she never been in any danger to begin with?

She hadn't made a wish on the stone yet, and she didn't really believe that any wish she made would come true. Still, Beth didn't see what harm could come of thinking about what she wanted most and saying it out loud. Maybe just making that determination and announcing it was all a person needed to do to make a goal real for themselves. And maybe once a goal was real, then the person could take the steps they needed to reach that goal. Maybe that's all the necklace was for. Maybe that was enough.

What did Beth want more than anything else? She wanted to figure out what was wrong with her experiment, that was certain. And she wanted to graduate and get a good job, something she would enjoy doing that paid well enough that she wouldn't have to worry about making ends meet. But those things would come on their own, she knew they would.

So, what did Beth want, then? What was more important than her educational goals?

The same vague thought she'd always had when pondering her life, her future, tugged at the edges of her consciousness. *I want to make a difference in someone's life.* She'd never said the words aloud, nor would she now, but she recognized the truth behind that feeling. The only way to make a mark on this world was to help someone in it. To be a positive influence. To make someone else's life better. That's what she'd always wanted, and that's what she wanted now.

But now that same unspoken wish looked like Thomas. All she had to do was close her eyes and there he was, looking at her with warmth and longing. Beth smiled. Was Thomas going to be part of her future? She'd known him for just over a week. Logic dictated that it was too soon to tell if whatever they had was something that would last, something real and substantial.

Still, Beth's instincts told her that what she felt for Thomas, and what he felt for her, was different than anything she had experienced before—with Ryan or anyone else. *He* was different. He always seemed to know what she was thinking, what she needed to hear. When she'd met up with him earlier that night and didn't know how to greet him, he had pulled her into a hug and kissed her. After the movie, when Thomas admitted he'd been lost in his thoughts, she had immediately concluded he was questioning their relationship, and he had *known* that. He had reassured her.

At the same time, she saw disappointment flicker across Thomas's face when she explained they couldn't meet the following day. Part of him doubted her feelings for him, and it was just enough insecurity to endear him to her even more.

Where would this road with Thomas lead? There was no way for her to know, but she had a feeling it was somewhere she'd never been before, somewhere worth going. She just had to relax, be patient, and take it day by day.

Beth closed her eyes and turned onto her side, still holding the necklace. First, she would get through tomorrow. She would focus on classes, study for her Lasers exam, catch up with Lin for dinner, do some work in the lab on her experiment, and then get a good night's sleep. Then on Wednesday, she would ace her test, get through her other classes, and do some more work in the lab. When she was done with all that, she would see Thomas again.

Just the thought of him made Beth grin as she drifted off to sleep.

Chapter Fourteen

The night could never last long enough, or so it had always seemed to Thomas. But that was before he had met Beth. Now it was only his time with her that seemed to slip by too quickly. The hours between their last goodbye and the oblivion of sleep that came with the breaking dawn seemed to stretch on and on.

Knowing he would not see Beth on Tuesday night, Thomas woke from a day of sleep particularly irritable. It didn't help that he hadn't had a decent feeding in days. A few sips from a homeless man here, a couple of gulps from a drunk frat boy there—it wasn't fulfilling in the least. Try as he might, the old satisfaction of selecting his prey, luring them to a private spot, seducing them, and enjoying the warm blood that pulsed from their bodies into his was nowhere to be found.

Now all Thomas wanted to do was quench his thirst, just a little. Just enough so that he wasn't ice-cold to the touch. So that he wouldn't lose all control of his faculties and attack the jugular of the next living thing that crossed his path. But feeding was hard to do when the act he used to find so pleasurable was now physically repulsive.

At least he'd had no dreams that night. No memories, no new feelings. Thomas ached to see Beth as it was. Had he endured another memory from his mortal life, he wasn't sure how he would have coped.

Thomas passed the night as best he could, opting to leave campus to find his meal. He finished quickly, disgusted with himself and angry at the change in his personality. Why should he find feeding so distasteful? It was still a necessity. Despite the human emotions that had awakened after being dormant for so long, he still required human blood to survive. It was in his nature. How could it be, then, that his body rebelled against the act? And to what end? He could not simply *decide* not to drink. The thirst was in him—it *defined* him. His body would compel him to feed, sooner or later. It was a contradiction, a struggle between compulsion and revulsion. How was he to deal with such a conflict?

As Thomas stretched out his limbs after an interminable night pondering the question, more than ready for sleep to overtake him, he wondered what Beth would say about his predicament, should he ever have the courage to tell her. What would she advise? A bitter realization rose like bile within him as he faded out of consciousness. He would never have Beth's counsel on the matter. Beth would never know who he really was. She couldn't.

Because if she ever learned the truth, she would run away from him screaming at the top of her lungs. And he couldn't bear to lose her. Not yet.

****

Thirsty. He was so thirsty. Even with his eyes closed, Thomas knew he was dreaming.

His head was spinning, and there was fire coursing through his veins. He knew nothing in that moment other than the thirst and the fire.

"Open your eyes, child."

He was not alone—he remembered that now. The creature was there, too.

Thomas slowly opened his eyes within the dream, as the gravelly voice had commanded, and his surroundings came into focus. Looking around, he saw more than the moonlight filtering into the hole in the ground where he lay should have allowed him to see. There was bright green moss on the large flat rocks near the entrance of the shallow cave, and above him tiny roots poked down, searching for moisture to feed the plants that grew above. He placed his hands on the ground and raised himself to a sitting position. Then, he lifted one of his hands to touch those roots, needing to confirm their existence.

Breathing in, he could smell things he had not smelled before—the sweat and disease that still clung to his skin and his clothes, the ammonia in the damp earth all around him, the earthworms that squirmed beneath the soil. Yes, the earthworms. They smelled good; delicious, in fact, because he could smell their blood.

Without thinking, Thomas clawed at the ground, feeling with his fingers for the plump, juicy body of an earthworm.

"No!"

The creature's voice stopped him instantly, and for the first time he turned his head to look at the thing he had sought out earlier that day, the being that had terrified him only slightly less than the knowledge of his impending death.

The creature was sitting on its knees against the wall at the far end of the tiny cave, watching him. It had been watching this whole time. It looked like a man, with jet black hair falling in waves to its shoulders. Its deep-set eyes were dark and contrasted starkly with its pale face, creating a falsely alluring effect, and its prominent nose sloped invitingly toward a wide mouth which, at the moment, bore a paternal smile.

Shaking its head slowly, the creature spoke again, more softly this time. "You need not stoop to eating worms from the ground. You are thirsty, child, I know. Go and quench your thirst. You know what to do."

Obeying, Thomas crawled to the mouth of the burrow, and his eyes caught the contrasting texture of an object in the dirt just outside. Still within the hole, he extended his hand through the opening to touch it, then recoiled when he saw that it was a wooden cross fixed on a length of twine. Curious, he studied the object, and slowly it began to look familiar. He had a hazy memory of having carried that cross once. Yes, the cross was his—had been his. It seemed like so long ago that he had worn it around his neck, praying with his brothers, hoping one day to tend his own flock of sheep.

But that was not him any longer. No, he was changed—he could feel it. He could no more pray now than a snake could fly to the clouds.

He had traded his soul for a new life, and now his body was strong, his senses sharp, his mind focused. And he was thirsty.

Breathing in the night air, Thomas picked up the scent of human blood. He stood up, suddenly frantic to find the source. Looking to the south, he spied a cluster of flickering lights in the distance. It was an encampment, just outside the city, where immigrants who could not yet afford city life had settled. He had known of the village in his previous life, had visited there, he was sure of it, though the memory had been replaced with a single conscious thought.

Blood.

Wasting no more time, Thomas ran in the direction of the lights. His legs were strong, carrying him swifter and more surely than they ever had before. He felt no fatigue as he dodged trees and leapt over rocks and streams.

An errant branch swiped across his cheek, stinging him, but only for a moment. Reaching up to his face, he touched a thin line of dampness—his own blood from the scrape. The wound itself, however, was gone in a matter of moments, his body healed. Just as the disease had left him, the injury had been erased, as though it had never existed. This was his body now.

Perfection.

The sound of human families settling in for the night reached his ears before the first of the makeshift shelters came into full view. Louder than the voices was the pulsating rhythm of the sweet liquid that flowed through their veins.

Thomas stopped and took refuge behind a tree. What would he do now? The people would surely see him if he went any closer.

Even as he asked himself the question, he laughed at his own folly.

Let them see him. Let them gaze upon him and let fear greater than any they had ever known fill their being. Let them scream and run and try to protect their wives and children.

It would make the feeding that much more satisfying.

****

Thomas woke from his dream on Wednesday

night, his body weak and trembling.

The vision had ended before he'd left his spot behind the tree, while he was still gazing at the immigrants sitting around their fires, talking and laughing, unaware of what was about to happen. But Thomas remembered what came next. He remembered his insatiable thirst and how he had ripped through one settler after the next, trying to quench it.

He remembered the look of terror in his victims' eyes, the pleading and begging. He remembered being amused at how weak and inconsequential each of them was. He remembered laughing as he killed every last one of them—man, woman, and child.

Even after his thirst had been sated, hate, darkness, and bloodlust had propelled him.

Oh yes, Thomas remembered how he had taken pleasure from every second of his feasting that first night as a vampire, and countless nights thereafter. He remembered, but now there was only…remorse.

Was this what his visions had been leading to? Was he expected now to feel sorry for the last century of his existence?

Moving slowly, still pondering the vision, Thomas rose to prepare himself for the evening, changing into a forest green sweater and pulling on a pair of dark blue jeans.

What purpose could remorse possibly serve, he wondered as he ran a comb through his thick hair, then teased it with his fingers. It had been many years since he'd killed anyone. Intentionally, that is. And since he'd met Beth, he no longer took pleasure in feeding. He fed now only out of necessity, to stave off the thirst, and even that he found difficult to do.

Because the pleasure was necessary.

There it was—if he did not *enjoy* feeding, then it was nearly impossible to take blood. And if he could not take blood, then he could not continue to exist. He would perish.

How, then, could he tolerate this new emotion, this guilt? How could he regret what was necessary for him to survive? To do so would be to deny his very self.

More importantly, how could he be with Beth, knowing what he was, allowing her to think he was anything other than the monster who had taken dozens of lives in that first night of his wretched existence, and countless nights thereafter? Was that the purpose of this latest vision, then? To remind him of how unworthy he was to share even one moment with Beth?

And then it struck him, a memory from his past, one that he did not need a vision to recall.

Confession.

How many times had he gone to confession in his human life? As a seminarian, he made use of the sacrament regularly, sometimes once a week, sometimes daily. Confession was, after all, good for the soul. Of course, he no longer had a soul to speak of. He had exchanged it for the power and immortality of his vampiric existence.

Even still, as he rushed out of his makeshift home and toward the Engineering buildings, Thomas wanted nothing more than to confess. To Beth. It was hardly a decision—he knew now, with his whole being, that it was what he was meant to do.

Thomas would confess who he was and all the evil of his past to Beth. He would tell her everything he had done—the countless innocent lives he had taken, the pleasure it had given him—and he would ask for her forgiveness.

But what then? How would she react? Would she truly believe he was a murderous vampire? And if she did believe him, would she run from him in terror?

Would he lose her?

It did not matter. He had no choice. He could not persist in his self-loathing, this complete and utter disgust with himself and his existence. Beth was the only person who could help him. She would be his absolution, or she would be his condemnation. It was up to her, and he would accept his fate either way.

Even as he stepped into the parking lot and found Beth's car, Thomas could feel the thirst of several days of meager feedings gnaw at his insides. He could not risk seeing Beth like this. He had to drink, even just a bit.

There was no one at the car, and Thomas surmised that Beth was still inside the building, finishing up her work. With a good twenty minutes before they were scheduled to meet, Thomas slipped into the woods behind the lot, hoping to come across a student taking a shortcut from the main campus to Collegetown.

He was not disappointed. Only a few minutes passed before Thomas heard the rustle of leaves and spied a young woman—a junior or possibly a senior—coming toward him, on the way to meet friends at a restaurant or a bar, no doubt. She carried a small red purse, the same color as the lipstick she wore, and her hair was teased into curls that framed her face.

She didn't see Thomas until she almost ran into him, looking up from the path just in time to see his charming smile. Disarmed, the girl smiled back.

Hating himself, Thomas reached for her.

Chapter Fifteen

Beth burst out of the Engineering building like a grade schooler on the last day before summer vacation, trying her best not to run and to stop grinning like an idiot. Although she had just spent another unproductive afternoon in the lab, she had done well on her exam earlier in the day, and now she couldn't wait to see Thomas to tell him about it. More accurately, she couldn't wait to see Thomas, period. It had been a long two days, and her body nearly hummed with excitement at the thought of that roguish, lop-sided smile and those strong arms pulling her in for a welcoming hug.

She rushed right past her car in the parking lot, relieved to see that Thomas wasn't standing there already. He had a tendency to be early, and though she ached to see him, there was something she wanted to do first.

In between problem sets and studying and unsuccessful experimental runs in the lab, Beth had been struggling to come up with a gift she could give Thomas. Something small, but meaningful, to show she had missed him, that she cared about him.

The idea had finally struck during her exam that morning. She had been thinking of the time she had spent with Thomas dancing the merengue, and of leaving the club to go next door for a drink. Thomas seemed to enjoy whisky, and a bottle of the stuff would make a nice present.

Crossing over into Collegetown, she entered the liquor store, a jingling bell above her head announcing her presence as she opened the door. The tiny store consisted of three aisles in the middle and walls with floor-to-ceiling shelving, holding a bottle of every type of alcohol imaginable. If she couldn't find a good whisky for Thomas here, she wouldn't be able to find it anywhere.

Not wanting to be late meeting Thomas, Beth stepped over to the counter, where a silver-haired store clerk was watching a guy who looked suspiciously under-aged hide out in the center aisle. She chuckled to herself as the old clerk shook his head and turned to greet her with a smile.

"How can I help you, Miss?"

Beth smiled back and hoped she wouldn't sound ridiculously stupid when she opened her mouth. She didn't know much about hard liquor, or alcohol in general.

"I'm looking to buy a bottle of whisky for someone, but I'm not sure what to get."

The old man nodded knowingly as he stepped out from behind the counter. "You've got a few options," he said, leading her to a shelf near the front door where bottles of amber-colored liquid were on display. "It all depends on how much you're looking to spend."

She certainly didn't want to get Thomas cheap whiskey that tasted like turpentine, but she didn't have that much money to spend, either. "How much would a good, middle of the road whisky cost?"

The man turned to look at the bottles, then reached for a short-and-stout one that looked pretty fancy to

Beth's untrained eye. "This is a popular one. It's smooth, flavorful, and well-regarded, but not what you would call top-shelf. On sale this week for twenty-five dollars. I can put it in a nice gift bag for you."

Beth nodded appreciatively. "That sounds perfect. Thank you."

As the clerk rang up the purchase, Beth wondered what Thomas would think when she gave him the present. There was no occasion—they had only gone out a few times, and it wasn't his birthday or anything. Then again, she had no idea when his birthday was. There was a lot she didn't know about him. But what she had discovered, she liked. He was kind, thoughtful, caring, and protective. And he was conflicted about something in his past. It was almost as though he didn't think he was good enough for her, but he wanted to be better. He was humble, and she liked that about him, too.

Beth thanked the man and left the store, checking the time on her phone. It was ten minutes to seven, and she knew Thomas would already be standing by the car, waiting for her. She quickened her pace.

Normally, Beth stuck to the sidewalk and took the long way around to the Engineering buildings. Eager to see Thomas even a few minutes sooner, she took the shortcut through the woods without hesitating.

The cloudy sky made the night seem darker than it should have, and Beth clutched the bottle of whisky to her chest, her purse tucked under her arm. She looked ahead, toward the clearing on the other side of the trees that she knew was the parking lot, and moved her feet even faster. It wasn't safe to be walking through the woods alone at night. Thomas would probably be upset when he saw her come out from behind the trees into the parking lot. The thought made her smile.

A low moan sounded from behind the trees to her right, and Beth stopped dead in her tracks, the hairs on the back of her neck rising. It hadn't been her imagination. Even in the quiet that followed, Beth knew what she had heard. A woman had made that sound, and the fact that there was no giggling, no hushed whispers or snapping branches, meant this wasn't a college girl just having fun with a guy.

Her moan had been silenced. The woman was in trouble.

For a moment, she thought about running to the car to get Thomas, but the eerie quiet that followed the woman's moan made her wonder if she had that kind of time. Perhaps just seeing her would make the evildoer release his victim. All she knew was that if she were the one in trouble, she wouldn't want the person who'd heard her cry for help to just turn around and walk away.

Reaching into the outside pocket of her purse and pulling out her pepper spray, Beth said a short prayer and moved toward the spot she thought the moan had come from. It was hard to know how far the source of the sound had been, or whether she was even going in the right direction. But she kept advancing, one step after the next, scanning the area for signs of a struggle.

The snow-packed ground was clean and undisturbed, and Beth wondered if she really was just losing her mind. Then, from behind some shrubbery, she caught a flash of movement. Focusing on the shrubs, she continued moving toward them until she could see the figure of a man, partially obscured by the low branches. He was hunched over, his back toward her, oblivious to her approach.

As she got closer, she heard another sound—a soft suckling, like the smacking of lips against a juicy piece of fruit. Something slipped from the man's lap and fell to the ground with the faintest crunch against the snow.

It was a red purse.

Realizing the man held a woman in his arms—the woman who had made that desperate sound minutes ago—Beth gasped. The man's head snapped up, so quickly that she hadn't seen him actually move. Then he turned around slowly to look at her, and her heart stopped beating in her chest.

It was Thomas, or some version of Thomas. His face was the same, except for the blood on his lips—he looked like Thomas. But his eyes were dark and soulless, empty and devoid of emotion. They reminded her of the man who had spoken to her that first night, when she thought she had run over a pedestrian.

They were not human.

Then he blinked, and his mouth formed a single word, even as her Thomas resurfaced.

"Beth."

Despite the anguish in his voice, the remorse for whatever he had done to the poor girl in his arms, Beth could not overcome the fear coursing through her body at the sight of the man she thought she knew. The man she thought she cared for.

She could not respond.

Instead, she dropped the bottle of whisky she had been holding, the sound of breaking glass as the bottle hit the ground not fully registering in her mind.

Then she ran.

****

A grainy, oak scent with just a hint of caramel hit Thomas with the same force the bottle had hit the hard, frozen earth.

Whisky. She had bought him a bottle of whisky.

A low growl of anger and frustration rumbled from his chest, and he almost cried out in pain. How could this happen? How could he let Beth see him like this, see what he had done?

He propped the drowsy girl up against the shrubs to keep her from lying in the cold snow and rose to his full height, turning his body in the direction that Beth had run.

Beth had broken out of the woods and was running for the safety of her vehicle. Panic, unlike any he had experienced in all his vampiric existence, gripped him as he imagined her driving away, never to see him again.

He couldn't let that happen. He couldn't let her go without explaining. It was what he meant to do that night anyway, wasn't it? Now that she had seen with her own eyes what he was, it was even more important for him to come clean. To confess.

In less than the blink of an eye, Thomas was standing in front of Beth, watching her fumble with her keys. It took her a moment to realize he was standing there, and she dropped the keys in shock, her mouth open to scream, but she made no sound.

Instead, she shook her head, the fear written on her face, her body trembling. And that hurt him most of all.

She thought he would harm her.

"Beth," he began, taking a step closer, wanting to touch her but afraid she would run, "I'm not going to hurt you."

Her gaze darted to the woods, and he knew what she was thinking.

"She's fine, Beth. I didn't kill her. I just needed..." He paused, suddenly not knowing how to explain. Not knowing how to tell her what he was. "I needed to drink. I took no pleasure in it. I can't anymore, not since I met you. But I still need it."

"Blood." She whispered the word, as though it were sacred, still shaking her head slowly.

"Yes, blood. I need it to survive. I wish I didn't, but I do."

"What are you?"

"You know what I am."

She looked at him for a long moment, holding his gaze, giving him hope.

"Vampire." Her voice was so quiet, he would never have heard it with mortal ears.

"Yes. Vampire."

Her body stilled and her breathing slowed, her eyes still fixed on him. Thomas took courage, stepping closer. Heat radiated from her body, and it took a heroic amount of willpower not to take her in his arms.

A tear slipped down her cheek, and he fought the urge to run his finger down the same path.

Her lips parted, and he leaned in closer.

"Leave me alone."

The weight of her words crushed his chest, pressing down on him, squeezing the place where his heart should have been.

She was rejecting him. Despite her promise that he could tell her anything and she wouldn't think less of him, she did. She wanted him to go away. It wasn't fair of him to hold her to that promise; he knew that. It was a promise made when she thought he was a man, not a mythical monster who fed on the blood of the innocent. Even still, part of him had believed her. Part of him had hoped.

Thomas had also made a promise, and it was one he intended to keep. Reluctantly, he nodded his head and turned away, fighting with each step he took against every instinct that told him to stay. Fighting with a strength even he should not have possessed. And somehow, as her anguished sobs reached his ears, he managed not to turn around for one last glance.

****

Beth fell into her bed less than an hour later, hair wet from a hot shower that did nothing to calm her, face wet from tears that refused to stop coming. Pulling the blankets up to her chin, she rolled over onto her side and curled up in a ball, hugging the pillow next to her for comfort.

It didn't make sense. None of it made sense. Vampires did not exist, and the man she was falling in love with was not one of them. But he was. She had seen it with her own eyes. The woman in his arms, the blood on his lips. The look in his eyes.

Was that the reason he frightened her the first time she'd met him? Did part of her know, at that first encounter, what he was? Or rather, what he was not?

She shook her head, her face burrowing under the covers. What if there was a reasonable explanation? Well, maybe not reasonable, but something short of her boyfriend being a soulless vampire. Wasn't there a mental condition where a person thought they were a vampire and that they needed to drink blood?

Renfield's Syndrome, named after Count Dracula's assistant.

Still, how was it better if Thomas thought he was a vampire and attacked helpless women to suck the blood out of their bodies? Was being psychotic better than being supernatural? Perhaps he could get therapy, or medication, if it was a mental condition.

She let out a groan at her own insanity. She was grasping at straws, trying to find some way to make the situation better, but there was no way to change the fact that Thomas was sucking blood out of that poor girl. Or that he'd reached her side in a split second when she'd run to her car.

There was no mental condition that gave you the ability to run at the speed of sound, she was quite sure of that.

Flipping over onto her other side, Beth grasped at the necklace that was tucked into her sweatshirt. Could she wish it all away? This immense feeling of loss, of confusion and helplessness? Could she wish that she had never met Thomas? No, she knew that was impossible. Despite the devastating absurdity of that evening, she couldn't imagine her life without the things that had happened over the past week and a half. Dancing with him, sharing dessert, kissing him in the museum—sweet, wonderful moments that she could never part with.

What did she wish for, then? That he was not a vampire, if indeed that's what he was? That he was just a man? That she could just love him, and that he could just love her?

She shook her head slowly from side to side, tears welling up behind closed eyelids. Vampires. Wishes.

Love. She didn't know which was the most irrational notion.

Tightening her hand around the smooth stone, she tried her best to fall asleep.

Chapter Sixteen

"You okay?"

Beth turned away from the computer screen she had been staring at and found Adam sitting in the chair next to her, a concerned frown on his bearded face.

It had been nine days since she'd seen Thomas in the woods. Nine days since she'd discovered he was not a normal guy she could have a relationship with. Nine days since she'd told him to leave her alone. And she had been thinking about him almost every minute since. Missing him, despite what she'd seen. Despite what he'd told her he was.

"Yeah, I'm fine. I still can't figure out why it's shifting like that." Beth pointed to the edge of the picture on the screen in a lame attempt to justify her lack of conversation.

"Are you sure? Because you haven't been yourself all week. Has anything happened?" His frown deepened. "Is there anything you want to talk about?"

Beth shook her head, trying to smile. "Everything is okay. I'm just distracted, I guess. Which doesn't help in the problem-solving department."

Glancing at the time, she let out a resigned breath. It was only six-thirty, yet she couldn't bear to be in that lab a moment longer. As she logged off the computer and reached for her coat, she could feel Adam's stare.

"Are we calling it a night?"

"Yeah." Beth shoved her notebook into the backpack by her feet, then looked over to find Adam still sitting there, looking at her curiously. "My head's just not on right tonight," she added, hoping to placate him.

"What about tomorrow?" He stood as she got to her feet and slung the backpack over her shoulder.

"Tomorrow?" Beth's brain was like mush, and she had to think hard to remember that the following day was Saturday, the day of the dance she had no desire to attend with her ex-boyfriend.

"Tomorrow," she continued, regaining some of her faculties, "I'll have to leave early to get ready for the Barrister's Ball. So, maybe just until three o'clock."

"You going to that with Ryan?"

Beth nodded. She was still hoping she'd develop a sore throat or a fever between now and then so she could have a legitimate excuse to bail on her ex.

"Are you two back together?"

"No." She practically interrupted him.

"Oh." Adam looked confused. "Why are you going with him, then?"

A frustrated sigh passed her lips. "Because I'm an idiot and I make bad decisions. He asked me to go when I was breaking up with him, and in a moment of weakness, I agreed. And additional moments of weakness since then have prevented me from backing out of it. But I've still got twenty-four hours to find some courage and text him a ridiculous excuse for why I can't go, right?"

Beth smiled weakly at Adam.

"Somehow, I don't see that happening," he replied, holding the door open for her, then following as she stepped out of the lab. Turning to lock the door, she shrugged. "It'll be fine. It's just one night, then it'll be over. And then I can focus my full attention on getting this god-forsaken experiment to work so I can graduate."

Adam chuckled, falling into step beside her. He had been making it a habit to walk her to her car lately, and she didn't really mind. In a way, it was good to have the distraction of small talk as she exited the building and looked out toward her parked vehicle, where Thomas used to wait for her. Although she knew he wouldn't be there, dark hair falling across his eyes, hands shoved casually in his pockets, Beth still couldn't help *wanting* him to be there. She wanted to see him so much that sometimes she could feel him, watching her. She would take her time unlocking the car door and getting in, just in case he might appear, just on the slim chance she might see his lop-sided smile. Just in case he decided to show up and pull her against him and kiss her.

"I haven't seen your friend with you in a while."

Beth tore her gaze from the car they had been approaching and shot a wide-eyed look at Adam.

"What?" Was he referring to Thomas?

"Your friend," he repeated, more slowly this time, "the guy I saw you with at the movies a week or two ago."

"Thomas?"

Adam nodded slowly, his eyebrows raised, as though he could see right through her act.

She fixed her eyes on the car again, which was only a few steps away now.

"Thomas has his own stuff going on. We only met

up a few times. It wasn't really anything."

Except that it was.

Adam didn't say anything as Beth found her keys and got into the car. He waved as she backed out of the spot, and she waved back, trying not to cry.

****

"Bastard," Adam muttered under his breath as he watched Beth drive away.

The back of his neck was tingling. He was sure the creature was nearby, watching. It was a wonder Beth couldn't sense him. The feeling was so strong when he was with Beth outside.

Turning slowly, Adam walked toward his own car, which was parked a couple of rows away, closer to the woods.

Instead of subsiding as it usually did, the feeling that he was not alone grew stronger. Adam dug his hands into both coat pockets and touched the smooth wood of the stakes he kept with him always. His crossbow was in the car. Only a few steps more.

Before he could reach the car, a rush of cold air across the back of his neck made him spin around. Yanking the wooden stakes out of his pockets, he jabbed at the creature who had come up behind him, but he was too slow. Easily, the vampire knocked the sharpened stakes out of his hands and shoved him hard against the car, making it rock. Its arm pressed against Adam's neck, and for a moment he couldn't breathe.

"What are you doing with Beth?" the thing asked calmly while Adam thrashed and tried to break free from the creature's grasp.

"Making sure *you* don't hurt her," hissed Adam, pushing against the vampire's arm with both hands to no avail.

"And how did you think you would protect her when you can't even protect yourself?"

The creature's eyes bore into him, but its face held no hint of violence, only pain. And possibly regret.

Adam stilled, allowing his arms to fall to his side, and almost immediately the pressure on his neck subsided, though the vampire still held him in place.

"Thomas," Adam muttered, more to himself than to the vampire. "Your name is Thomas."

"Yes. And you are Beth's laboratory assistant, Adam."

As though the re-introduction made them friends, Thomas released his hold.

Glancing at the wooden stakes on the ground, Adam silently recognized that he was ill-equipped to kill the vampire on his own. The creature—Thomas—was faster, stronger, and in all likelihood, smarter than he was. Alone, without his mother and her weapons, Adam was powerless against it.

If he couldn't kill the creature, perhaps his time would be better spent learning something that would help him defeat it, later. After all, it didn't seem like the vampire wanted to harm him. At least, not at the moment.

"Why are you following Beth around, Thomas? If you'd wanted to hurt her, you could have easily done so at any time."

"I would never hurt Beth."

The way Thomas spoke her name, with reverence and sadness and excitement combined, made Adam think of how Thomas had pushed Beth behind him at the student center when Adam had come upon them and

Thomas had thought he was a threat. And suddenly, Adam *believed* him.

"Do you…do you care for Beth?"

Thomas straightened his back and cocked his head slightly to one side, as though assessing whether Adam could be trusted. All the while, Adam said nothing, waiting for the vampire to come to his own conclusions.

"Yes," said Thomas, finally. "I care for Beth very much."

There was agony behind his words, and Adam felt a twinge of sympathy, which he promptly pushed aside. The creature before him was blood-thirsty and evil. It was a cold-blooded killer, relishing in inflicting pain and suffering. It was not worthy of sympathy or compassion. It was not worthy of anyone's love, let alone Beth's.

"I know what you are. I know what you've done." It was a risk to tell the creature that he knew it was a vampire, but Adam did not sense any violence in the creature's manner. Which was odd, to say the least.

The creature gave him a sidelong glance. "How would you know?"

Adam panicked for a moment. He hadn't anticipated this question, and he couldn't tell the creature the truth about his family's connection to the vampire or that he and his mother were out to kill it.

"I've heard stories," Adam finally replied, "and I've seen the messes you've left behind. A sorority girl at a frat party here. A homeless man at the bus depot there. I know."

The vampire seemed to accept this response. It lowered its gaze, appearing almost contrite.

"Does Beth know?" Adam asked, finding courage

in the creature's vulnerability. "Does she know what you are?"

"Yes, she knows. Which is why she told me to stay away from her."

"But you aren't staying away from her, are you?"

The creature kept its gaze to the ground. "No."

"What do you want from her?"

"Nothing." The creature paused. "Everything."

Adam's body tensed with rage, and he balled his fists, trying to keep his hands from trembling.

"Stay the hell away from Beth," he spat out, not thinking about how foolish it was to incite the vampire.

Immediately, the creature snarled, baring its teeth. "Watch yourself, Adam." Then, with a low growl, it walked past him, deliberately slamming against Adam's shoulder as it headed toward the woods.

Adam lowered his head and closed his eyes, letting out a slow breath in relief. When he looked toward the woods once more, the creature was gone.

Chapter Seventeen

The night air was warm Saturday evening, hinting at spring, though the only reason Thomas noticed was because Beth wore a knit shawl over her black cocktail dress rather than her usual heavy winter coat and scarf. He almost smiled at the memory of her standing next to Lin outside the club a few weeks ago, looking like she was ready for an arctic expedition. Now, she looked…well, divine.

Her hair had been curled and gathered at the sides with two diamond clips to keep it away from her face. In the back, the brown curls fell just past her shoulder blades.

That dress—Thomas swallowed hard, drinking in every detail as she walked up the stone steps to her ex-boyfriend's front door. The neckline was square and scooped low enough to reveal the enticing curves of her breasts, but in a tasteful way. And the dress hugged her body as though it had been made just for her.

Tearing his eyes away from the dress and the body within it, Thomas noted the grimness of Beth's expression as she waited for the door to open. Vainly, Thomas wondered if she missed him, if perhaps getting dressed up and going to a party held no joy for her because she wasn't going with him.

He almost laughed out loud as soon as the thought crossed his mind. It was delusional to think the beautiful woman he was watching wanted anything to do with him when she had told him in no uncertain terms to leave her alone. Still, when her body stiffened as her ex-boyfriend opened the door and leaned in to hug her, Thomas couldn't help but wonder.

Like the soulless, depraved creature he was, Thomas watched as Ryan put his hand on the small of her back and guided her down the steps to a silver car that was parked along the street. The click of the car doors unlocking echoed in his supernatural ears, and he focused his gaze on the asshole's hand as it moved slightly lower under the guise of helping Beth into the passenger seat of his car. Thomas growled low in his throat but stayed rooted to his spot on the roof of the house next door. He would not interfere. He had promised Beth to stay away, and while she likely wouldn't consider his shadowing her every move "staying away," it was the best he could do given the circumstances.

Tonight, of all nights, something compelled him to keep a careful watch on Beth. Whether it was her somber demeanor and half-hearted smiles or the glint in her ex-boyfriend's eye as he hopped into the driver's seat and started the car, something was off.

The car pulled away from the curb and moved in the direction of the law school where the soirée was to be held. Looking around to make sure he would not be seen, Thomas jumped down from his perch and landed on the lawn between the two houses. Slowly, he walked to the spot where Beth's ex-boyfriend had been standing before getting into the car and breathed in the air.

Tequila. The asshole had been drinking tequila. He

may not have been drunk yet, but he was well on his way.

Letting out another guttural sound, Thomas looked down the road the car had just driven. And he followed.

****

Beth was suffocating. The grand hall on the first floor of the law school building was jam-packed with law students and their dates, and the bright overhead lights and heat blasting in through the vents were not helping the situation.

She took another sip of her water.

"Are you sure you don't want something else to drink?"

Beth smiled politely, feeling a twinge of guilt at her present lack of enthusiasm.

"I'm okay with water, but thanks."

Ryan shrugged sympathetically, draining the last of his soda, then setting the empty cup on a high-top nearby. "I need to take a piss. I'll be right back." He leaned in to kiss her cheek before walking in the direction of the double doors that led into the hallway.

She was so relieved that she had would have a few minutes without him that she forgot to dwell on the fact that he shouldn't have kissed her, even just on the cheek.

Raising her cup to take another sip, she spied two of Ryan's classmates approach—both pretty brunettes. Beth smiled weakly as they came and greeted her with hugs. She was pretty sure she had only met them once or twice, when she and Ryan had first dated.

"Beth, it's so good to see you!" It was the one with wavy hair who spoke, but for the life of her, Beth couldn't remember her name.

"Thanks," Beth replied, pretending she was equally pleased to see them.

"Yeah," the other one chimed in, raising her hands to check that her updo was still in place. "When Ryan told us you guys had broken up, we didn't think we'd get to see you anymore. It's so great that you came."

The girl's smile was genuine, but Beth didn't remember her name, either.

"I told Lydia you two would get back together. Ryan was really into you. He still is. It's not hard to notice how he looks at you. He wants you."

"And Ryan always gets what he wants."

Lydia, the one whose hair was up in a twist, smiled playfully as she made the comment, but Beth was not amused. She didn't care what Ryan wanted. They were *not* back together, and she didn't want anyone to think that they were.

"I'm just here with Ryan as a friend," said Beth, trying not to be too harsh or defensive about the matter.

"Oh, Beth, don't worry!" Lydia squeezed Beth's shoulder. "With a dress like that, you two will be an item again in no time. He still talks about you."

A dress like that? She hadn't worn the dress to impress Ryan, or anyone.

Beth was about to explain when she noticed Ryan push through the double doors. Lydia and her friend saw him, too.

"Speak of the devilishly handsome," said the one who was not Lydia in a wistful tone.

"Come on, Jen. Ryan's going to think we're trying to sabotage their love if we stick around talking to his girlfriend all night."

The two of them, *Lydia* and *Jen*, giggled and said

bye to Beth just as Ryan reached them.

"Bye, ladies," he said to their backs as they walked away. Jen raised a hand and wiggled her fingers at him without even looking back.

"Were they keeping you company while I was gone?" asked Ryan, putting a hand on Beth's waist.

"Yeah, I guess so."

Beth's gaze traveled from his hand on her body, which she wanted him to remove, to his face so that she could tell him as much. At seeing the glazed-over look in his eyes, she asked instead, "Are you okay?"

Ryan smiled that prince charming smile she used to find so endearing. "I'm good. How can I not be? You're here with me."

Beth lowered her eyes. Did he think they were back together again, too? Was she going to have to break up with him a second time?

"Hey, will you dance with me? Just one dance, so that Lydia and Jen don't make fun of me tomorrow for standing in the corner all night with you talking and not dancing."

She was about to say she didn't feel like dancing when he added, "Please? It's okay for two old friends to dance one dance, isn't it?"

Beth chuckled half-heartedly, glad to hear him acknowledge that they were only there together as friends, but not so glad when Ryan's fingers kept moving along her side. It was time for her to go home.

"Please, Beth? For old time's sake?"

Taking in a deep breath, she relented. "Okay, one dance. Then I think I'll head home. I'm not feeling great."

It wasn't even a lie.

His hand tightened around her waist, then dropped to grasp her free hand. "Understood. I'll take you home after our one solitary dance. I promise."

"You don't have to drive me. I'll just walk. It's not that cold out tonight."

He took the water cup from her other hand and set it down. "Don't be ridiculous. I'm not letting you walk home by yourself in the dark. I'm taking you home. But first, we dance."

Beth let him lead her out to the ten-by-ten laminate dancefloor, and the music changed to a slower, more sultry rhythm. A couples' dance, of course. She cursed her bad luck as Ryan wrapped his arms low around her waist and stepped closer. Reluctantly, she put her hands on his shoulders and began moving in time to the slow beat of the song.

"I've missed you, Beth." He spoke the soft words into her ear, his cheek grazing hers, his hands pulling her closer. And she felt nothing for him, not even a single flutter in her stomach at his nearness.

Part of her had wondered if the old feelings would come back tonight. Thomas was no longer a possibility, and she had cared for Ryan before. Ryan had touched and kissed and held her, and she had enjoyed his attentions. She'd enjoyed being with him, talking to him, hearing about his day, and sharing stories about hers. And, back when they were dating, she had thought about him when they were apart and looked forward to the next time she would see him.

But now? Well, now Beth looked forward to the end of the song. She didn't want Ryan's hands on her, and she certainly didn't want his cheek warming hers. All she wanted was to go home and crawl into bed. She wanted to bury herself in blankets and cry and think about Thomas and how good it had been when they were together. Even knowing what she did, Beth preferred him in her life over Ryan. Without a doubt.

The song mercifully ended, and Ryan kissed her cheek again, his lips lingering on her skin a little longer than before.

Taking her hand, Ryan led her slowly off the dancefloor and toward the double doors. As they passed through the doors, Ryan turned to her and smiled shyly.

"I won first speaker at the moot court competition last week," he said, looking down as though he was embarrassed to brag about himself.

"Really?"

He nodded, grinning. "Yeah, really."

"That's wonderful, Ryan. I hope this doesn't sound condescending, but I'm proud of you. I know how hard it is to speak in front of people like that. They had real judges listening to the arguments, didn't they?"

"Yeah. I mean, two of them were real judges. The others were professors."

"Still, that's quite an accomplishment. I'm sure there were a lot of talented students up against you, and you beat them all. That's pretty amazing."

He looked over at her, his gaze admiring and appreciative at the same time.

"It means a lot to me that you think so, Beth."

They paused in front of the doors to leave the building, and Ryan looked down the long, dimly lit hall to the stairs.

"There's a plaque with my name on it in the Moot Court Room downstairs. Would you let me show it to you?"

A niggle of worry worked its way up from her stomach, but she pushed it down, replacing it with sympathy. Who else did Ryan have to boast to of his accomplishments? His friends were probably jealous of him, and he didn't have another girlfriend yet. Nor did his parents live near enough to come visit.

"Sure," she replied with a reassuring smile.

He squeezed her hand, then tugged on it gently to draw her toward the staircase.

The muffled sounds of revelry faded fast as they walked down the flight of steps to the basement floor of the building, where the Moot Court Room was located.

Ryan flipped on the lights as they entered, illuminating the newly refurbished room that looked just like a courtroom with a witness stand and jury seating off to the side. The door clicked closed behind them as she followed Ryan down the aisle between the audience seating toward the judge's bench.

"There," he said, pointing to an engraved golden plaque mounted to a glossy wooden base.

Beth stepped around the judge's seat to where Ryan stood and read the words out loud. "Criminal law mock trial. First speaker. Ryan Corbin."

She turned her head to find that Ryan had moved closer. His eyes were fixed on hers, but something about the way he was looking at her sent a chill up her spine.

He put his hand on her back, then moved it lower, until it was just above her tail bone.

"Thanks for showing me this, Ryan," she said, careful to keep the fear from her voice, "but I think I should get home. I'm really not feeling well."

"God, you're so beautiful, Beth," he groaned, his

hand creeping downward and his head lowering toward hers. Recognizing his obvious intent to kiss her, Beth instinctively backed away.

"Come on, Ryan. Let's go."

"We were so good together," he continued, ignoring her request. "Everything about us was right. Well, almost everything. But I know how to help you. It's going to be perfect this time."

He moved toward her again, and again she inched away until her side hit the other wall. He placed a hand on each wall, caging her in the corner with his body, and lowered his head once more for a kiss.

"Ryan, no." She spoke firmly but did not yell. Ryan wouldn't hurt her. He had cared for her once, and perhaps he still did. "I don't want to kiss you, Ryan," she added, putting her hands on his chest and trying to create some distance between them. "We came as friends, that's all. And now it's time to leave."

"Friends," he whispered, frowning. He grabbed her face with both hands and kissed her mouth roughly. She pounded on his chest until his mouth broke away from hers, but he didn't release her. "I don't want to be friends. I love you, Beth. And I want you more than I've ever wanted anything in my life."

Beth's heart was pounding now, her pulse loud in her ears. There was no one down there to hear them, and his friends all thought they were leaving the ball after the dance. No one would be looking for them.

"You can't have me, Ryan. Let go of me!"

He squeezed his eyes shut and shook his head. "You're just saying that because you're scared. I remember how you used to kiss me, Beth. You love me just as much as I love you. You want me inside you, but you're scared. Once we do it, though, once you know how it feels, you won't be scared anymore. I promise. I'll take such good care of you, Beth. You'll like it, I promise."

In one swift move, Ryan grabbed her by the waist and knocked her off her feet, setting her on the floor with surprising ease. His body immediately covered hers, his hands holding her down as she twisted and bucked against him. "I'm going to take care of you, Beth. Just trust me."

"Are you high, Ryan?" she screeched, feeling helpless against his weight. "This isn't you. You're not—" He cut off her protest with another kiss, swallowing her screams.

Moving her hands up above her head so he could secure both wrists with one of his hands, he ran the other hand down the side of her body. As he released her mouth, she heard him undo his zipper.

"Oh my God, Ryan—no!"

Panic coursed through her, taking over her whole body, and she struggled harder, almost kneeing him in the balls when he shifted his weight.

"Not like this, Ryan, please," she pleaded, knowing she couldn't win on strength. Her only chance to protect herself was to convince him to stop, to make him see reason. "This is a crime, you're committing a crime. How are you going to sit for the bar exam if you do this?"

He said nothing in response, and his silence frightened her more than his ludicrous statements about them belonging together. Because silence meant he was focused on doing the unthinkable to her.

His free hand found the hem of her dress and

pulled it upward. When his fingers found the waistband of her panties, she gasped in horror and her mind went blank, save for one thought, which she whispered as he began to pull her underwear down.

"Thomas, please help me."

Suddenly, Ryan was across the room, shoved up against the wall, his feet dangling inches above the ground. The man who held him by the neck had his back toward her, but she didn't need to see his face to know who he was.

Tears streamed down her face as she got to her feet and arranged her clothes, her joy at laying eyes on Thomas for a moment overshadowing the relief of being saved from her ex-boyfriend's attempted rape. She swiped at the tears, her gaze fixed on her rescuer as she stepped softly to his side.

Thomas was as still as a statue, the bulged biceps straining against the white fabric of his dress shirt providing the only indication that he was exerting any effort to hold Ryan in place. His lips were a thin line of concentration, his eyes laser-focused on Ryan's face despite the distraction of Ryan's gasping pleas and flailing limbs.

Slowly, Beth placed her hand on Thomas' raised arm, and he turned his head to look at her.

"It's okay, Thomas. I'm okay."

****

Beth's words broke through the red haze clouding Thomas' vision, and he drew in an unnecessary breath.

"Are you sure, Beth?" he replied, keeping the degenerate scum up against the wall.

"Yes. You came before he could do anything." Her eyes left his as she threw a narrow glance at the son of a bitch, but only for a second.

"Do you want me to kill him?"

"No." Her reply was calm and immediate, and he had no choice but to obey.

Reluctantly, Thomas lowered the asshole until his feet touched the ground, but he kept hold of his neck.

Forcing himself to look away from Beth, Thomas turned his attention to his captive. "Do you understand that I could kill you right now with less effort than it took you to piss yourself?"

The scumbag looked down at his wet, unzipped pants where he had, indeed, urinated in fear minutes ago, then looked back up at Thomas and nodded frantically. "Yes, sir, yes, I do."

"Do you understand that I could tear off your dick and shove it down your throat faster than you can blink your eyes?"

He nodded again, his face scrunched up in a terrified whimper. "Yes, sir, I do."

"I will be watching you for the rest of your short, worthless life. And if you ever treat anyone like you treated Beth..." Thomas paused, swallowing down his emotions. "If you ever try to force yourself on anyone like that, you will *not* live to regret it. Because I will end you. Violently. Painfully. And without mercy. Do you understand?"

"Yes, sir. I understand."

Remembering the fear in Beth's voice when she called his name, and the image of her ex-boyfriend holding her down with his hand up her skirt, Thomas reconsidered snapping the son of a bitch's neck.

"Most importantly," Thomas continued, collecting himself, "if you so much as look at Beth from this point forward, I will disembowel you with my teeth. Do you understand?"

"Yes, yes, I understand!" he cried out, shutting his eyes, as though he didn't want to risk looking at Beth and suffering the fate that was just described.

"Let's go, Thomas."

Beth's hand was still on Thomas' arm as he released her ex-boyfriend and allowed him to curl up into a sobbing ball on the ground. He resisted the urge to kick the sack of shit as Beth slid her hand down his arm to twine her fingers around his.

Without a word, the two left the room and found their way up the stairs and out into the cool evening. They were walking toward North Campus, in the direction of Beth's apartment, when Beth suddenly stopped.

Thomas spun around to look at her. "Are you al—"

Before he could finish his question, Beth had thrown herself into his arms, and he held her tightly, burying his nose in her hair. The feel of her body on his warmed him to the core, cracking through the icy stone shell of his existence to reach something soft and pulsing with vigor underneath.

"I don't know why I called for you," she whispered into his shoulder. "I don't know what made me think you would hear me, that you'd come for me, but you did. Thank you, Thomas. Thank you."

He said nothing in response, not wanting to ruin the perfection of that moment, but kept her in his embrace. How could he explain that he had been circling the law building in frustration since the moment she had disappeared inside with her ex-boyfriend, fighting the growing urge to rush into the hall and rip the asshole's arms off his body so that he couldn't touch Beth? How could he tell her that he'd been watching them, that he'd sensed her ex's ill-intentions? Or that the second his name had passed her lips, he'd been pulled to her side as though she had yanked an invisible string connecting them?

Feeling her grip on him loosen, Thomas released her and took a step back.

"May I take you back to your apartment?" he asked, almost shyly.

Nodding, she reached for his hand again, and they continued walking.

He didn't ask her what it meant, that she had called for him, that she had embraced him. That she was holding his hand now. Had she forgiven him for not telling the truth about what he was? Had she forgiven him for *being* what he was?

Fear that her actions now were simply a by-product of her harrowing experience minutes earlier gripped him, and he decided he preferred not to know the answers to those questions. He preferred to keep her hand in his for as long as possible. Because he rather liked the human emotion of hope.

When they had reached the edge of the driveway to her apartment building, she stopped again and turned to face him.

"Thank you for protecting me tonight," she said softly, keeping her hand in his.

He reached for her other hand.

"Do you thank a bird for flying? It does what it is meant to do."

She crinkled her nose in an adorable expression of doubt. "So, you were meant to protect me?"

Kathryn Amurra

"I've grown to believe I was meant to love you, Beth."

Her eyes widened at his admission, and he suddenly felt very vulnerable. What had happened that evening did not undo her command that he leave her alone. It did not change the fact that Thomas was a vampire. To expect that she would accept him, his bloody history and flawed, unnatural existence, was unreasonable. And yet, he knew he was wishing for just that.

Unwilling to abandon that hope so soon, Thomas released her hands and took a step back.

"Go inside, get some sleep. I'll stay here until I'm sure you're safe in your apartment and the door is locked."

"How will you know the door is locked?"

He smiled. "I'll hear it. One of the benefits of being undead."

Her lips quirked up slightly, and she nodded. Thomas wanted to kiss her, but after what she had been through that night, he thought it best to let her be.

"Go on," he prompted gently, still hoping—fool that he was—that Beth would crash into his arms again and tell him never to leave her side. That she would say she loved him, too.

Instead, she lowered her eyes and turned to walk up the drive.

Thomas watched the graceful sway of Beth's hips as she approached the door and opened it. She cast one more glance in his direction, then disappeared inside, locking the door with a deafening click.

****

Adam walked the quiet path from North Campus

210

back to the law building, where he had left his car, puzzling over what he had witnessed. He had been watching the vampire closely that evening, concerned about the creature's seemingly agitated state. He'd never seen the creature distraught before. The vampire had been so preoccupied with the scene of Beth and Ryan together that it hadn't even sensed it was being observed. Then, inexplicably, the vampire had disappeared in a blur, entering the building faster than Adam had ever seen any person move. Its motion was as fast as the beating of a hummingbird's wings. If Adam hadn't known what he was dealing with, what the vampire was capable of, he would have doubted he had seen anything at all.

Fearing the worst, Adam had scrambled inside, looking for Ryan and Beth, hoping it wasn't too late. By the time he'd found his way to the Moot Court Room downstairs, Beth and the vampire were gone. Ryan was muttering unintelligibly to a small group of friends, saying something about a demon exacting vengeance on him, asking to be taken to the Campus Police. He said he had tried to rape Beth and wanted to confess. He thought he would be safer in the Campus Police's custody than left alone to face the wrath of the demon.

Adam hadn't seen what had happened between Ryan and Beth, but he had been able to catch up to the vampire as it walked Beth back to her apartment. Alarmed at first that the vampire would harm her, Adam had kept close to the pair, his hand on the crossbow hidden within his overcoat. He was close enough to hear Beth thank the creature for its intervention.

The vampire, Thomas, had apparently saved Beth from being the victim of a horrible crime.

Getting into his car, Adam tried to wrap his head around the facts as he understood them. Ryan had tried to rape Beth. Thomas had somehow known this and rushed to her defense. Thomas had *not* killed Ryan—had not even drawn blood. And Thomas had walked Beth home, waited to make sure she was safe inside, then quietly left. He hadn't even kissed her goodnight.

He had been kind.

What the hell was going on?

Chapter Eighteen

Beth pressed her forehead to the cold windowpane and closed her eyes. It had been two days since the Barrister's Ball. She had gone to the Campus Police the day after Ryan had attacked her to file a report, only to find that he had turned himself in. The fear of Thomas' wrath had apparently outweighed everything else, or maybe it had reminded Ryan that he had a conscience. Whatever it was, she was glad it was done. Ryan would be dealt with. He wouldn't be able to hurt her or anyone else. And with Thomas watching over her, she wasn't afraid. She wasn't afraid of anything.

Putting her hand on the glass, she raised her head and looked outside, scanning the parking lot outside her bedroom window, looking across the street to the woods beyond. Thomas was out there. She knew he was. She could feel his eyes on her, feel his movements as he followed her from the dining hall to the lab, then home.

His presence gave her comfort, but at the same time filled her with longing. Regret.

He had told her he loved her, and she had said nothing. He hadn't pressed, hadn't asked to see her again. He had stayed in the shadows, respected her wishes, and watched over her.

She heaved a sigh, reaching for the stone at the end of her necklace. Passing her thumb across its face, Beth wondered for the hundredth time if she should make her wish. Now that she knew what she wanted, what was stopping her from saying the words? Was she afraid it wouldn't work? Or was she afraid that it would?

Tucking the amulet back into her sweatshirt, Beth stepped away from the window. It was almost midnight. She should get some sleep. She was bone-tired—she had been since that night Thomas walked her home. The problem was that even when she'd gone to bed at a reasonable hour, she couldn't fall asleep. She'd lay there, eyes closed, thinking. Thinking about him. About his arms around her, his eyes looking into her soul. About what he was, and what it meant. About why she sensed his absence so acutely.

She sat on the edge of her bed, then turned her head toward the window once more. Was he still out there? Would he hear her if she called to him?

As soon as the thought entered her mind, she knew she would get no sleep until she found out the answer. She rose and almost ran back to the window, her heart pounding. Undoing the lock on her window, she lifted it open, letting the cold breeze gust onto her face through the wire screen.

"Thomas," she whispered, looking around outside. "Are you there?"

She waited, hoping. Praying.

"Thomas," she tried again. "I want to see you. I…" She wondered how much she should say, speaking into the wind as she was. "Would you come to me, please?" Almost under her breath, she added, "Would you forgive what I said, and what I didn't say, and let me be with you now?"

"There is nothing to forgive."

His low, smooth voice startled her, and she took a step back before rushing to the window and dropping to her knees so she could be eye level with Thomas, who was crouched on the ledge outside.

"Oh, Thomas."

Beth raised the screen panel and reached for his face. He closed his eyes as her fingers caressed his smooth cheek, then covered her hand with his.

"I'm so sorry," she uttered softly as he moved her hand to his lips and kissed it.

"I told you, there is nothing to be sorry about."

"But there is, Thomas. I was wrong to tell you to leave me. I was scared of you, and I shouldn't have been. I was wrong."

He smiled warmly even as he shook his head.

"You were right, Beth. That instinctual feeling you had when we first met, that was right. That is who I am."

"But I'm not afraid of you anymore. When I look into your eyes now, it's not the same. Where there was nothing before, now I see something."

She put her other hand through the open window, and he held both her hands in his.

"What do you see, Beth? What is so different now?"

"I see warmth, Thomas. I see…love."

He closed his eyes, as though her words had caused him pain.

"I don't know how it's possible. I'm not supposed to feel love. I never have, in over a hundred years." His eyes opened, and his gaze went straight to her soul. "It's you, you know. It's as though you've reminded me of all the things I used to be, the things I used to feel.

Before. You've reminded me of my humanity."

How he could balance himself on that narrow ledge, Beth had no idea. Then again, she didn't know how he'd gotten there in the first place. There were no trellises or ladders to get up to her second-floor window. Had he jumped?

She let go of his hands and moved aside. "You can't be comfortable out there. You should come—"

"No." His firm tone stopped her mid-sentence, but the harshness of his face softened a moment later. "Don't invite me in. Once you do, I'll be able to come into your home whenever I please, and you will not have the security you have now."

"So that's true, about vampires? You have to invite them in?"

He nodded. "It's true. Many things are. Legends and myths usually stem from some sort of truth. Truth that's gotten lost over time."

Beth reached for his hand again, and he took it, his thumb rubbing the back of her hand as though he needed the contact. As though he craved more of her touch.

"What if I want to invite you in? We can't talk like this, and I don't want you to go. Not yet."

"Just…" He paused, as though searching for what to say. "Just wait before you do it. Let me tell you more about what I am, and what I have done. Then you can decide whether you really trust me to be in your home. It's what I should have done from the very beginning. For that, and so many other things, I ask your forgiveness."

It was Beth's turn now to shake her head as she repeated his words. "There is nothing to forgive."

"Wait until you've heard what I have to say. Then you can decide on that, as well."

If he wanted her to know more about him before accepting her invitation, she would respect that. What mattered most was his willingness to open up to her.

"There's a little balcony off the living room. You can see it if you look to your left. I can meet you out there in a minute."

He nodded, then was gone.

Beth reached for her fluffy bathrobe and put it on over her sweatshirt and sweatpants. It was cold outside, and though she didn't know how long she would be out there talking to Thomas, she hoped it would be awhile.

Thomas was sitting in one of the metal lawn chairs on the balcony when Beth slid the door open and stepped outside. Closing the door behind her to keep the cold air from entering the apartment, she glanced at Thomas. He was watching her every move, and she couldn't stop herself from blushing in response.

She took a seat in the chair next to his and folded her hands in her lap, unsure of what to say.

"I'm glad you're here." She raised her eyes to his. "I've missed you. A lot."

"I've missed you, too." He looked at her hands, as though trying to decide if he should reach out and touch her. She wanted him to, wanted to hold his hand and kiss his soft lips, but she knew it would be a distraction.

So instead, she smiled encouragingly. "You can tell me anything, Thomas. Anything you want to tell me, I want to know."

He closed his eyes and bowed his head slightly, in a gesture of conceded defeat, then opened them, a tiny wrinkle of doubt forming between his dark brows.

"I don't know where to start."

"Well," she hugged her robe tighter around herself, thinking aloud, "would it be easier if I asked you questions and you answered them?"

The corner of his mouth turned up in a heart-melting half-smile. "You mean, like an interview? With a vampire?"

She chuckled, glad to have inadvertently lightened the mood. "Yes, an interview with a vampire. Not terribly original, I'll admit. Would that be okay?"

"Yes. I think that would be easier."

Beth leaned back in the chair and pulled her legs up to hug them, hoping the more compact position would keep her warmer.

"Okay, great. Well, here are the things I've been wondering since…" She paused. "Since I came upon you in the woods near the Engineering building."

He dipped his head in acknowledgement.

"Do you have to drink blood to survive?"

"Yes," he answered simply.

"And it has to be human blood?"

"Yes."

She hesitated before asking her next question, unsure of how she would feel after hearing his answer. But she had to know.

"Do the people you take blood from…do you have to…I mean, do they…die?"

"No," he answered unequivocally. "I do not kill my victims. Not anymore, at least." He sighed, and she knew he had more to say.

"Look, Beth, I don't want to give you the wrong impression. I am not a 'vampire saint.' I have killed people in the past. Hundreds of people. And I enjoyed it. The only reason I stopped is because it became too dangerous—for me. I didn't want to be found out, and the more bodies I left in my wake, the easier it would have been to discover me."

"How long has it been since you killed someone?"

He closed his eyes and leaned his head back, as though counting the years. "Longer than you've been alive. But it took a while for me to learn how to stop drinking—how to stop myself from draining my victims. And just because I didn't kill them doesn't mean I didn't want to."

"Do you want to kill now, when you drink?"

"No, not anymore. Not since I met you." Again, his answer was quick and firm, and Beth had no doubt he was telling the truth. She hoped that meant he would answer her next question truthfully, as well.

"Did you ever want to kill me?"

****

Thomas should have known this question would come up. Beth was incredibly smart, and the thought that the blood-sucking vampire sitting next to her had probably wanted to kill her at some point had, of course, crossed her mind. And, being the sweet, genuine person she was, she had figured the best way to learn the answer was to ask.

He had no choice but to answer truthfully and let the cards fall where they would.

"Yes." He could only form the one word in response.

To his surprise, Beth chuckled. "You can't possibly think I'm going to let you off the hook with a simple 'yes.' I'm going to need more details. When did you want to kill me? Why didn't you? Do you feel that way now—"

"No," he cut her off, answering the last question first. "I do not want to kill you now. I cannot bear the thought of anything harming you."

Unable to keep his distance any longer, he reached for Beth's hands and held them tightly, willing her to feel how strongly protective he was when it came to her safety and wellbeing.

"When I first met you," he continued, "when you hit me with your car—"

"I knew I'd hit something!" she exclaimed, making him smile.

"Yes, you mangled my leg—momentarily. In any case, when I first saw you, I could tell how pure and innocent you were, and I wanted to corrupt that innocence." He knew he risked destroying the fragile connection between them with his next admission, but something compelled him to be completely honest. "You were a challenge to me, Beth. I knew I frightened you, and I found that thrilling. It gave me a sadistic kind of joy. I wanted to overcome that fear, to seduce you into desiring me. I wanted to take your innocence in every possible way, and then I wanted you to know what had happened to you, what I had done. I wanted to take your body and drink your blood, and I wanted to be there when you realized it, to witness you feeling hurt and betrayed. And yes, I wanted to kill you."

He dropped her hands and rose from the chair to step to the railing. He sullied her just by touching her. He was deplorable—selfish and vicious. He was pure evil, and now she knew it. How could he have thought he could be with someone who was the complete opposite of what he was?

"Thomas," she whispered, the nearness of her voice making him turn his head to find her standing at the railing with him, their shoulders brushing. "It's okay. I know you wouldn't hurt me now. Heck, you saved me from Ryan, and I could feel you watching over me all those nights. You were protecting me."

"But that doesn't erase the fact that I wanted to hurt you less than a month ago."

"In a way, it does."

She put her hand over his, and the effect was instant. She was a comfort to his soul. Which made no sense because he didn't even have a soul.

Tugging on his hand gently, she led him back to the lawn chairs and sat, drawing him down with her.

Her lovely eyes studied him, and he knew before the words were uttered what her next question would be.

"Tell me about how you became a vampire."

Chapter Nineteen

Boston, May 1890

Blood.

Thomas looked at the handkerchief again, just as another fit of coughing seized him, adding more crimson to the white fabric.

He was coughing up blood.

It had been four weeks since the coughing had started, two months since he had attended Edith's funeral. He had visited over a hundred ailing men and women in the three years he had been in the seminary, comforting them with Bible passages and words of peace and hope for the eternal life to come. And yet now, transfixed by the blood on his handkerchief, Thomas could find no peace for himself. No hope.

Thomas was dying; he knew this with more certainty than he knew his own name. How long had Edith lasted in her feverish state? Three, maybe four weeks?

His own illness would follow the same course. There was no denying it, no escaping it. The coughing would get worse. He would develop a fever and become bedridden. He could be dead in another month. And then what? What would become of him?

When asked that question by the many to whom he had ministered, his reply was always the same. *The body is transient. The soul is eternal. Fear not, for God is with us always. For the wages of sin is death, but the gift freely given by God is eternal life in Christ Jesus our Lord.*

Thomas had believed those words, uttered them with the deep conviction of a faithful servant of God. But though he remembered those words now, he felt nothing—nothing but fear.

What if God did not exist?

The more he thought about it, the more convinced he became. *God was not real.* Thomas had been doing God's work, after all, had he not? He had made numerous sacrifices for his Lord—given up the woman he loved, lived simply as a seminarian with no possessions, prayed constantly, shepherded God's own people. If there was a God, how could He have allowed Thomas to fall ill? Why would He have stopped the good works Thomas did every day in His name?

The answer was simple, as clearly visible as the blood on his handkerchief—*because there was no God.*

Thomas had devoted his life to perpetuating a lie. And now his life was about to end.

Withdrawing from his pocket the small book of prayers he always carried, he hurled it at the door of his modest bedroom. He watched as three of the pages came loose and fluttered slowly to the floor, near where the book had landed.

Father, Son, Holy Spirit.

He did not want to die. He did not want to become nothing, a rotting corpse in the ground.

Ash. Dust.

Everything he had done in his life had meant nothing. There had been no purpose to any of it. The men, women, and children he had visited were dead. Edith was dead. His mother and father, dead. Soon, he would be dead, too. There was nothing he could do, no way to stop this death from coming.

Unless—

He can save us, you know. He can save us.

Edith's voice came back to him, as clear as though she were speaking the words in his ear at that very moment.

He will take away my fever and the coughing. I will live with him forever.

At first, Thomas had presumed Edith's fever was the cause of her ramblings. During each of his visits, she had spoken at length of the man who lived in the woods, the one who had visited her.

The one who lived forever.

Thomas had tried to gently guide her away from blasphemy, but she had refused to listen. She had continued to speak of that man, had described every detail of his appearance and manner, down to the earthy smell of his skin and the deep timbre of his voice. Eventually, Thomas had stopped trying to correct her, allowing Edith the momentary peace of recounting the mysterious man's visit and his promise of eternal life.

Eternal. Life.

Was it so far-fetched to believe such a thing was possible? Up until a few weeks ago, he himself had believed in eternal life, though he had credited it to a different source. And based on what? Words written over a thousand years ago in a language he could not read? Why, then, should it be more difficult to believe in what the woman he once loved had seen with her own eyes and heard with her own ears?

If he chooses to give you the gift, Thomas, you must accept it. You must invite him to drink your blood. He will give you his blood in return, and it will change you. You will become immortal, as he is. You will be beyond pain, immune to sickness, stronger than death. You will no longer need your God. You, yourself, will be God.

Before the decision was fully formed in his mind, Thomas was rushing to the door. He had to find the man in the woods, and he had to find him soon. Who knew how long Thomas would have the strength to hunt for the man who could possibly save him? Edith had run out of time—bedridden, feverish, weak. All she had to cling to was the hope that the man would come to her again. But he hadn't.

Thomas would not make that mistake.

The woods Edith had spoken of were about three miles northwest of the seminary, but it took him almost two hours to get there. Already, the sun was starting its slow descent toward the horizon, and Thomas knew he had no time to waste. Besides the darkness, he feared his own exhaustion, which was overtaking him.

Without knowing what he was looking for, Thomas headed deeper into the woods, stopping now and again to lean against a tree for a few moments of rest. His quest was the definition of madness, and he knew it. Still, he found madness preferable to hopelessness.

As the sounds of small, unseen animals scurrying through the dry leaves and brush underfoot faded and the chirping of various birds died away, Thomas noticed a shift in the shadows around him. Something had changed. There was an unnatural stillness where he was—a darkness that he could feel more than see.

He was getting close.

Scanning the area for movement, his gaze found a mound of earth about two feet higher than the land surrounding it. A crooked elm rose from the base of the raised area and shook its leaves at him, though there was no wind.

Come, my son.

It was not a voice but a *feeling* that beckoned him, and Thomas found himself stepping toward the elm. Only as he approached did he notice the narrow opening in the mound, framed on one side by the tree. He was about to step through the opening when the wooden cross around his neck grew inexplicably heavy and Edith's voice came to him once more. *He won't like that.*

Without a second thought, Thomas pulled at the leather cord around his neck and tore it off, letting the cross fall to the dirt.

He looked into the darkness beyond the opening he was about to step through. He could feel a presence within, and he knew it was the man he sought.

What would happen when the man saw that Thomas had entered his home? Would he grant him the gift of eternal life that Edith has spoken of? Or would the man just kill him? It was a distinct possibility. Then again, Thomas already had one foot in the grave. Should the man choose to end his life, perhaps it would be a mercy. It was better than the death that Edith had experienced—the slow descent into madness and desperation, lying feverish and helpless in a bed as his body slowly surrendered itself.

He really had nothing to lose.

Lifting his head, Thomas peered into the darkness and stepped forward.

****

"So, you see, I was a coward."

Beth couldn't help but stare at Thomas. His beautiful face. His sad eyes. His downturned mouth.

He had been coming to her every evening for the past three nights, and each time he would tell her a little more about how he came to be a vampire. She had listened in rapt attention, speaking only when he needed encouragement to keep going. And so she spoke now.

"You were not a coward. You were just…human."

"Not only a coward," he continued, "but also a hypocrite. For all my zealous proclamations about the love and mercy of God and the transitory existence we have on Earth when compared to a lifetime in Heaven, when it came right down to it, I couldn't take the chance. I didn't want to die, regardless of the cost. I chose, instead, to become this." He gestured to himself, as if he were some detestable creature.

Beth saw only a man filled with regret and self-loathing.

"You made a mistake, I'll give you that," she replied, wrapping her bathrobe tighter around herself to ward off the chill in the air. "But you're not the only one who's ever been afraid to die. It's innate, despite faith and religion. No one wants to die. That's why we have the will to survive. It's just how we were made. Most of us don't have a choice in the matter. But it seems that you did."

"Yes. And I chose poorly."

She said nothing in response but reached over to where he sat and placed her hand on his.

He looked up at her and smiled, almost serenely. "The funny thing," he added, "is that I never thought about the choice I made before I met you. The life I had chosen, this thing I had become, suited me. I had no regrets."

A wry smile tugged at her lips. "So, I've brought you shame and remorse?"

He raised her hand to his lips, and closing his eyes, kissed it. "Yes. And with them, a measure of peace I never knew I lacked."

Squeezing her hand briefly, Thomas released her and rose to his feet. "It's late. I should go."

He turned toward the rail to jump down, but Beth stood quickly and grabbed his arm.

"I don't want you to go yet."

Her bathrobe had come loose, and she shuddered at the cold as she tried to wrap it around herself once more with her free hand.

"You're freezing. You should get inside."

"I'm fine. I want to keep talking to you." Her teeth chattered as she spoke. Why did it have to be so cold?

"I'll come again tomorrow," he replied. "I promise. You need to get warmed up."

"Come in with me. Just for a little while."

He froze at her words, and she realized she had just invited him into her home. She had relinquished the only power she had. She had put herself completely at his mercy.

And she wasn't the least bit afraid.

Quietly, Beth moved to the sliding glass door and pushed it open. "Come in, Thomas," she said again, looking him squarely in the face. "I invite you in."

The panicked look on his face was almost enough to make Beth feel sorry for putting him in this awkward situation. She knew he was trying to protect her from himself. But she also knew he would never hurt her. So, she stood there, hand outstretched, waiting for him to come to the same realization.

It took several seconds, but finally Thomas reached for her hand and let her pull him inside the apartment. As he looked around the living room, she shut the sliding glass door and shivered again, glad to be back in the heated space.

"I still have a lot of questions," she said, sitting down on the dull gray couch and looking over at him expectantly. He followed and sat down beside her.

"What do you want to know?"

He had left a space between them big enough for another person to sit. Was he worried it would make her uncomfortable to have him near? What would he think if she slid closer?

"I've just been wondering about some things. About vampires, in general."

He nodded. "That's understandable. Just ask, and I'll tell you what I know."

"Well, for one thing, do you eat food? I mean, I've seen you eat, and drink. I just want to know if I should I offer you a drink or some chips or ice cream or something. I wouldn't want to be rude."

The corner of his mouth quirked, and she was happy to have teased a smile out of him.

"I can eat food, but it is tasteless, and my body does not metabolize it. I don't need it. Like everything else, I only eat food as a survival mechanism, to fit in."

"I thought you enjoyed whiskey, though. I mean, it seemed that way to me, watching you drink it."

"Whiskey is the one thing I can almost taste. The smell of it, the moment just before the liquid touches my tongue. It's like a memory, or a memory of a memory. I don't know. It's just different for some reason. It always has been, since before I met you, even."

Beth nodded. "I could tell. I bought you some, that night—"

"I know." An apologetic frown had formed on his brow. "I'm so, so sorry for what happened that night. I know you were going to give me a bottle of whiskey, for no reason at all, and I ruined it. I ruined the whole evening. I ruined any chance you might care for me."

"No, you didn't ruin that."

His gaze held hers, and he seemed to draw closer, even though she didn't see him move.

"What do you mean?" he asked in an uncharacteristic whisper.

His vulnerability made her heart pinch, and she wanted to give him a hug.

"It means," she began, reaching for his hand, "I care about you. I never stopped caring about you. Even after I saw…what I saw. I admit that it scared me, and I didn't know what to think. But I said those words, told you to leave me alone, out of fear. Not revulsion."

When he didn't respond, she moved to sit closer to him, and his hand tightened around hers.

"I'm sorry for what I said, Thomas. I've been sorry for it every minute since the moment I uttered the words. I didn't like not being with you. It seemed empty, like I was constantly missing something. And having you with me now feels good and right."

He touched her cheek with his other hand. "Oh, Beth, how can you say that, knowing what you know about me? How can you say that anything about me is good or right?"

She shrugged. "It's not who or what we are that defines us. It's the decisions we make."

"But the decisions I've made in my life have been quite awful. Selfish and depraved."

She was quiet for a moment, thinking. "What would you have told someone who came to you and confessed something terrible that they had done, Thomas? I mean before, when you were a seminarian?"

Thomas closed his eyes, and Beth knew he was trying to recall what must have seemed like another life so that he could answer her question. She watched him in silence, curious to hear what he would say. When he finally opened his eyes and looked at her, his expression was calm and hopeful.

"I would have said that if the past sin was confessed, then it was forgiven. Even if the person remembered the sin, that's all it was, a memory. It didn't exist anymore. And it shouldn't be dwelt upon."

Beth nodded. "That sounds wise. And for what it's worth, I think it's true. I know I'm not a priest or anything like that, but in a way you've confessed your sins, haven't you? You're sorry for what you did. So, maybe all you have to do now is just move forward and do better. Make new decisions, ones you will be proud of."

Thomas looked down at the hand she still clasped in her own. "I'm on the verge of making a terrible decision right now," he said, his voice raw with emotion.

For a second, a prickle of fear raced down her spine, but when his eyes found her face once more, the fear dissipated.

"What terrible decision are you on the verge of making?"

He closed the gap between them and, gently withdrawing his hand from hers, reached up to cradle her face. "I'm on the verge of kissing you."

Beth smiled, leaning toward him without a conscious thought. "And what would be so terrible about that?"

"Are you sure you want a vampire kissing—"

She brought her lips to his before he could get the words out, and he pulled her body closer as he took control of the kiss. It was sweet and gentle, and hungry and powerful at the same time. His fingers were in her hair, his thumbs caressing her cheeks as his mouth thoroughly claimed hers.

When he pulled away, his hands dropped to her neck, then her shoulders. She caught her breath, then surprised herself by laughing. Immediately, her hand came up to cover her mouth.

He grinned as he brushed the hair out of her face. "What have I done to make you laugh? Tell me, so I can do it again."

Her laughter became a smile as the tenderness of his words struck her. She shook her head and looked down, suddenly embarrassed. "It's just that I was wondering about, you know, your teeth."

Thomas looked perplexed. "My teeth?"

She reminded herself that he wanted her to ask him questions. He wanted her to know everything about him. "I thought vampires had, I don't know, fangs or something. To help them with the whole drinking blood thing. But…" she knew she was turning a bright shade of crimson "…I've never seen any fangs. And I haven't *felt* any."

Understanding, his smile widened. "You mean, you've never felt any when we've kissed?"

She nodded, shyness taking over again.

"Vampires don't have fangs," he explained. "You can break the skin to drink just as easily with your teeth as I can with mine. It's all about the pressure you apply."

As he said this, his hands squeezed her upper arms gently, as though he wanted to reassure himself that she was actually there. His eyes held hers with a mixture of affection, gratitude, and…something else that made her need to catch her breath again.

"I missed your kisses," she murmured, moving close enough to rest her head against his shoulder. He put his arms around her and kissed the top of her head as she added, even more softly, "I was afraid you weren't going to kiss me again."

His arms tightened, telling her he missed their kisses just as much as she had. "I didn't want to kiss you again until you knew what you were kissing."

"You mean 'who.'" Beth turned her head to look up at him. His perfect lips were pressed into a thin line, his eyebrows drawn together in thought. In pain.

"Haven't you been listening, Beth? I am not like you. I am not good. I'm not even human."

There was no reproach in his words. Only sadness.

She lifted her head off his shoulder, so that her eyes were level with his. "I am listening, Thomas. I've heard every word you've said." She racked her brain, trying to find a way to make him see he wasn't the monster he may have once been. That he had changed. That he could keep changing, be whatever he wanted to be.

Before she could think of something brilliant to say, a yawn overtook her. Thomas chuckled softly as Beth tried to cover her mouth.

He ran his fingers through her hair lovingly as he gave her an indulgent smile. "The spirit is willing, but the flesh, though beautiful, is weak."

"I don't think that's how it goes."

He grinned, placing a brief kiss on her lips. "I may have taken some liberties with the original text to better suit the circumstances."

The way he said "liberties" had her thinking about other liberties he might take, and she shivered in anticipation.

Moving her aside gently, Thomas stood. "I should leave so you can get some sleep. It's late, and you're tired."

"I'm not tired," Beth protested, even as she stifled another yawn.

Without warning, Thomas scooped her up from the couch and strode toward the closed door at the end of the hall. The warm feeling of being held against his chest, wrapped up in his arms, was greater than her indignation at being carried to bed like a child.

"How do you know where you're going?" she teased as he reached for the doorknob.

"Just a wild guess."

He stepped into the room and turned toward the double bed. His lips curled in a victorious smirk. "Looks like I was right."

He pulled back the light blue comforter and set her down gently on the sheets.

"Do you always make the bed?" he asked with a

playful lilt to his voice.

"It's the best way to start the day."

As Thomas moved to pull the comforter back over her, she grabbed his wrist to stop him.

"Stay with me, just a little while longer. Just until I fall asleep. Please?"

A part of her understood she was playing with fire, that inviting a handsome man she was already drawn to into her room was risky. That she should not put herself in the path of temptation. But she trusted Thomas. Above all else, she trusted him and knew he would never hurt her. And the heady feeling of being with him, of having him close to her, made any other concerns seem trivial.

Thomas said nothing for several long moments, though his fingers seemed to grip the comforter more tightly. With Beth's hand still on his wrist, he finally moved again, pulling the covers over her.

"I'll sit at the foot of your bed," he said softly, "seeing that the only pieces of furniture that fit in this tiny room are your bed, a nightstand, and a dresser."

She knew he was teasing her again, but there was an edge to his voice that bordered on fear.

All Beth wanted to do was hold him in her arms and take away all his fear. Have him understand how much she cared for him, how special he was, and how good. She wanted him to know himself as she knew him.

Lifting the edge of the comforter back up, she surprised herself with how confident and bold she sounded when she spoke her thoughts out loud. "Come lie down next to me. I just want to be close to you."

"This is not a good idea," he said, his voice low

and almost gruff. But already, he had kicked off his shoes and was slipping into bed with her.

"Wait."

Thomas froze at her command, and she couldn't help giggling. Sitting up, Beth shrugged off her thick robe and tossed it onto the ground. "There's not enough room in this bed for two people *and* my thick robe."

Seeing that he remained as still as a statue, Beth pulled him down until he was lying next to her. She pulled the covers over both of them and reached for his hand. He seemed to need reassurance, and at that moment she was in possession of an overabundance of certainty that lying there, next to him, was the perfect thing to do and the only thing that made sense.

"Your hand is so warm," she said, closing her eyes and reveling in the feel of his skin against hers. "I thought vampires were supposed to be cold to the touch."

Thomas didn't reply right away, and she was about to open her eyes to look at him when he finally spoke.

"I always feed before I come to see you. That's why I'm warm. Even a bit of blood will warm me for a while."

"I like that you're warm." Her voice sounded breathy. She almost didn't recognize it.

She scooted closer to him and put her head in that perfect spot between his arm and his chest. That place that seemed to be made just for her.

Throwing her other arm across his chest, Beth sighed contentedly. She was so relaxed, so comfortable being there with him, tucked into his side.

"I don't deserve to have you here with me. Like this."

His voice startled her, and she realized she had almost fallen asleep.

"As flattering as that is to hear, Thomas, you couldn't be more wrong."

He turned his head to look at her, and suddenly his face was very close to hers. "How can you say that, Beth? I'm a soulless, depraved creature that feeds on the blood of the innocent. It doesn't get more evil than that."

Suddenly, she found the argument she had been seeking earlier.

"Everything you've told me since that night I learned you were a vampire, has it all been true?"

Without hesitating, Thomas replied, "Yes."

"Do you remember when you said that you believed you were meant to love me?"

He was quiet, but only for a second. "Yes."

"And do you know what love is?"

Thomas turned his head to look back up at the ceiling and let out a long breath. "I had forgotten what love was, for the longest time. But the visions I've had, the ones I've been having since I met you, they reminded me. So, yes. I know what love is."

Beth raised her hand from his chest to caress his cheek, making him look at her again. Even in the darkness of her bedroom, she could see the whites of his eyes. She held his gaze, trailing her fingers through his hair as she asked her final question.

"Do you love me?"

Chapter Twenty

"Love does not begin to describe what I feel for you."

Thomas knew his response was a horrible cliché, but to answer with a simple "yes" seemed inadequate. From the look on Beth's face, she hadn't expected that reply. But it pleased her. She brushed his lips with her finger and crinkled her nose. If he didn't know better, he would have thought she was about to cry.

"I love you, too, Thomas. Not because you just said that. I've loved you for a while, I think. Do you understand now? Do you understand why what you said about being soulless and depraved cannot possibly be true?"

Seconds passed, her hand on his cheek, her thumb on his lips, and he couldn't respond. The truth was that he *didn't* understand. He didn't understand any of it. He didn't understand how this remarkable, intelligent, beautiful, compassionate woman could be lying here with him, or how she could have no fear knowing what he was. She *loved* him—how was that possible? Harder still was to fathom how *he* could have developed feelings for *her*. Not just feelings, but deep, gut-wrenching, life-changing feelings. He would have done anything for her, been anything for her. He would change his very existence to please her, if only such a thing were possible.

But it wasn't.

So, in the end, he made the only reply he could.

"No. I don't understand. Do you?"

A tear streaked down her cheek, but she was laughing.

"How can you be so old and yet so stupid?"

He couldn't help laughing himself. And he couldn't help kissing her still-laughing mouth.

"Explain it to me, Einstein."

She gave a final chuckle and took a breath. "How could I love something that didn't have a soul, Thomas? More importantly, how could something without a soul love me?"

He felt as though he had been punched in the gut, but in a good way. How could he argue with her logic? He knew what he was before, and he knew he had no care or concern beyond his own survival and pleasure before he met Beth. Before the visions. But now he was different. He *knew* he was different. It had been the source of all his recent problems and frustrations, this conflict between the nature of what he was and the desire to be something more. Something better.

Someone good enough for her.

"Do you really believe that, Beth?"

She nodded against his shoulder. "I do."

Her breath brushed his lips as she spoke, and then she leaned in for a kiss. It was as though she poured all her love into that kiss, and his mind went blank. There was only her and only him. He was a man, and she was a woman, and they were made for each other. Nothing else mattered because nothing else existed.

"I want to be closer to you," she murmured into his mouth.

Without thinking, he reached for the bottom edge of his sweater and, nudging her off him gently for a moment, took the sweater off, along with the shirt he wore underneath. Her hands touched his bare chest, tentatively at first, then with purpose.

"You're beautiful," he heard her say, half in a daze from the sensations her fingers on his skin wrought. "And so warm."

Abruptly, her hands were gone, and there was space between them. He almost reached for her to bring her back but then realized why she had pulled away. As her sweatshirt landed on the floor beside the bed, he found her tugging her black camisole up.

His hands stopped her, and she looked down at him.

"You're taking off your shirt." He was stating the obvious, but he didn't know what else to do.

"You took off yours. And I want to feel your skin on mine. Please?"

It was the "please" that would have killed him, had he been alive, and he found himself helping to tear the cami off her body. As soon as it was off, she wrapped her arms around him, holding him so that every inch of her bare skin was touching every inch of his. He had never felt anything so good in his entire existence.

Rubbing her back, he kissed her again. It was different this time, hungry and wanting, fueled by the electric sensation the contact of their bodies had generated, and he wanted more. His hands moved lower, down her back, but were stopped by the elastic waist of her sweatpants. It was the reminder he needed of her purity and goodness, and he pulled away from their kiss, struggling to collect his thoughts and summon the strength to resist the urges he felt so deeply.

Before he could bring himself to speak his concerns or put distance between them, she shattered what little restraint he had managed to gather with seven words.

"I want to feel more of you."

Again, his hands took over without consulting his brain, and the rest of his clothing was off. He didn't have a chance to consider helping Beth with her clothes when she rolled on top of him.

She was completely naked.

He was only going to hold her. He repeated it in his mind, over and over again.

He was only going to hold her.

He was only going to touch every part of her, have her smooth, soft skin under his fingertips and against his body, feel the beating of her heart against his chest and pretend it was his own.

As they kissed again, his hands moved to cup her bottom, and she started shaking.

"I'm sorry," he said, immediately sliding his hands up to her back instead.

"No, no, it's okay. It's just adrenaline, or something. I don't know. But it's not...I mean..."

She reached one arm behind her and moved his hand down again, still shaking.

"Don't stop."

Everything melted away as she covered his face, neck, and shoulders with kisses. He wondered vaguely how he had never experienced such exquisite pleasure in the past. Not as a human, certainly, but also not as a vampire. For all the things he had done, all the women he had seduced and taken pleasure from, and all the different ways he had done so, nothing had ever made him feel so alive. He had never felt so *good*. It was pure bliss.

He had lost himself in the weight of her body on his, the green-apple scent of her hair, the curve of her beneath his hands, when from somewhere in the haze her voice broke through to him again.

"Closer. I want to be closer to you."

He opened his eyes, which he hadn't realized were closed, and found her looking at him intently, her hair forming a curtain around both their faces.

"Beth," he managed to croak, "there's only one way to be closer than this."

A fierce pride filled him as she boldly looked into his eyes and replied, "I know."

"Are you sure, Beth? Because once we do that, we can't go back. And I know how much it means to you to wait until you get mar—"

She stopped his ramblings with her mouth, kissing him deeply, then nibbling on his lower lip in a way that made him ache with need.

Finally, when she was done torturing him, she lifted her head.

"I'm sure."

Without another word, he shifted, gently rolling her beneath him, his weight pinning her softly into the mattress.

And he obeyed.

****

Beth's eyes fluttered open as she stifled a yawn. Reaching for the bedside table, her hand instinctively found her cell phone, and she looked at the time. It was ten minutes before her alarm would go off.

She had been having a wonderful dream. A scandalous dream, really. She smiled as she remembered Thomas's eyes looking into hers, the warm weight of his body covering her, melding into her. Kissing her and whispering endearments. Gentle and strong. Protective and possessive.

She'd never had a dream like that before. Nothing that real, a dream she could recall so thoroughly in the morning.

He had held her afterwards, in the dream. Held her and asked her if she was okay. Brushed the hair from her face and kissed her nose, as though she were the most precious thing in the world to him. She had drifted off to sleep in his arms, comfortable and content and relaxed. And as she'd fallen asleep, he had whispered that he would stay as long as he could, but that he'd have to leave before the sun broke the horizon.

Beth sat up in bed, suddenly aware of a dull soreness in a place she'd never been sore before.

Slowly, she turned her head to the other side of the bed. The sheets were in place, but slightly crumpled, and a piece of lined paper, folded into quarters, sat on the indented pillow.

It hadn't been a dream. Of course it hadn't been a dream. She had slept with Thomas. She was no longer a virgin.

With a shaky hand, she picked up the note and unfolded it. The black ink struck a contrast against the whiteness of the paper, the lines bold and gentle at the same time. He had lovely handwriting, she found herself thinking as she read the brief message he'd penned in long, elegant strokes.

My Dear Beth,

Never have I detested what I am more than I do at this moment, knowing that the sun will rise in an hour and that I cannot be with you as you open your eyes to a new day. I would give anything to wake at your side, to watch the morning's rays filter through the blinds and make your rich brown hair glow golden. That when the memory of our night together comes rushing back and fills you with doubt, I would be there, ready to hold and reassure, confirming that I love you as I've never loved anyone else.

What we shared last night was perfect. I have never felt so complete in my entire existence. But I worry about what you must be thinking, how you might feel about yourself, now that dawn has broken. If you must blame someone, blame me, not yourself. I should have been stronger. Perhaps I am more human than I thought.

I hope my weakness does not change how you feel about me. How you feel about us. I wish to see you again, tonight, but I will not come to your apartment. I do not want to impose myself on you. But I cannot help the overwhelming desire to talk to you, to have you smile at me, to be with you. If you are able and willing, meet me at the art museum, in the gallery overlooking West Campus. Half an hour after sunset. I'll be waiting for you. Hoping.

All my love,
Thomas

Sighing, Beth folded the note and held it between her clasped hands. Any notion she might have harbored that Thomas had seduced her or somehow manipulated her into having sex with him dissipated as she read his words. Thomas hadn't done this. She had. She remembered it clearly, the heady feeling of being near him, touching him, feeling his skin everywhere she possibly could. She had asked for more, repeatedly. He'd tried to remind her of her ideals, but she hadn't listened. She had wanted all of him, and he had given it to her.

What was most confusing was that she didn't regret her actions. Not exactly. Was she disappointed in herself for not following through with the promise she'd made to remain a virgin until she was married, to live by her beliefs? Yes. But was she sorry it had happened? Did she wish it hadn't? That was a more difficult question to answer.

Pushing aside the heavy covers, she padded to the bathroom to get ready for the day. It didn't matter if she did or didn't regret sleeping with Thomas. The fact was that she had, and she couldn't undo it. Now she had to figure out what to do next.

Beth had never been more thankful for her light class load on Fridays than she was that day. After barely managing to get through her mid-morning lecture and a brief meeting with her advisor, she texted Lin. She felt bad burdening Lin with her transgressions—not to mention a little bit ashamed after all her talk about how wrong she thought premarital sex was. But Beth had to talk to someone, and she knew Lin would understand.

Still, as she spotted Lin standing under a tree outside the North Campus dining hall, Beth had second thoughts.

"Hey stranger," Lin greeted her, picking her backpack up off the ground and walking with her toward the building. "I haven't heard from you in a few days. Everything all right?"

At that, Beth's eyes welled up with tears.

Lin stopped short when she saw Beth's reaction, and a trio of students almost ran into them.

"What happened?" asked Lin, steering her toward a path by the side of the building rather than into the dining hall, where they were originally headed. "Seriously, Beth, tell me what's wrong."

Beth had no choice but to tell her now, what with all the waterworks.

"I'm sorry, Lin, it's really not that bad. I just made a mistake."

"What kind of mistake?" One of Lin's eyebrows shot up, and Beth chuckled even as more tears streamed down her cheeks.

She took a deep, calming breath, let it out slowly, then wiped the tears off her face.

"I slept with Thomas."

Lin's eyes grew to twice their original size.

"You mean you had sex with him?"

All Beth could do was nod her head.

"You? You had sex with Thomas?"

"Lin, stop saying it, please. Yes. I did. I had sex with Thomas."

For some reason, it sounded much worse when she said it that way.

Lin's expression softened, and she reached over to thread her arm with Beth's before guiding the two of them down the dirt path that led to a walking trail behind the dining hall. "Tell me everything," said Lin, gently patting Beth's arm.

Beth had met up with Lin the day after the

Barrister's Ball to tell her what Ryan had tried to do and how Thomas had rescued her. So, Beth filled her in on her talks with Thomas since then, leaving out the vampire stuff, of course, and ending with the two of them in bed together.

When she had finished getting Lin up to speed on her transgressions, Beth sighed and looked away from Lin's sympathetic stare. "I'm a hypocrite," said Beth, giving voice to what had bothered her the most about everything.

"No, you're not."

Lin's emphatic statement, with no additional explanation, made Beth look at her again.

"Yes, I am. You know I've been proclaiming how I don't believe in premarital sex and then I go and do this. It's the very definition of hypocrisy."

"No, it's not. Do you believe premarital sex is wrong?"

Beth nodded. "Yes. I should have had some self-control."

"Are you going to go around sleeping with every guy with a pulse while you tell everyone else not to have sex?"

Beth frowned. "No, I guess not."

"Then you're not a hypocrite. You're just human."

Lin was so adamant, so sure about what she was saying, that it made Beth stop and think.

"I shouldn't have put myself in that position," said Beth, a minute later.

"Do you love him, Beth?" The tender look on Lin's face meant she already knew the answer.

"Yes."

Lin sighed. "For what it's worth, I don't think what

you did was so bad, but if you do, then do something about."

"Do what? What can I do?"

Lin threw her hands in the air and shrugged, almost making Beth laugh. "I don't know. You're the one who's Catholic. Isn't this the type of thing you're supposed to go to church and confess? Confession is good for the soul and all that? Just go and tell a priest you had sex with a hot visiting researcher and then you're done, right?"

Confession. Lin was right. That's what Beth needed to do. Just get it off her chest, admit she had done something wrong, and start over again. She didn't need to carry the guilt with her, not when it would keep her from being the person she wanted to be.

"You're right," she replied.

Lin chuckled. "Of course, I'm right. I took an undergrad course in comparative religions last semester, just for fun. I know what I'm talking about."

Beth smiled and hugged her friend. "Thank you, Lin. You're always there for me. You always know what to say. You're the best friend."

Lin shook her head as she pulled away from Beth's embrace.

"I'm not, Beth. I...I feel bad about something, too."

Lin's eyes shimmered with unshed tears, and Beth reached out to squeeze her arm.

"Oh, Lin, what is it? What's wrong?"

Her friend took a step back and looked down at her feet.

"I haven't been completely honest with you, and it's been eating away at me."

"Lin, you can tell me anything."

Lin looked dubious for a moment, then sighed.

"Do you remember when I told you that Tyler and I slept next to each other naked, but we didn't have sex?"

Beth nodded, and it dawned on her. "You had sex with him?"

The tears Lin had been trying to keep in fell freely now, and Beth pulled her into another hug.

"Oh, Lin," whispered Beth, still holding her. "I'm so sorry."

"He told me that I wasn't his first, but that I would be his last. And I'm so stupid, Beth. I actually believed him."

Beth stroked her back until her friend calmed down a little. "Why didn't you tell me before, Lin?"

Lin breathed deeply against her and loosened her grip. Wiping the tears from her face, Lin shrugged. "I guess I was scared. I know what you think about sex, and you warned me not to sleep with Tyler. I thought if you knew what I had done, then you would…"

Fresh tears made Beth's throat close up with sympathy. And shame. "I would what?" asked Beth. "I would stop being your friend?"

Lin nodded timidly. "Yes,"

"Oh, Lin, I'm the one who's sorry if I made you feel like I would judge you for that. That I wouldn't want to be your friend because of that. Because of anything. I love you like a sister. I just feel bad you went through all of this with that lying sack. And I wish you hadn't. But it doesn't make me think any less of you. It's just like you said. We're all human, and we make mistakes. And that's okay."

The two were quiet for a few minutes, watching the squirrels scurry through bushes and up trees, listening to the sounds of spring in the bird songs around them.

"Thomas isn't like Tyler, is he?"

Beth smiled, so touched by the concern in Lin's question that she almost started tearing up again.

"No. He's nothing at all like Tyler."

Feeling as though she had to prove that point, to make Lin see that there were good, decent men in the world despite her horrible experience with Tyler, Beth pulled out the note she had tucked into her jacket pocket before heading to class that morning.

"He left this for me," she said, handing the folded paper to Lin. "Read it."

Lin devoured the note, then turned to look at Beth, her mouth hanging open.

"Beth, this guy's in love with you. Like, serious, kill-anyone-who-stands-in-his-way kind of love. This stuff in the beginning about detesting himself is a little over the top, but I think he was just still reeling from whatever you did to him last night."

Beth could feel herself blushing, but she knew any protest would only trigger Lin to ask more in-depth questions about the night before.

Lin looked at the note again before folding it up and handing it back over to Beth. "So, what are you going to do? Are you going to meet him at the museum tonight?"

Stuffing the note into her pocket, Beth nodded. "Yes. I thought about it all morning, but despite all the guilt I have about, you know, what we did, I can't not see him. I love him, and I want to be with him. I don't know how it's going to work. It seems impossible. But how can we not try?"

"Impossible? Why? Because he's a visiting researcher?"

Beth froze. She could never reveal to Lin exactly what Thomas was and why there was absolutely no way she could have the relationship she wanted with him. So, swallowing down more guilt from not telling her friend the whole truth about Thomas, Beth nodded. "Yes. He'll be leaving campus soon, I'm sure."

"You never know what's going to happen," said Lin, linking arms with Beth and leading them toward the dining hall once more. "I say give it a shot, and just take it day by day. That's all any of us can do, right?"

Letting herself be pulled toward the entrance of the dining hall, Beth said nothing in reply. What had seemed so joyous and wonderful a moment ago now filled her with sadness and dread. It really was impossible. How could a human and a vampire be together? In every love story ever written about such a relationship, the human had to turn. He or she had to become a vampire in order to spend the rest of their existence with the one they loved. She couldn't do that. She loved Thomas very much, but she knew what he thought about his vampiric state. She wanted to save him. She couldn't do that if she was just like him.

There had to be another way. Thomas had been having visions of his human life. Glimpses of his past human experiences. What if there was a way to undo what he did all those years ago? Make *him* like *her*? Would he do it? Would he want to?

Even if he did, she'd never heard a vampire story where the vampire could become human again. And myth was born from truth—Thomas had told her that.

Did that mean, then, that such a thing was impossible?

How she wished she could find a way…

Beth stopped walking abruptly, nearly taking Lin's arm out of its socket.

"What happened? Why did you stop?"

Beth shook her head to bring herself back to the present.

"Oh, nothing. I just thought of something. I hadn't thought about it before, and it just came to me."

"For your experiment?" Lin looked at her expectantly.

"Kind of. Come on, let's eat. I have a problem set due today that I haven't even started yet, then I have to get ready to see Thomas."

Lin gave her a knowing smile. "Maybe you should wait a few days before going to confession. Just in case you have a couple more sins you want to get out of your system first."

Chapter Twenty-One

There were only a few people wandering around the museum. Thomas hoped they would leave soon so that he and Beth could have the place to themselves, like the first time she'd brought him here.

If she decided to come at all.

From the moment he woke that evening, Thomas had been running through different scenarios of how Beth's day had gone, or rather what she had been thinking as she went about her day. Had she been angry at him for taking her virginity when he'd known her beliefs about such things? No, he couldn't picture her being mad at him. More than likely, she was mad at herself. She had probably spent the day riddled with guilt, disgusted with herself for succumbing to temptation. To him.

There was no way she would want to see him again. He was a reminder of how far she'd fallen. She would stay away, try to forget it had ever happened. Try to forget him. And she would succeed.

And he would be alone again, hating himself. Soulless, depraved, but now fully realizing it. How could he continue to exist in a world where—

"Thomas?"

Beth's voice jolted him out of his maudlin thoughts and he turned to look at her, his body electrified by the reality of her presence.

"Hi," she continued, reaching her hand toward him. He grasped it, as though it was his only connection to sanity.

Perhaps it was.

"Were you having dark thoughts?"

Her lips hinted at a smile. How could she know him so well already?

"What gave me away?" he teased, watching her smile grow.

"You were staring at the only blank wall in this place."

"Ah, yes. A telltale sign."

He led her to one of the benches along the wall near the windows and they sat down, their bodies so close that their thighs were touching.

"Are you all right?" he asked, wondering what was going through her mind. She seemed at peace, which was a relief. Still, he had no idea what had brought about that peace, and that fact alone worried him.

"I'm fine. How are you doing?"

"I'm…glad you came." Glad was an understatement.

He raised her hand to his lips and kissed it, making her smile. He loved making her smile.

"Before you distract me too much with your charming ways, I want to talk to you. About last night."

His stomach suddenly filled with lead. He lowered her hand, placing it on his knee and covering it with both his own. "Go on," he said softly, preparing himself for the worst.

Beth let out a long breath. "First, I want you to know that my feelings for you haven't changed. I mean, if anything, I feel closer to you. But I have been thinking a lot today about what I want and what I believe is right and how I want to live my life." She looked down and shook her head. "I'm not making any sense."

"It's okay," Thomas replied, both moved by her vulnerability and fearful of what she truly intended to say. "Just keep going."

She nodded, her gaze finding his again.

"What I want is to be with you. As much as I can."

"I want that, too. More than anything."

She smiled at him, but the moment was brief, and the smile was quickly replaced by a look of concern. She had more to say.

"I didn't intend for what happened last night to happen. I didn't want that to happen until I was married. But it did, because it was you and I underestimated how strong my feelings for you were."

He was suddenly grateful that they were sitting down. Realizing he was squeezing her hand too tightly, he released her to grip the edge of the bench instead. Instead of pulling her hand back, she kept it on his knee, and he was grateful.

"I want to be with you, Thomas, but I don't feel right doing that again. We're not married, and despite how wonderful it was to be with you, like that, I can't."

"We will never be married, Beth. I can't marry you—" he gestured to himself "—like this. I'm sorry."

"I know, Thomas. I understand. And I understand if you don't want to see me anymore because of this—"

He grasped her arms, stopping her words. "I never said that. You've given me your terms, and I accept them. I can be with you without that happening again. I will respect your wishes."

Beth's big blue eyes opened wide in disbelief. She clearly hadn't expected that response.

"You love me," he went on, trying to explain himself, "and you want to spend every moment you can with me?"

She nodded, and it was as though the organ that used to be his heart could beat again.

"That is the only thing I want," he continued. "The only thing I need."

Relief flowed from her as she relaxed her shoulders and reached up to touch his face lovingly. She had doubted his response. She'd thought he would reject her once he learned he could never have all of her as he'd had the night before.

She had no idea how much he truly loved her.

He covered the hand on his cheek with his own, then slid it over to his mouth and kissed her palm. "Thank you," she whispered, bringing his hand to her lips and kissing it in return.

A surge of raw emotion overcame him as her eyes welled up with tears, and he took her in his arms, crushing her to his chest.

"I love you," he said softly, feathering kisses in her hair. "That's all I know. That's all that matters."

They held each other for several long moments before he felt her squirm. He chuckled as he released her. "I didn't mean to hold you so tightly. Are you all right?"

She beamed at him. "Of course. I love holding you like this. But I have something I want to give you. And it will require some explanation."

Beth reached for the silver chain of the necklace she wore around her neck and pulled it out of her shirt, where it had been tucked away, revealing a large blue stone on a thick, silver mount.

"I think it's turquoise," she said, holding the jewel in the palm of her hand.

"It looks old," he replied. He guessed there was a story connected to the piece, something she wanted to share with him. Though he wanted to put his arm around her and pull her back into the crook of his arm, she looked deep in thought, and he did not want to interrupt her musings.

A moment later, she pulled the chain off and pooled it into the same hand that held the stone. Then she extended her hand toward him.

"I want you to have this."

He put out his hand, and she carefully placed the necklace in his palm. It was heavier than he had expected it to be, and he couldn't help running a finger over the smooth blue stone.

"Did it belong to someone in your family?" He was honored that she would trust him with an heirloom. Then again, she had trusted him with so much more already.

"In a way, yes. My cousin gave it to me just before my sophomore year." She lowered her head and blew out a breath, looking up at him as though she were about to say something off-the-wall and wanted to gauge his reaction.

"Do you know what you want more than anything else? If you could have anything you wished for, do you know what that wish would be?"

The question caught Thomas off-guard. It had been a long time since he'd wanted something he couldn't just take. He could satisfy any desire easily. Sex, the thrill of the hunt, domination over others. Blood. Being a vampire allowed him to take. It required that he do so. But lately his humanity had been creeping back up on him, preventing him from taking. Making him want things he couldn't have *because* he was a vampire.

"Yes," he finally answered. "I know."

She smiled broadly, putting her hand on the amulet and closing his fingers around his.

"Good. Because this stone is supposed to give it to you. Whatever your heart desires most. That's what my cousin said. And you'll have what you wish for as long as the amulet is yours. Which, in your case, could be a very long time, depending on what you wish for."

"You believe that? You think this amulet is magical?"

Beth shrugged. "I don't really know. My cousin believes, and I'm sitting here talking to a vampire, so who's to say? It's probably worth a shot, don't you think?"

He opened his hand to look at the necklace again. It was plain and unassuming, but at the same time it possessed a unique sort of beauty. Who knew?

"Haven't you tested it? To see if it truly does grant wishes?"

She shook her head. "I haven't been able to decide on something to wish for. It feels like cheating a little bit, to wish for better grades or to pass a final, and a bit of a waste, too. I wanted to have something important to use it on. Something I could never do on my own. Something grand that would change things for the better." She looked at him thoughtfully before continuing. "I've been thinking more about using it lately though…"

Her voice trailed off, but she smiled brightly and squeezed his hands before letting go and rising from the bench they were sitting on. He stood and moved to follow her as she walked toward the large windows overlooking the campus.

"Why are you giving it to me, Beth? If this is real—if the necklace really can grant you a wish—then why not keep it for yourself? You said there is something you've been thinking about. Why not wish for it?"

He had hoped she might be wishing for him to be with her always, but he couldn't ask her outright. The idea was laughable. Still, he hoped.

"It's better this way," she replied, avoiding the question. "I want you to have the wish. I want you to have what you want most for yourself."

"Do you want me to wish that I wasn't a vampire? Do you want me to be human, like you, so that we can be together?"

She shook her head slightly, then closed her eyes. When she opened them again, her face was peaceful, and the same peace filled him. Whatever her response, he would do as she asked. Her wish was his.

"I can't tell you that, or else what was the point of giving you the power to decide for yourself?"

Power. She was giving him, the most powerful creature ever to exist, the power to decide. As absurd as it sounded, it was true. And suddenly, Thomas didn't know what to do with it.

He stepped toward her and pulled her into his arms once more, holding her, feeling her body move against his with each breath she took in his embrace.

This was what he wanted.

The thought came from nowhere. And everywhere. But he couldn't make the decision yet. What if she didn't want the same thing? Or what if she thought she wanted him now, but in a week or a month or a year she realized the folly of choosing him over any other man she could have had? Could he really give up eternity for the chance of a moment with Beth?

"This is a huge gift you have given me. This choice. I believe I know what I want, but I will not rush to make the wish until I'm sure it's the right thing. For me. And for you. Do you understand?"

She nodded, her face glowing with some new emotion.

"I trust you, Thomas. You know I do. Plus, you always seem to be right about things," she teased, shifting to lean her head against his shoulder as they stared out onto the lights of West Campus below.

"What have I been right about?" In his mind, he had only ever been wrong—wrong to be afraid of death, wrong to choose this empty existence, wrong to make himself part of Beth's life…

"I talked to Lin today."

He turned his face to kiss the top of her head. "Oh? Did you tell her about…last night?"

Her head moved slightly against his shoulder in a shy nod.

He would have killed to hear how that conversation had played out. Metaphorically speaking, of course.

"What did she say?"

Beth sighed and hugged him closer. "She listened, and she tried to understand how I felt. She doesn't believe the same things I do, you know, but still, she said what I needed to hear. She told me it was okay not to be perfect. It didn't mean I was a hypocrite. And it was okay to regret something and not regret it at the same time."

She was looking at him, worried he would misunderstand, so he nodded at her, smiling. "A person can regret an action but cherish the experience. I know that better than most, Beth."

Her expression softened. "I haven't been the best friend to her. You were right about her and Tyler. She slept with him, but she was afraid to tell me. She thought that if I knew, I wouldn't want to be friends with her, because I was always against doing that stuff. So, she kept it all in."

"She was wrong not to trust that you would be there for her, Beth. Just because you have differing beliefs doesn't mean you would judge her so harshly. I haven't known you as long as she has, but even I know that."

"You're a special case." She laughed softly, making him smile.

Thomas turned his body to face her, wrapping his arms around her waist. "You are not so rigid in your convictions that you lose sight of what is at the heart of those beliefs. Love, compassion, mercy, hope. Those are the things that first drew me to you, though I didn't realize it at the time. Those are the things that persist. They are the reasons for the rules, what governs them. Rigid things break, they don't work as they should. But you…" —he pulled her closer, lowering his head to her neck to punctuate each word with a kiss— "you are soft, tender, kind, loving. You are not perfect. But you are good. And wonderful."

He had made his way from her neck to her mouth

by this point and could no longer resist claiming a real kiss. She welcomed him, kissing him back passionately, making him wonder how she expected they would be able to keep from doing the things they'd done the night before again. And again, and again.

"Thomas!" she exclaimed suddenly, pulling away and making him think that perhaps she had heard his wicked thoughts.

But the bright gleam in her eyes told him that she was far from angry at him.

"What is it?"

"You just gave me an idea about my project. Will you come to the lab with me so I can see if it works?"

If kissing gave her ideas for her project, he would need to encourage more brainstorming sessions. He grinned at the thought.

"Sure. Let's go."

Chapter Twenty-Two

Beth hadn't noticed her mouth hanging open until Thomas gently nudged her chin up, closing it. She looked away from the computer screen to find him observing her, a crooked grin on his face, his hand lingering on her cheek.

"I take it the results are better?"

They had been in the lab for almost two hours, taking apart the experimental apparatus and removing the tiny fasteners that held the camera in place. She wasn't sure they would find the springs she remembered coming across weeks ago, the remnants of another student's experiment, but they did. And she'd replaced the rigid fasteners with the springs, then put the housing back together.

Then she had held her breath and said a silent prayer as she set the apparatus at the launch point and hit the button to release it into freefall.

They had rushed back to her workstation to look at the digital photos. Thomas had laughed at her when she jumped so quickly into her chair that she almost slid off.

And now, this. A perfectly spherical fuel droplet, perfectly centered on the screen.

"Yes. The results are better. The results couldn't *be* any better. Look at this." She pointed to the dark ring around the droplet in the first image at the top of the screen. "I've never seen the boundary so clearly. And do you see how the droplet is in the same position, from the first picture to the last? That's what I've been trying to do since October."

She turned away from the screen to look at him, a wide smile and bright eyes evidencing the excitement of her success. "I kept thinking that the camera had to be fixed tighter to the housing, that it was shifting the image because it wasn't secured to the housing. But that wasn't it at all. There was nothing to absorb the shift in force when the apparatus was released. There was no give. Rigid things break, just like you said. Sometimes you have to have a little flexibility to get the clearest picture."

"The springs?"

She nodded. "The springs."

Thomas reached for her hand and pulled her out of her chair and into his lap. "You figured it out. My little genius."

He brushed the hair that had come loose from her ponytail off her neck and kissed her there.

Taking his face in her hands, she kissed him square on the mouth, and he growled as his arms tightened around her.

She laughed at his reaction and got to her feet. With catlike grace, he rose and followed her. It was as though he wanted to be near her at all times. Which was more than fine with her.

Beth put on her coat, grabbed her backpack, and turned to Thomas, extending her hand. Throwing a devilish half-smile at her, he took her hand and led her out of the lab.

"You didn't eat dinner before you met me at the

museum, did you?"

"No," she replied, touched that he would be concerned about her hunger when it was something he hadn't experienced in over a hundred years. At least for food. "The meeting with my advisor was later than usual, and I didn't want to keep you waiting."

He squeezed her hand, then pulled her closer as they walked down the hall toward the exit that opened out to the parking lot.

"Let's go to Collegetown and get dinner, then. You can leave your car in the parking lot here and we'll walk down."

"I can just grab a sandwich or something, Thomas. You don't have to pretend to eat with me anymore."

"I know," he said abruptly, almost interrupting her. He took a breath, pausing a second before continuing. "I know I don't have to sit and pretend to be human around you, Beth. But I want you to eat a good meal, and I want to be with you. It doesn't hurt me to eat food. But it does hurt me not to be near you every moment I can."

Beth rolled her eyes teasingly. "There you go being overly dramatic again."

He chuckled, but his laughter sounded a little hollow. He was worried about something.

"What's wrong?" Beth asked, looking up at him as he pushed open the door to the parking lot. "There's something bothering you."

"I wouldn't say that, exactly. I'm just…concerned."

Beth could feel her face scrunch up in a frown. "Concerned about what?"

"About you. About whether you know what you're

getting yourself into, being with me. About whether you've thought through how it's going to work, what it's going to look like."

He paused, and she waited.

"You don't have to stay with me because of what happened last night. It does not bind you to me."

"I know that, Thomas. I'm not that naïve. I *want* to be with you."

"But this is never going to be *normal*. It can't be."

She had to make an effort not to roll her eyes again. "I don't want it to be normal. I don't need it to be."

A few steps later, she stopped and turned to look at him. "Do you?"

"No."

"Good. Then we'll just take it one day at a time and see what happens. Because we don't know what will happen, Thomas. What we do know is that something is changing. You're not the same as you were."

He was looking at her, seemingly transfixed, and her face flushed under his gaze. Then he shook his head. "No, I'm not the same."

"Neither am I," she replied, leading him across the parking lot. "So, let's see what happens. Let's see where we end up. Doesn't that just make sense?"

"I guess so. I've never measured my existence in days. Not since I was turned, in any case."

He sighed heavily, and she found herself repressing a chuckle. "I suppose being immortal might have something to do with that."

They had reached the other side of the parking lot when Thomas suddenly stopped, pulling her closer and turning her body to face him. He touched her cheek with his hand, his lips turning up slightly at the corners. His eyes were a warm brown color that told her he was content in the moment. The thought made her smile in return.

"Thank you," he said softly, tucking her hair behind her ear.

"You have nothing to thank me for, Thomas. We're only a couple of days into this. I could decide to break up with you after dinner."

His smile grew, and she laughed at her own statement, which was, of course, ridiculous.

"Even if you do," he replied, his tone solemn despite his smile, "I am more than I was before I met you. And that will never change."

****

Adam jumped to his feet and ran to the door, his head still pounding from whatever it was his mother had slipped into his drink. A glance at the clock on the wall told him he'd been out for almost an hour, which meant she'd had an hour's head start.

Please don't let her find them.

His mother had gone into a rage when Adam had told her they should let the creature live. He'd never seen her that angry before. Adam had tried to explain that the creature, Thomas, was not the monster they believed him to be. He was not the vampire that had murdered her ancestors. They had either tracked down the wrong creature, or he had changed. Regardless, Thomas did not deserve to die, and Adam refused to allow his mother to take any action against him.

His mother had laughed at his speech, all the while recounting the horrors of the murders that had occurred so long ago. Then, quite suddenly, she'd stopped. She had gone off into the kitchen without another word, and when she came back, she was carrying two glasses of lemonade.

Adam should have known better than to accept the peace offering. But ever since he'd been a child, his mother had reconciled her differences with her son over a tall glass of lemonade. He should have known better, but he didn't. He'd taken the glass from her and drunk the whole damn thing while she calmly told him that she admired his capacity to forgive. It was only when he'd put the glass down, his head already starting to spin, that his mother had confessed she did not share his perspective.

She would kill Thomas, with or without her son's help. And she would do it tonight.

The car was gone, of course, so Adam ran to the closest bus stop, thankful to see a bus coming just as he approached. He flashed his bus pass at the driver and found a seat by the windows, all the while trying to figure out how he would stop his mother from exacting her revenge.

Two stops later, Adam was running up Collegetown Avenue, toward the Engineering buildings. His mother had taken his cell phone, too, and he didn't have Beth's number memorized. But her number was written down in the lab, and he could use the phone there to call her. He was sure she would be with Thomas, but even if she wasn't, she might know where to find him.

He only hoped he wasn't too late.

****

"After you."

Thomas held the budding branches back from the path and gestured for Beth to pass. She rewarded him for the sweet gesture with a smile. The truth of the matter was that she couldn't stop smiling when she was with him.

As the worn dirt path widened, Thomas fell into step beside her and grasped her hand, not-so-subtly pulling her closer.

"I don't know how you are going to eat an entire meal with me if you can't taste it or enjoy it."

"Oh, I'll enjoy it," Thomas replied, squeezing her hand.

Beth chuckled, then grew quiet as the thought of all the human joys Thomas couldn't experience hit her.

"What do you miss the most?"

Thomas looked at her with a puzzled expression. "What do you mean?"

They had reached the edge of the woods and stepped onto the sidewalk, turning to head toward the main street where many of the restaurants were located. It was a nice evening for a stroll, especially one with Thomas.

"I mean, what do you miss most from your human life? I think, if it were me, it would be food. I enjoy eating. The different flavors and textures, the aromas, even the memories that come with certain dishes. It would be a lot not having that anymore. But maybe you haven't thought about it in a while." She shrugged, suddenly feeling stupid for bringing it up. What was she trying to do, rub salt in his wounds? "I'm sorry, I don't know why I said all that. Let's talk about something else."

"Feeling the warmth of the sun on my skin."

The quickness of his answer surprised her, causing her to lift her gaze to his face.

He smiled wistfully. "Our home was not large growing up," he continued, "but my parents took pride in keeping it clean and inviting. There was a chair in our kitchen, near the window, where I would sit sometimes while my mother cooked. She would hum songs from her childhood and tell me stories. The sun would slant through the glass in the mornings, filling the kitchen with brightness and warmth, even on the coldest, snowiest winter day. I loved sitting there, watching her and listening to her stories and songs. I felt safe and loved. Warm, inside and out. I miss that."

Thomas was staring straight ahead as he spoke, his words tugging at her heart as she imagined the little boy in the scene he described.

"You loved your mother very much," she replied softly, not knowing what else to say.

He nodded. "And my father. I had siblings, but they were almost grown by the time I was born. Even now, with all the memories that have come back to me, I don't remember much about them."

"But you do of your parents?"

"I do. And every day I remember more. I think if I'd had these memories all along, I wouldn't have done the things I did after I turned. Those unspeakable acts—they are more easily committed in the absence of fond memories. When you can't remember what it is like to feel safe and loved, you think nothing of destroying it for others. I suppose that's why the memories were taken away when I was turned. They would have only been a hindrance to becoming the creature I had chosen to become."

She waited a moment before asking her next question, half afraid of the answer.

"Are you glad to have them back? The memories?"

He turned his head to look at her, a genuine smile forming on his lips, giving her the answer before he could confirm it with words. "Yes. I am glad to have the sun back in my life."

Releasing her hand, he put his arm around her back and hugged her closer as they continued walking, and she knew in that moment he truly had changed. He may still have been a vampire in technical terms, but his heart was human. He was a man in all the ways that counted.

Beth was about to suggest one of the restaurants ahead as a good place for dinner when a soft whimper reached her ears.

"Somebody, please. Someone, help me!"

It was closer to a whisper than a voice, but she'd heard it. A quick glance at Thomas confirmed that he'd heard it, too.

"I think it's coming from there," he said, pointing to an alley on the right, just a few steps ahead of where they stood.

She rushed forward, but Thomas blocked her with his arm. "Let me go first. Stay behind me."

Beth nodded, though she wondered what danger a woman in trouble could pose.

The light from the streetlamps did not reach into the alley, and Thomas stopped at the entrance, scanning the area. "Is someone there?"

"Please, sir, I'm hurt. Please, someone, help me!" the whisper came again. It was definitely a woman's voice.

A few large trash containers lined one side of the alley, and it was difficult to see past them. Slowly, Thomas inched forward, Beth's hand clutching the back of his shirt, half a step behind him.

A brief flash of movement as a shadow emerged from behind one of the dumpsters caught Beth's eye, and the hairs on the back of her neck stood on end. Without thinking, she jumped in front of Thomas, conscious of the sound of something cutting through the air before pain tore through her left side. She would have crumpled to the ground if not for Thomas's strong hands around her waist.

"No!" he cried out, his anguish palpable.

"Shit!" she heard the woman say before her footsteps faded. She had run out the other side of the alley.

Beth closed her eyes, suddenly feeling very tired. Thomas was on the ground with her, cradling her head in his lap, rocking her back and forth as his hand searched for the wound.

"It's a wooden arrow, Beth," he whispered, his voice cracking. "It was meant for me. She was aiming for me, but you stepped in its path. You shouldn't have done that! It wouldn't have killed me—she aimed too low. Now, look at you. My beautiful Beth, look at you…"

Beth took in a breath. It was as though something pressed down on her chest, keeping the air from fully entering her lungs. She opened her eyes briefly to find Thomas's face close to hers. He was crying.

Somehow, she found the strength to reach up with one hand and touch his cheek. "You're too handsome to cry, Thomas," she managed to get out, taking several breaths in the process. "I'm fine. I'm fine."

Already, she was feeling better. Not heavy anymore, but quite the opposite. Had Thomas picked her up? No, she could still feel the ground beneath her.

Thomas shifted her in his arms, and she could feel his breath on her neck.

"I can save you, Beth. I can turn you."

Beth's eyes shot open, and she shook her head frantically.

"No, Thomas, no," she gasped. "I won't be the same if you turn me. You said it yourself, you became something different when you were turned. You forgot your humanity. I don't want that. I don't want to forget how much I love you."

"But you'll die, Beth. You'll die," his voice cracked, and Beth's heart broke for him. "You'll die, and I can't exist without you in my life."

Beth managed a smile, even as her face and limbs began tingling into unconsciousness. "You will exist. You'll be fine. Stay this way, Thomas. You've found the humanity that you had lost. Keep it. Don't go back to what you were. Stay good, as you are now. And then we'll be together again."

Her eyelids were heavy, but she raised them one last time to look at Thomas. So beautiful. So sad. "I love you, Thomas. Don't ever forget that."

****

Panic gripped Thomas anew as Beth closed her eyes and let out a long breath. His throat closed in fear, and he tightened his arms around her, pulling her against his chest. "I can't let this happen," he whispered, pushing the hair from her neck.

He would turn her. He had to. It was inevitable.

He'd been a fool to think they could be together otherwise. Even if she had not been shot with an arrow, even if she was not bleeding to death in his arms, he would have had to turn her eventually. How else would they have been able to be together?

Putting his teeth against the smooth skin of her neck, he closed his eyes. He could still hear her voice in his ears, could still see her desperate look as she pleaded with him not to make her a vampire.

No, Thomas, no.

An anguished sound he did not recognize as his own spilled out of him, and he withdrew, only to lower his lips to her neck once more, this time in a tender kiss. He could not go against her wishes, even if he did not agree with her reasoning. She was convinced she would not remember the love they shared if he turned her, that she would become soulless, emotionless. Inhuman. But if her love could bring him out of the darkness that was his former vampiric existence, why couldn't he do that for her? How else could they possibly be together?

He hugged her limp body to himself, willing life into her limbs, but he knew it would be to no avail. She had left him. The only thing he could do was to heed her final instruction.

Don't go back to what you were. Stay good, as you are now. And then we'll be together again.

And yet, how could he be good without her? How could he be anything more than the creature he had chosen to become so many years ago? Oh, how he wished things were different...

A wish—the amulet! The realization struck him like a bolt of lightning, and he carefully withdrew his right hand from under Beth to reach into his pocket where he'd been carrying the gift she had given him.

Grasping the chain and pulling it out of his pocket, he clutched the blue stone at the end of the chain between both his hands, holding them up as if he were praying. Perhaps he was.

He thought of how happy he had been with Beth, how kind and understanding and forgiving she was. She had made him feel like a person with a heart and a soul, and he never wanted to be without either again. He never wanted to be without *her*. She was the purpose for his existence, and if he had to spend the rest of his days paying for his sins to deserve her, he would. All he needed, all he wanted, was to be with her.

"Please, I wish for Beth to be well. I wish for her to survive and be whole and to overcome this injury. I wish for her to be healed. Please, please…"

His voice tapered off, and he lowered his head to whisper in her ear. "Beth, wake up. Please, Beth. I love you. Please wake up."

Seconds passed, then minutes, the bloodstain on her shirt growing larger.

With trembling hands, Thomas moved Beth off his lap and gently placed her on the pavement. He closed his eyes, fisting his hands as the growl that had been rumbling in his throat burst forth from him in an ear-shattering roar.

It had not worked. The damn necklace wasn't magical. It was just a necklace. Beth was dead. He would never hold her again or hear her sweet voice. She would never laugh again or kiss him into oblivion. He had lost her. He had lost himself.

Rising to his feet, he turned toward the far end of the alley, where the woman had run. Sniffing the air, he caught her scent—a foul mixture of pasta sauce and cheap deodorant.

She would pay for what she'd done. He would find her, and he would make her suffer, long and hard, for what she'd done to his Beth. Then, as the sun began to rise, he would kill her.

And he would feel the sun on his skin, one last time.

Chapter Twenty-Three

An anguished cry ripped through the still night air, making Adam's blood immediately run cold. It was an arresting sound, and he instinctually froze mid-step, turning his head toward the source.

It had to be the creature. And the creature was not happy.

Beth.

Less than a second later, Adam was running down the street toward the building where he thought the sound had come from. He had been walking in the opposite direction minutes ago, toward the lab to find Beth's phone number, but there was no need for that now. If he found the vampire, he would find Beth, and he could warn them both.

If he wasn't already too late.

He would have run past the alley if not for a group of bystanders standing at the entrance, looking at something, and the car his mother "borrowed" from him parked across the street. Shoving past a guy taking a picture of the scene with his cell phone, Adam stopped short when he caught sight of Beth laid out on the hard ground in a pool of blood he feared was her own.

He rushed to her side and searched frantically for a pulse along her neck.

God, please.

He had all but given up hope when his fingers sensed a tiny movement under the corner of her jaw. She was alive!

"Someone, quick, call an ambulance. She's alive, but she needs help. Now!"

To his credit, the guy who had been taking pictures made the call right away. Adam didn't pay attention to what the guy was saying into the phone, but instead put his hand on Beth's side, pressing the flesh around the wooden arrow that pierced her abdomen.

His mother hadn't done this on purpose. He was sure of it.

"You tried to save him, didn't you?"

Beth was completely still. It hardly seemed like she was breathing.

"Where is your vampire boyfriend now, Beth? Where is he? Did he run and hide, leaving you here to bleed to death, all alone?"

As soon as he'd said the words, Adam remembered the cry of despair that had led him to Beth. The vampire, Thomas, hadn't run away to save his own hide. He'd thought that Beth had died.

And he was going to seek his revenge.

His mother was in danger. Thomas would kill her. She would die an excruciating death at his hands. He would make her suffer.

Adam looked over his shoulder, where his car was still parked, then down the alley to the next street over. If his mother hadn't been able to get to the car, then she would have doubled back to his apartment on foot. It was a two-mile walk—not impossible.

Sirens blared in the distance, getting closer.

"Hang in there, Beth." He pushed the hair away

from her face.

The ambulance would arrive, and he would make sure Beth was taken care of.

Then he would find his mother. Hopefully before Thomas found her.

****

Tears streamed down Thomas' face. Hot tears of sadness and rage.

Vampires weren't supposed to cry. They weren't supposed to mourn. But Beth, with all her goodness and sweetness, was gone, and he couldn't do a damn thing to bring her back. All the strength, all the power, all the years of supernatural existence he'd had, they all meant nothing. Beth's life had still slipped right through his fingers. Even the amulet, which was supposed to be magical, had failed. And now he was alone.

But there was something he could do, something he *would* do, and it would feel good and right. And this time, for the first time, his taking of a life would have meaning, a purpose. It would be *deserved*.

She had moved fast, that insane woman who had wanted to kill him, who had instead taken Beth's innocent life. But not so fast that Thomas couldn't follow her scent.

Having crossed the pedestrian bridge into downtown, where the locals lived, Thomas sniffed the air once more, tilting his head to the left. He moved in the direction of the scent, faster than any human being could, careful to stay in the shadows where he wouldn't be seen. As he rounded the corner, the woman came into view. She was running, though it was obvious she was tired. And scared. She kept looking over her shoulder.

She was right to be frightened.

Thomas dashed behind a two-story brick industrial building to avoid being spotted, then, looking up the side of the building, scaled the wall with hardly any effort to land on the roof. Soundlessly, he moved forward, jumping from one building to the next, until he'd gotten ahead of the woman. Then, he jumped down, landing in her path.

"You took an innocent life," said Thomas to the woman, his voice low and menacing.

The woman stopped so abruptly that she nearly fell forward. Her mouth hung open in shock. Despite apparently knowing what he was, she had not expected to see him again that evening.

Thomas closed the distance between them in the blink of an eye and wrapped his fingers around her throat. Her pulse was rapid beneath his hand, the blood pumping to her limbs in a fight-or-flight response.

Neither would be possible for her.

With no desire to drink the blood of Beth's murderer, Thomas pushed her to the ground and watched as she scrambled to her feet and backed farther away from him.

"Why did you have to kill her?" he asked, his voice sounding foreign to him.

The question seemed to elicit a strange response in the woman, and instead of turning to run, she laughed ironically.

"*You* want to know why *I* killed her? Well, isn't that the pot calling the kettle black. *You* are the killer, Vampire. Not me."

Again, he was at her throat in an instant, but this time was she unafraid.

"I wasn't trying to kill her, you bastard," she gasped. Thomas relaxed his fingers slightly to allow her to continue speaking. For some reason he couldn't understand, he *wanted* to hear what she had to say.

The woman obviously knew exactly what he was and how to kill him. Had he met her before? The color of her eyes and the line of her face looked familiar, but he was certain he had never seen her before that night.

"How do you know about me?" he finally asked.

The woman would have tossed her head back and laughed, had Thomas not been holding her in a vice-like grip. As it was, the choked sound of her derisive response only filled Thomas with a greater rage, and he began to wonder if what she had to say was worth the trouble of hearing her speak.

"I've known about you my whole life, Vampire. You are part of my family's history. In the year 1890, you killed the grandmother of my own grandmother. Do you even remember? You've killed so many, after all. Brutal, vicious killer that you are. You murdered an entire encampment of Italian immigrants just outside Boston, but you left a four-year-old little girl alive. A mistake, I'm sure—she was hiding. Watching how you coldly took the life of each member of her family and countless others."

"A four-year-old girl…" Thomas frowned, the memory stirring within him, and he could see the carnage he had wrought that night. His first night as a vampire.

"Yes. A four-year-old girl. One who would survive and grow and become a woman. A mother. My grandmother's mother. She told the story to my grandmother, and my grandmother told me. And I am here to kill you, you bastard."

Thomas would have laughed at her bold proclamation, considering her throat was seconds away from being crushed by the powerful fingers he had wrapped around it. But he didn't. Instead, he asked, "Then why didn't you kill me? Why did you kill Beth?"

Her brow wrinkled in confusion. "Adam said you had a fondness for the girl. He gave you more credit than you deserve. I think he grew to believe you had more man in you than monster. But you don't. You are evil, pure and simple."

"You killed Beth!" he screamed at her, his temper flaring once more, his fingers tightening around her throat. "She was innocent. She was good."

"She got in the way," the woman answered in a choked voice, her hands clawing at his in desperation. "She didn't know what you are. She tried to save you. I wasn't aiming to kill her. It was her own damn fault."

Raising the cursed woman in the air by her neck, Thomas groaned in fury. "You killed her! And you will die for it."

As the woman flailed her arms and legs, fighting for another breath, Thomas shook his head, the woman's words coming back to him. "You're wrong," he admonished the woman. "Beth did know what I was. She knew what I'd done. But she could see past it to what I've become. She loved me in spite of my sins, because she could see my heart, and she knew I had changed."

The woman's eyes fluttered as she teetered on the edge of consciousness, and her lips parted to mouth a voiceless response. "Have you?"

Her words hit Thomas like a stake through the

heart and he released her. She fell to her knees and rolled over onto her side, wheezing and trying to catch her breath. All Thomas could do was stare at her. Had he changed?

Curled in a ball on the ground, the woman had her hands at her bruised neck. She gasped noisily for breaths, one after the other, and Thomas knew he had been seconds away from ending her life. He had *wanted* to end her life, to make her suffer for what she did to Beth. Truth be told, he still wanted to. Did that mean he was still a monster, after all?

He closed his eyes and conjured the image of Beth's smiling face. She had seen good in him, had loved him, knowing who and what he was. *Don't go back to what you were*, she had warned. *Stay good, as you are now. And then we'll be together again.*

Together. That was what he desired. More than vengeance. More than blood.

Thomas reached into his pocket and pulled out the amulet. It held no magic, but it would remind him of Beth. And perhaps if he could remember Beth, how much he loved her and how much she loved him, he could be what she thought he already was.

A good man.

Slipping the chain around his neck and dropping the amulet under his shirt, so he could feel it there against his bare skin, Thomas turned away from the sniveling woman and was about to walk away when he thought of something.

Turning toward her again, he said, "You were right in what you said. I have done unspeakable things. I am sorry for killing your ancestors. I am sorry for what the child, your great-grandmother, saw and had to endure."

He knew it was not enough. The words he'd said in apology to the woman would not rewrite the past, but it was all he could offer. That, and the sparing of her life. It was what Beth would have wanted him to do.

As he walked away from the woman, the pain of losing Beth rose again inside him, threatening to take away what little composure his anger had managed to provide just moments before. Beth was gone. He would never see her again, never again hear her sweet voice or see her face blush at something ridiculously innocent or inconsequential.

"Vampire!"

Pushing aside his thoughts, Thomas spun around to face the woman again. By the time his mind registered the sight of the wooden arrow flying toward his heart, it was too late to move. Or perhaps he hadn't wanted to.

The arrow shattered the amulet in its path and pierced his flesh, sending a wave of searing pain throughout his body. His limbs useless, Thomas fell to the ground like a lifeless puppet whose strings had been cut. As his vision blurred, he closed his eyes, choosing to see Beth one last time rather than the woman on her knees ten feet away, staring in shocked glee at what she'd done.

His consciousness blowing away like ash in the wind, he said a prayer to the God he had abandoned decades before. *Forgive me.*

In his last moment, he thought of Beth. Then, with a peaceful sigh, he let go.

Chapter Twenty-Four

"Da, why do you drink that so slowly? Are you not thirsty?" Thomas, a boy of six, hopped up onto the wooden chair next to where his father sat at the kitchen table, sipping amber liquid from a short glass.

"This isn't water, boy. It's whisky. Good whisky, at that. It's made to be drank slowly. Savored. So that the enjoyment lasts. So that it can be properly appreciated."

"Does it taste good, then, Da?"

His father nodded, running a hand through his short-cropped ruddy hair. "It does to me. You may not like it, though."

Thomas stared at the drink for a few moments, contemplating what it might taste like. Finally, he asked, "May I have some?"

His father chuckled, pushing the glass toward him. "Here, take a small sip."

Clutching the glass with both hands, Thomas raised it to his lips. The strong, grainy aroma he inhaled made him crinkle his nose, and his father laughed again. "Go on. You won't know until you try it."

Determined, Thomas stuck out his little pink tongue and dipped it into the liquid. Grimacing at the strong flavor, he immediately put down the glass and pushed it back toward his father. "I don't like it," he announced.

His father slapped him on the back, still laughing, and took the cup to enjoy another sip.

Setting the cup back on the table, the man smiled kindly at his son and touched his cheek lovingly. "You'll remember your father when you smell whisky again, won't you, son?"

Thomas nodded solemnly. "It's hard to forget, Da."

"Good. Then maybe you'll remember this, too. Life is like whisky. It's meant to be savored and enjoyed. At times, you'll want to drink it fast to get to blissful oblivion, but that, my son, is a damned foolish thing to do. There's only so much whisky in the glass, you see, and the sooner you drink it, the sooner it's gone. But if you drink it properly, the way it's meant to be drunk, it'll last longer. And that feeling of contentment will last, even after the liquid's gone."

Thomas stared at his father, trying not to look confused.

Finishing off the last of his drink, his father laughed again, then plucked his son out of the chair and placed him on his lap. "Give your Da a hug, son."

Without hesitation, Thomas flung his arms around his father's wide torso, squeezing him tightly and burying his head against his strong chest. His father held him close, dropping kisses in his hair. It was the best feeling in the world, to be hugged by his big, strong Da. Nothing could harm Thomas here. He was safe, and he was loved.

Thomas felt a tear slide down his cheek. He didn't want to wake up. He didn't want to leave the warmth of this memory to face whatever hell awaited his vampire soul. It made no sense, really, that he was dreaming. Did the dead dream? It made even less sense that he was dreaming of his father. His father's love. He couldn't even remember the last time he'd thought about the man who had raised him. His father had died and left his mother a widow when Thomas was twelve. Thomas had taught himself to enjoy whisky not long after, at first simply dipping his tongue in the potent liquid, then, slowly, taking one very small sip. Then a larger one. It was all just so that he could remember his father, remember that feeling.

But he had forgotten both, just as he had forgotten everything else, when he had turned. That is, until Beth came along and reminded him. Now she was gone, too, and he would have to bear the memories alone. Was that what Hell was, then? Had the Devil finally claimed his soul?

"Beth." Her name escaped his lips on an anguished sigh, and another tear slipped past his closed eyelids.

A hand touched his face, wiping away the tear. "I'm here, Thomas. Everything is all right. You're going to be all right."

A jolt of awareness shot through him, and his eyes popped open. At first, the overhead fluorescent lights and white walls and floor were blinding, and Thomas had no choice but to squeeze his eyes shut against the brightness. Again, the hand touched his face, smoothing his eyebrow, caressing his cheek.

He heard the scrape of a chair against the floor, then the shuffle of feet, even as the hand remained to comfort him. There was a soft click, and, with eyes still shut, Thomas could tell that the light was no longer so bright. He opened his eyes.

At first, his vision was blurry. He blinked a few times to remove the film of tears and residue that blocked his sight.

Slowly, she came into focus. And she was smiling.

"Beth—am I somehow in Heaven, then?"

She reached for his hand and he grasped it, telling himself that if he could feel her, it meant she was truly there.

"There you go, being overly dramatic again. This is far from Heaven. It's just a hospital room. You were rushed to the hospital after your run-in with Adam's mother. You had an arrow in your chest, but you're going to be fine." She squeezed his hand and repeated the last part, as though reassuring herself. "You're going to be fine."

Scrambling to sit up so that he could take her in his arms, Thomas quickly discovered that small plastic tubes connected him to machines on either side of the bed where he lay, and a painful ache in his chest made him aware of a very important detail he had almost overlooked.

"I'm not..." He couldn't say the word. "I'm not what I was before, am I?"

She shook her head slowly, a dubious look on her face.

"Are you...upset?" she asked, making circles on the back of his hand with her thumb that were meant to soothe. Instead, her touches made him want to tear the tubes out of his arms, wrap himself around her, and kiss her senseless.

He settled for bringing her hand to his lips and placing a long kiss on her palm, then on her wrist, then on the back of her hand. She blushed, and his blood grew even hotter.

"No. I am the very opposite of upset."

She was still standing over the bed, looking down at him, but he managed to move his body to make some room and motioned for her to sit by tilting his head in her direction. She perched herself on the edge of the bed, pulling his hand into her lap and clutching it with both her own.

"I thought you were dead," he whispered, still unable to convince himself fully that this was not another dream. "You were unresponsive, and there was so much blood..."

His voice trailed off as he remembered again the horror of holding her bleeding body, watching her life slip away.

"Since when are you afraid of a little blood?"

The absurdity of her statement made him laugh, and she laughed along with him. As their laughter faded, she kissed his hand and held it against her heart. "I didn't think you were going to wake up, Thomas. I was so worried."

A tear fell onto his hand as she bowed her head, and he was about to console her when a movement by the closed door at the far end of the room drew his attention.

Thomas growled, low in his throat, as he realized it had been Adam who had turned off the lights a few minutes earlier. He had been standing by the door the whole time, watching.

"It's okay." Beth touched Thomas' face, drawing his attention back to her. "Adam knows what you were, and he knows what you've become. He tried to stop his mother from coming after us because he knew you had changed. When her first arrow hit me instead of you and she ran, he found me and saw to it that I was brought here. He went after his mother, afraid you would kill her, and he watched as you caught her, then let her go. When she shot her second arrow at you and fled, he made sure you wouldn't die. He saved us both, Thomas. He saved us both."

Thomas narrowed his eyes as Adam cautiously approached the bedside, a dopey look on his face.

"How are you feeling, man?" he asked, his expression more sober.

"I've been better," Thomas replied. Then, casting a look in Beth's direction, he couldn't help smiling. "And I've been worse, much worse."

"I don't think I've ever heard of a vampire turning human." Adam scratched his shaggy head of hair.

"You know a lot about…vampires?"

Adam shrugged. "It was required reading when I was growing up. To help with the vengeance my mother, and her mother and grandmother, were always talking about. They were ecstatic when they finally tracked you down. I was sent here to see if I could find you. And…well, you know the rest."

"You no longer want vengeance?" Thomas had all but destroyed Adam's family. How could he not wish to subject Thomas to the same pain and torment?

To his surprise, Adam shrugged again. "I'm not sure I ever wanted vengeance, really. I had heard the story, and I had seen my great-grandmother's horror when she recounted it. I didn't want what she had suffered to be inflicted on anyone else." Adam's gaze shifted to Beth, then back to Thomas. "I don't think you're capable of doing those things anymore."

"Why?" asked Thomas, trying to keep his tone even. "Because I am no longer a vampire?"

Smiling, Adam shook his head. "No. Because you're in love."

The look on Thomas' face must have been amusing because Adam stifled a laugh. He patted Thomas on the shoulder, twice, then turned and opened his arms toward Beth. She obliged him with what appeared to be an emotionally-charged hug, and Thomas could feel another possessive growl bubbling up from inside him.

With a nervous look back at Thomas, Adam released Beth and cleared his throat. "I'm going to get out of here before that one" —he gestured to Thomas— "jumps out of that hospital bed and rips my head off." He leaned toward Beth and added in a whisper meant to be heard by Thomas, "You don't have to be a vampire to kill someone."

Beth chuckled, and Adam squeezed her arm. Thomas repressed another territorial urge.

As Adam reached the door to the hallway, he paused and turned to face them. "My mother thinks you're dead, Thomas. She's gone back to Boston. I'll be leaving here soon, too."

"Back to Boston?" asked Beth.

"No," Adam replied, scratching his dark mop of hair. "Somewhere else, where I can start over. Good luck to you two. Maybe we'll see each other again someday."

As Adam reached for the door, Thomas called out, "Adam, wait." He hadn't been a human again for very long, but even Thomas knew that he owed his life to the young man. More importantly, he owed Adam Beth's life, which was a much larger debt.

Adam looked back at Thomas, waiting for him to speak, but despite all the thoughts swimming in

Thomas' head, he found it hard to vocalize any of them. Instead, he simply bowed his head in the young man's direction. "Thank you, Adam."

Nodding in acknowledgment, Adam left.

"Are you okay?"

Beth's sweet voice drew Thomas out of his thoughts and back to the present. He smiled. "My chest hurts when I move, but I'll live." The import of that statement—*I'll live*—struck him as he said the words. He was alive again. His existence was finite once more, which made every moment between now and that inevitable ending more meaningful. More precious.

No doubt sensing the direction of his thoughts, Beth caressed his cheek tenderly. "I love you," she whispered, as though those words could heal all wounds, mind, body, and soul. Looking into her eyes, Thomas believed they could.

"Kiss me," he commanded softly, putting his hand over hers.

Perched on the edge of his bed, she leaned over him, approaching his mouth so slowly and carefully that Thomas couldn't stop himself from reaching for her face and pulling her lips into his to hasten the contact.

The kiss was long and languid—his first kiss as a human, and yet he could have sworn his heightened vampiric senses were still functional because he was aware of everything as she kissed him. Her soft, full lips moving over his, tasting and teasing, as though she, too, were savoring the moment. The smell of generic soap coming from her hands and face, unreasonably exotic and enticing. The subtle sound of her breathing, her little sighs of satisfaction as he moved his hands from her face to wrap around her waist, drawing her body closer to his. She was everything good and right in the world, everything he wanted to experience. Everything he wanted to believe in.

As she drew back from him slowly, smiling, it dawned on Thomas what a terrible position this turn of events would put her in, just *because* she was such a good person. He knew they had to talk, so she would understand what it all meant before she did something she would regret.

Before he could get out the words, Beth traced his cheek with her finger, an adorable wrinkle forming between her lovely eyebrows. "Are you sure you're okay with not being immortal anymore?"

Thomas nodded, trying to smile. "Of course, I am. My wound isn't fatal, is it?"

She laughed, shaking her head. "No. Adam's mother had good aim, and the arrow *should* have pierced your heart and ended you, vampire or human. But that amulet you were wearing happened to be over your heart. The amulet was shattered when the arrow hit, but it slowed the arrow down. I think it knew what my wish would have been in that moment, had I been there, and it granted it all the same."

"I made my wish as I held your bleeding body in my arms, but I didn't think it worked. I was just too late." Thomas brushed the hair away from Beth's face and tucked it behind her ear. "I should have thought of using it sooner. But when I was holding you, watching you grow paler as you lost blood, I couldn't think at all. Then, when it finally occurred to me to pull out the amulet, the only thought in my mind was that I wanted to be with you. Selfish, selfish creature that I am. My wish was for me, not you. Even when I thought you had died."

Beth wiped the tears he hadn't noticed he was shedding. "I had only passed out. You know I have a problem with that sometimes."

He nodded, chuckling, her grin contagious. "I know."

Instinctively, he put his hand over his chest, where the amulet had been, and thought back to the first vision he'd had. "The first time I remembered my human life was the night I met you. I've often wondered why—why that particular night? The more time we spent together, the more visions I had, the stronger my belief became that it was you—had to be you. You were the catalyst for my change. And now, knowing about the amulet, I just can't help thinking that maybe the amulet also played a part in my redemption."

Beth looked puzzled. It was a far-fetched theory, to be sure, but no more far-fetched than the rest of the events that had brought him to this moment.

"I didn't know you then," she replied, "or what you were. How could I have wished that for you? I never wished anything at all, although…"

As she paused, her expression changed, and Thomas suddenly needed to know why.

"Although what?" he urged gently, rubbing her arm. "What are you remembering?"

Beth sighed, shaking her head slowly. "I never made a wish while I had the amulet, Thomas. At least, not out loud. But every time I held the amulet and wondered what I *should* wish for, I had the same thought—I wanted to make a difference in someone's life. I wanted to make someone's life better. It didn't even matter whose life it was. I wanted that person to be better because of me. Which is really a very vain thing to wish for, if you think about it."

"No. No, it isn't. Not the way you wished it."

She smiled at him then, and he realized that, even without the amulet or her wish, she would always make him a better man. And he loved her for it.

"Your wish, my wish, in the end they became one and the same, Thomas. We're together now, truly together. Everything is going to be fine, for both of us."

Her words reminded Thomas of what he had meant to say to her, and he took her hand from his face and placed it on his bandaged chest.

"You have a choice, Beth. You will always have a choice."

She frowned, obviously confused. "What are you talking about?"

"What I mean is that you don't *have* to be with me. You—"

"I *want* to be with you," she interrupted. "Didn't you hear what I said before you told me to kiss you? I love you."

"I know, Beth, and I love you, too. But I don't want you to think that you have to be with me for the rest of your life, just because you changed me. You don't owe me anything. You are free to be with me." He paused, the pain in his chest growing, though he knew it was not from the wound. "You are free *not* to be with me, as well. It's your choice—now, a week from now, a year from now. You are free to be with anyone you want to be with. And that person doesn't have to be me."

There, he had said it. As much as he dreaded the

outcome of his declaration, he knew it was the right thing to do. He couldn't allow her to hold herself captive to him for the rest of their lives out of a misplaced sense of obligation.

He looked up from their entwined hands to find Beth staring at him with a puzzled expression.

"Is that how you feel, Thomas? Because I would understand if it is. You've just regained your former life. It's only natural if you want to travel the world, meet new people as a human, find someone special that—"

He moved toward her with only a fraction of his former speed, but it was fast enough to cut off her words with a searing kiss. Ignoring the burning pain of the wound in his chest, he let go of her hands and reached for her face, holding her there until he had thoroughly kissed her.

As he attempted to catch his breath, he shook his head slowly. "You misunderstand me, Beth. I want nothing more than to be with you for the rest of my human days. It is you I worry about."

"Then don't," she replied, looking him squarely in the eyes. "This is where I want to be. And if that ever changes, you'll be the first to know."

He smiled, nodding. Hoping he never would.

"So, what happens now?" she asked, grabbing hold of one of his hands again. "Will you stay with me on campus until I finish up the semester? Will you come with me wherever I end up working? Will you—"

"Yes. To all of that. I will be wherever you are." He glanced down at his bandaged chest. "As soon as I'm healed."

She laughed, touching his chest through the

bandage and making him want to pull her in for another kiss. "I'll be released tomorrow, and you should be released soon, too. I have to finish working on the report for my senior project. It's due before spring break. I was going to go home for spring break. Maybe you could come with me? Meet my parents?"

He grinned. "I would love to."

"Then we'll figure out the rest."

Bringing her hand to his lips, he kissed it tenderly. "Yes, we will."

Chapter Twenty-Five

"Are you ready?"

Five days had passed—five glorious days of lying in an uncomfortable hospital bed, eating hospital food that, to his newly regained taste buds, didn't seem all that bad, and spending every moment possible with Beth. When he woke, she was at his side, ready to wish him a "good morning" with a mischievous grin that told him she understood how strange it was for him that he was no longer opening his eyes to the setting of the sun. In between their meals and long conversations, she worked on her senior design project report. Even then, when her attention was on the computer screen in front of her, Thomas didn't mind. He could watch her work for hours, forehead creased in concentration, hair continually falling into her face.

She was lovely.

She would catch him staring at her sometimes, and immediately she would set aside her laptop and come over to kiss him.

The last five days had been perfect.

"Yes, I'm ready," he replied, reaching for her hand as they moved forward, allowing the glass doors to sense their presence and slide open to let them out of the hospital.

The sun was high in the sky, and Thomas felt a twinge of fear as its rays hit his pale skin. Beth's fingers tightened around his, and she smiled encouragingly.

"You're not going to burst into flames," she whispered, making him laugh.

"I guess not," he replied. "But it was a distinct possibility."

She leaned into him and kissed the side of his mouth. "Come on. We need to work on your tan."

The weather for Thomas' first day outside as a human was wonderful—sunny, dry, and a little warmer than was typical for mid-March in upstate New York.

Back at Beth's apartment, they sat out on her small balcony and spent the afternoon working on their respective tasks—Beth with her laptop, working on the report that was due in three days, and Thomas with Beth's smartphone attempting to navigate the internet to find an apartment he could rent for the next couple of months. Of the two tasks, Thomas was beginning to think his was the more difficult one.

"You could just stay here," Beth suggested as she closed her laptop a few hours later and stood up to stretch.

Immediately, Thomas pictured waking up in bed next to Beth, reaching for her, and making her late to her first class. Possibly also her second.

"Not a good idea," he answered simply, though the grin he was trying to suppress must have given away his thoughts because she started laughing.

"Well, you can't go back to wherever you used to hole up during the day."

"The basement of the Admissions building," he clarified.

She stared at him, wide-eyed. "That's where you've lived this whole time? I thought you were in the woods behind the Engineering Quad, or maybe that old, decrepit house on Jetton Street."

He shook his head. "Too many people wander around those woods. And that house you're talking about is being renovated. The Admissions building seemed the most reasonable choice."

"Well, you can't go back there." Her eyes suddenly lit up with an idea. "Hey, maybe Lin has room at her house. I can text her and ask."

"How many people does she live with? Aren't they all women?" In some ways, Thomas was more apprehensive about staying out of trouble in his new human form than he had been in his vampiric one. He had known his temptations, his strengths and weaknesses, as a vampire. But now, as a human, he was still re-discovering his vices.

"It's an international house with ten students, and yes, they're all women, but I think I remember her telling me there's a separate entrance for the room in the basement. They use that extra room to accommodate visiting students. It has its own kitchen and bathroom, and I don't think they have any visitors at the moment. They may be done hosting for the rest of the schoolyear, I'm not sure. But I'll ask her and confirm."

"Are you sure?"

"Yes, I'm sure. What are you worried about?"

The question gave him pause. What *was* he worried about? He wasn't a vampire any longer, so he knew he would not hurt them that way. But there were so many ways humans could hurt each other...

"Tell me what you're thinking."

Beth was standing in front of his chair, looking

down at him. He hadn't even realized she had gotten up.

He rose to his feet and wrapped his arms around her, the motion hurting his chest but improving his mood.

"I don't want to do anything wrong," he finally answered, resting his cheek against her head.

"You won't," she replied. "And you will. That's the point. From now on, you're alive, and you're going to make mistakes. Just try not to make any big ones. So don't seduce any of those impressionable young foreign exchange students, for example—"

"That," —Thomas kissed away her next words— "you don't have to worry about. Ever."

"Well, good. Then let me call Lin and just make sure it will work out. And then I have a surprise for you."

He pulled her back into his arms as she attempted to pluck her cell phone off the chair where he had set it.

"What surprise? I don't want a surprise. I don't want secrets. I want to know all your plans for us, so I can look forward to them. I want to enjoy every moment I have with you."

Beth grinned and, forgoing the phone, placed her hands on either side of his face and pulled him in for a delicious kiss.

"Mmmm," he uttered when she released him. "Was that the surprise? Because I could learn to live with frequent surprises if that's the case."

"No," she laughed, "that wasn't it. I have dinner reservations for us at a rooftop restaurant in downtown. I asked for a table with a view of the sunset. It's time you saw one. And tomorrow, maybe I can get up early enough so that we can see the sunrise together, too."

Thomas watched as she passed through the sliding glass door, cell phone in hand, to call Lin. He wondered if she had chosen to talk to Lin inside, rather than out on the deck with him, because she knew Lin would ask her questions about the two of them. Girl talk, about him. The thought made Thomas feel warm and happy. Another human feeling he rather enjoyed.

Beth had done this to him. Changed him. Every vision he had experienced as a vampire since meeting Beth had brought back the capacity to experience emotions he thought would weaken him—sympathy, guilt, despair, anxiety, anger, fear—and he knew he would feel all those emotions over and over again throughout his new life. Such was the human condition. But also through those visions his heart had been revived, and other feelings could now take root, feelings that could help him through the dark times. The friendship of his brothers at the seminary. The soothing comfort of his mother's presence. The wisdom of his father's loving guidance.

Beth was already all those things to him—a friend, a nurturer, an advisor. And yet, she was something more, something he could never have remembered through a vision because it was something he'd never experienced before. She was his heart and his soul.

As he turned to the sliding glass door to see if Beth was done with her call, a pinch in his chest where his wound was still healing reminded him of his new state. It also reminded him of what the doctor had said before he was discharged. A small shard of the stone that had saved his life had lodged itself deep under his skin upon impact. The doctor had offered to try to remove it, but

Thomas had declined. If the amulet really did grant wishes, then the amulet would have known that what Thomas wanted more than anything else was to be with Beth. From the time they had shared dessert in that café, when Lin had stood her up, to the moment he held Beth's bleeding body cradled in his lap, until now. He'd had the wish even before he could recall or understand the feelings she had created inside him. And if that wish remained only as long as the amulet, or a portion of it, was in his possession, then it was worth keeping that small shard of the jewel exactly where it was. Close to his heart.

"Ready?"

Thomas raised his gaze to Beth's, finding her standing in the doorway to the living room, the love he felt reflected in her eyes. He couldn't help the smile that curved his lips in sweet anticipation of all that was to come.

"I'm ready."

A word about the author…

Winner of the Georgia Romance Writers' 2020 Maggie Award for Excellence in the Unpublished Historical Romance category, Kathryn Amurra is the author of sweet and sensual romance stories with mystical and historical elements. Her newest series, Heart's True Desire, revolves around a ring and a necklace from generations past, each of which has the power to grant the bearer his or her deepest desire. Amurra is also the author of the independently-published Soothsayer's Path series set in Ancient Rome. An intellectual property attorney by day, some of Amurra's best writing takes place between the hours of 10PM and midnight (or later), when she has "logged off" from her day job and her hubby and three girls are asleep. https://www.kathrynamurra.com

Thank you for purchasing
this publication of The Wild Rose Press, Inc.

For questions or more information
contact us at
info@thewildrosepress.com.

The Wild Rose Press, Inc.
www.thewildrosepress.com